His skin is covered by tattoos of murder victims. Each tattoo is the story of one destroyed life and Monk's desire to hunt those killers down, even if it costs him his sanity and his soul.

Monk is a former Special Ops soldier turned private investigator. He mostly hunts bail skips, but sometimes he's called to darker work—tracking down savage killers, abusers, and psychopaths at the request of their victims. Justice comes at a terrible cost, though.

Mystic collects old and new stories and poems about Monk Addison—a dangerous and deadly hunter who is haunted by the ghosts of everyone he's avenged.

With a foreword by Jim Butcher.

MYSTIC

THE MONK ADDISON CASE FILES

JONATHAN MABERRY

WFP
WordFire Press

EBook ISBN: 978-1-68057-697-9
Trade Paperback ISBN: 978-1-68057-698-6
Dust Jacket Hardcover ISBN: 978-1-68057-699-3
Library of Congress Control Number: 024934142
Cover design by Lynne Hansen Art
Kevin J. Anderson, Art Director
Vellum layout by CJ Anaya
Published by
WordFire Press, LLC
PO Box 1840
Monument, CO 80132
Kevin J. Anderson & Rebecca Moesta, Publishers
WordFire Press eBook Edition 2024
WordFire Press Trade Paperback Edition 2024
WordFire Press Dust Jacket Hardcover Edition 2024

Printed in the USA
Join our WordFire Press Readers Group for
sneak previews, updates, new projects, and giveaways.
Sign up at wordfirepress.com

This one is for my crew from high school all those years ago. Friends—some gone, others still here—who shared some wild adventures in and around Frankford High School way back in the 1970s. Michael Sicilia, Christina Seeling, Tom McCann, Bernardo Dickerson, Carolyn Lynn, Sarah Landis, and the rest. One of these days I'm going to put all of you into a novel. Not sure if it'll be drama, comedy, horror, or something else as yet undefinable.

And, as always, for Sara Jo ...

CONTENTS

FOREWORD

BY JIM BUTCHER

The world of storytelling is a world of wizards, invoking the most potent powers of the human mind with spells of words. As such, it can be a place of sweetness and light, of bold, heroic adventure, or of dark shadows and grim paths.

In these darker tales, there is often a figure who warns the characters involved to turn back, to look away, to avoid the horror and perilous trials which await them if they should continue on their path. This harbinger's appearance is often foreboding, and though his intentions might seem benign, his purpose in the story is to provide a sense of grounding for what the poor fools toddling along the twilight path are about to undergo.

Hello, my name is Jim. I'll be your harbinger today.

The tales contained herein, dear reader, are neither sweet nor light. If you continue along this path, you will find yourself in a world of gloomy streets and benighted alleys, lit only intermittently and in flickering uncertainty by what few weary streetlights remain unbroken.

The people who live there are tough and wary. The predators who make it their business to stalk them are vicious and clever. It is a world of true mean streets, where the law fights a desperate holding action against entropy and the darkest hungers of the mortal world; where the light of human kindness must be held close and kept safe against the uncaring cold.

Here, where pain and suffering can turn people into monsters, their victims can do little but fight for their lives. When they fail, their spirits rail against the eternal night, while the police do what they can, collect what remains, a human being reduced to component parts and a data point. For those poor souls, nothing remains.

Except, perhaps, some kind of primal redress. Some kind of balance. Something which, at times, might almost resemble justice.

Enter Monk Addison, private investigator. He is no knight in shining armor. He's not even in rusted, dented armor. This knight's mail is as dark gray as makes no never mind next to black. He's tough, hard, jaded, and ruthless. He's seen too many demons and chased them away with too much whiskey.

But he's there.

And his eyes can see into the darkest shadows.

When no one else cares about your horrible death, he's there. When no one else can find your killer, he can. When no one else can deliver justice, when another predator has slipped quietly away into the night leaving carnage behind, there is someone who can track the monster back to its lair—and make sure that no one else will suffer the same fate, ever again.

Monk isn't nice. No one in his position could be. He isn't a friend of the broken hearted. He's haunted. He's grim. And he refuses to turn aside from avenging those whose voices have been eternally silenced, no matter the cost.

He's brilliantly written, ugly and fascinating and pure as a gargoyle, and he lives and breathes in the dark, seething, vibrant world my colleague Jonathan Maberry has created for us.

If you've been to the terrible place yourself, you'll recognize someone with whom you wouldn't want to have lunch—but you'd want him next to you the next time you go down a dark alley.

Still, dear reader.

Beware.

If you turn these pages, you may not be able to stop.

You have been warned.

—Jim Butcher, April 2024

ABOUT MONK ADDISON

Welcome to the world of Gerald "Monk" Addison. Along with Joe Ledger, Monk has become my favorite character to write. He's the kind of character I can drop into almost any kind of story, and he'll find his way.

For those new to Monk, the short background is that he's a former soldier who saw too much, did too much, and that burned out all his wiring. He was a too-Special Operations shooter who became a PMC—Private Military Contractor—and then he cast himself loose on his own version of the pilgrim role. He went looking for some answers to make sense of the world and found answers he didn't expect. In Tibet, Vietnam, and other countries, he sat with mystics and healers and tried to rebuild his soul.

Instead of finding redemption he learned that he had a special gift. He can communicate with the ghosts of recently murdered people. The ghosts seek him out now, but helping them takes a terrible toll on Monk's soul.

In the early Monk stories, he lived in New York and in the wrong part of that City, working as a bounty hunter and skip tracer. In the more recent stories he's living in Pine Deep, the semi-fictional town I introduced in my first three novels, *Ghost Road Blues*, *Dead Man's Song*, and *Bad Moon Rising*. I returned to that town in *Ink*, a semi-sequel to the NYC-based *Glimpse*. He is in Pine Deep for *Burn to Shine*, the latest novel in my Joe Ledger thriller series. And even though I love having him in novels, I feel he's at his best in the more solitary and moody short stories and, more recently, poetry.

Monk's gig as a skip tracer takes up most of his work life, but every once in a while he's hired for special investigations. The ghosts of murder victims want him to find their killers. To do this, Monk recovers some of their blood from the crime scenes and has it mixed with ink so that the faces of the dead can be tattooed onto his skin. This allows him to experience the last few minutes of the victims' lives and get clues about who killed them so the murderers can be stopped before they destroy more lives. Solving these murders comes with a terrible price, both for Monk and his "clients." Once the tattoo is complete, the ghosts will forever after haunt Monk. They can't pass on and only he can see them. Monk Addison is a man haunted by more than his memories of war.

Most of the stories in this collection have been—typical of collections—previously published. Most have been in anthologies here or there. However, there are new tales and poems of Monk Addison, including the novelette that closes this volume.

Though originally created as a possible comic book character, Monk came to life first in the short story, *"Mystic,"* the first in this book. And he *is* a mystic. Though moody, damaged, and dangerous, Monk is still looking for that understanding, that bit of personal redemption. I *get* Monk. I understand scars, damage, and bad decisions. Just as I understand the need to rebuild one's life after that existential car has been totaled.

I hope you enjoy these tales and become friends with Monk, Patty Cakes, and the rest of the cast of his bizarre dramas.

—Jonathan Maberry
San Diego, 2024

MYSTIC

—1—

I see dead people.
Make a joke. Go ahead, people do.
Fuck 'em.
I see dead people.
Not all of them. My life would be too crowded. Just some.
The ones who need to be seen.
The ones who need me to see them.

—2—

The diner's name is Delta of Venus.
Most people think that's a pun of some kind, or a reference to Mississippi. It's not. The owner's name's not Venus. One of her girlfriend's was. It's like that.
I had my spot. Corner of the counter, close to the coffee. Out of the line of foot traffic to the john. Quiet most of the time. I dig the quiet. Kind of need it. My head is noisy enough.
It was a Thursday night, deep into a slow week. The kind of week Friday won't make better and Saturday won't salvage. Me on my stool, last sip of my fourth or fifth cup of coffee, half a

plate of meatloaf going cold. Reading *The Waste Land* and wondering what kind of hell Eliot was in when he wrote it. World War I was over, and he wrote poetry like the world was all for shit. Like he'd peeled back the curtain, and the great and powerful Oz was a sorry little pedophile and Dorothy was going to have a bad night. Depressing as fuck.

The coffee was good. The day blew.

Eve, the evening waitress, was topping off ketchup bottles and not wasting either of our time on small talk. Not on a Thursday like this. These kinds of days don't bring out the chattiness in anyone who's paying attention. Outside, there was a sad, slow rain and most of the people who came in smelled like wet dogs.

Then *she* came in.

I saw the door open. Saw it in the shiny metal of the big coffee urn. Saw her come in. Watched her stand there for a moment, not sure of what she was doing. Saw her look around. Saw nobody else look back.

Saw her spot me. And *know* me. And chew her lip for a moment before coming my way.

Little thing, no bigger than half a minute. Sixteen, maybe seventeen. Slim as a promise. Pretty as a daffodil.

Lost and scared.

Looking for me.

People like her find me. I never ask how they heard of me. In my line of work, the referral process is complicated. I get most of my standard clients from asshole law firms like Scarebaby and Twitch. Yeah, J. Heron Scarebaby and Iver Twitch. Real names. Some people are that fucking unlucky, and that dim that they won't use a different name for business. Or maybe it's a matter of rats finding the right sewer. Not sure, don't care. They hire me for scut work. Skip traces, missing persons. Stuff like that. Pays the light bill, buys me coffee.

They hadn't sent her, though. She found me a whole other way.

I signaled Eve and tapped the rim of my coffee cup with the

band of my wedding ring. Still wore the ring after all this time. Married to the memory, I suppose. Eve topped me off.

"Gimme a sec," I said.

She looked around to see what was what. Looked scared when she did it, which is fair enough. People are like that around me. Then she found something intensely interesting to do at the far end of the counter. Didn't look my way again.

There were five other people in the Delta. Two were regulars: a night watchman on the way to his midnight shift and Lefty Wright, who was always topping off his Diet Coke with liberal shots of Early Times. Neither of them would give a cold, wet shit if a velociraptor walked in and ordered the blue-plate special.

The other three were a gaggle of hipsters who must have gone looking for one of those no-name clubs, or the kind of dance party that's only ever advertised by obscure Internet posts. Probably got bad directions and brought iffy decision-making capabilities with them because they lingered here in this part of town long enough to order pancakes at a place like this. That or they were hipster wannabes who thought the Delta was retro cool. It's not. And pretty soon they were going to let common sense trump their peer pressure and then they'd fade away.

That left me and the girl.

I didn't turn, but I patted the red Naugahyde stool next to me. Maybe it was the color that drew her eye. I'm pretty sure it's the only color people like her can see. That's what one of them told me. Just red, white, black and a lot of shades of gray.

That's fucked up.

The girl hesitated a moment longer, then she seemed to come to a decision and came over. Didn't make a sound.

She stopped and stood there, watching me as I watched her in the steel mirror of the coffeemaker.

"It's your dime, sweetheart," I said.

She didn't say anything.

I picked up the Tabasco sauce and shook it over the meatloaf. Used enough of it to kill the taste. The Specials sign over the kitchen window doesn't say what kind of meat is in it and I'm not brave enough to ask. I'm reasonably sure that whatever it was ran on four legs. Beyond that, I wouldn't give Vegas odds on it being a cow or a pig.

"You want to sit down?" I asked.

Still nothing, so I turned and saw why.

Her face was as pale as milk. She wore too much makeup and clearly didn't know how to put it on. Little girl style—too much of everything, none of the subtlety that comes with experience. Glitter tube top and spandex micro mini. Expensive shoes. Clothes couldn't have been hers. Maybe an older sister, maybe a friend who was more of a party girl. They looked embarrassing on her. Sad.

She had one hoop earring in her right ear. The left earlobe was torn. No earring. No other jewelry that I could see. No purse, no phone, no rings. That one earring damn near broke my heart.

"You know how this works?" I asked.

Nothing. Or maybe a little bit of a nod.

"It's a one-way ticket, so you'd better be sure, kid."

She lifted her hand to touch her throat. Long, pale throat. Like a ballet dancer. She was a pretty kid, but she would have been beautiful as a woman.

Would have been.

Her fingers brushed at a dark line that ran from just under her left ear and went all the way around to her right. She tried to say something. Couldn't. The line opened like a mouth, and it said something obscene. Not in words. What flowed from between the lips of that mouth was wet and in the only color she could see.

She wanted to show me. She wanted me to see. She needed me to understand.

I saw. And I understood.

—3—

Later, after she faded away and left me to my coffee and mystery meat, I stared at the floor where she had stood. There was no mark, no drops of blood. Nothing. Eve came back and gave me my check. I tossed a ten down on a six-dollar tab and shambled out into the night. Behind me I heard Eve call goodbye.

"Night, Monk."

I blew her a kiss like I always do. Eve's a good gal. Nice. Minds her own business. Keeps counsel with her own shit. Two kids at home and she works double shifts most nights. One of those quiet heroes who do their best to not let their kids be like them. I liked her.

It was fifteen minutes past being able to go home and get a quiet night's sleep. The rain had stopped, so I walked for a while, letting the night show me where to go. The girl hadn't been able to tell me, but that didn't matter. I'd seen her, smelled the blood. Knew the scent.

Walked.

And walked.

Found myself midway up a back street, halfway between I Don't Know and Nobody Cares. Only a few cars by the curbs, but they were stripped hulks. Dead as the girl. Most of the houses were boarded up. Most of the boards had been pried loose by junkies or thieves looking to strip out anything they could. Copper pipes, wires, whatever. Couple of the houses had been torn down, but the rubble hadn't been hauled off.

What the hell had that little girl been doing on a street like this?

Fuck me.

I had a pocket flashlight on my keychain and used it to help me find the spot.

It was there. A dark smudge on the sidewalk. Even from ten feet away I knew it was what I was looking for. There were footprints all over the place, pressed into the dirt, overlapping.

Car tire tracks, too. The rain had wiped most of it away, smeared a lot of the rest, but it was there to be read. If I looked hard enough, I'd probably find the flapping ends of yellow crime scene tape, 'cause they never clean that stuff up. Not completely, and not in a neighborhood like this. Whole fucking area's a crime scene. Still in progress, too, for the most part.

Doesn't matter. That's me bitching.

I knelt by the smudge. That was what mattered.

It was dried. Red turns to brown as the cells thicken and die. Smell goes away, too. At first, it's the stink of freshly sheared copper, then it's sweet, then it's gone. Mostly gone. I can always find a trace. A whiff.

And it was hers. Same scent. If I was a poet like Eliot maybe I'd call it the perfume of innocence. Something corny like that. I'm not, so I don't. It's just blood. Even the rain couldn't wash it away.

I squatted there for a few minutes, listening to water drip from the old buildings. Letting the smells sink in deep enough so I could pin them to the walls of my head.

Back in the day, before I went off to play soldier, before I ditched that shit and went bumming along the pilgrim road trying to rewire my brain, smells never used to mean much. That changed. First time I didn't die when an IED blew my friends to rags, I began to pay attention. Death smells different than life. Pain has its own smell.

So does murder.

I stopped being able to not pay attention, if you can dig that. I lost the knack for turning away and not seeing.

There was a monk in Nepal who told me I had a gift. A crazy lady down in a shack near a fish camp in bayou country told me I had a curse. They were talking about the same thing. They're both right, I suppose.

A priest in a shitty church in Nicaragua told me I had a calling. I told him that maybe it was more like a mission. He thought about it and told me I was probably right. We were drinking in the chapel. That's all that was left of the church. They don't call them Hellfire missiles for nothing.

The girl had come to me. Couldn't say what she wanted because of what they'd done to her. Didn't matter. She'd said enough.

I dug my kit out of my jacket pocket, unzipped it. Uncapped a little glass vial, took the cork off the scalpel and spent two minutes scraping as much of the blood as I could get into the vial. Then I removed the bottle of holy water, filled the dropper, and added seven drops. Always seven, no more, no less. That's the way it works, and I don't need to fuck with it. Then I put everything away, zipped up the case and stood. My knees creaked. I'm looking at forty close enough to read the fine print. My knees are older than that.

Spent another forty minutes poking around, but I knew I wasn't going to find anything the cops hadn't. They're pretty good. Lots of experience with crime scenes around here. They even catch the bad guys sometimes.

Not this time, though, or the girl wouldn't have come to me.

It's all about the justice.

The vial was the only thing that didn't go back into the case. That was in my pants pocket. It weighed nothing, but it was fifty fucking pounds heavy. It made me drag my feet all the way to the tattoo parlor.

—4—

Patty Cakes has a little skin art place just south of Boundary Street, right between a glam bar called Pornstash and a deli called Open All Night, which, to my knowledge, has never been open. Someone nailed a Bible to the front door, so take that any way you want.

The tattoo joint was open all night. Never during the day, as far as I know. It wasn't that kind of place. I saw Patty in there, stick thin with a purple Mohawk and granny glasses, hunched over the arm of a biker who looked like Jerry Garcia. Yeah, I know, Jerry's been dead for years. This guy looked like Jerry would look now. His name was Elmo something. I didn't care enough to remember the rest.

"Hey, Monk," said Patty, when she heard the little bell over the door.

"Hey, Mr. Addison," said Elmo. He was always a polite SOB.

"Hey," I said, and hooked a stool with my foot, dragged it over so I could watch Patty work. She was half-Filipino Chinese, with interesting scars on her face. Lot of backstory to her. I know most of it, but almost nobody else does. She knows a lot about me, too. We don't sleep together, but we've stayed up drinking more nights than I can count. She's one of my people, the little circle of folks I actually trust. We met the year I came back, and she spotted something in me from the jump. Bought me my first meal at the Delta.

She was working on green tints for a tat of climbing roses that ran from right thumb to left. Dozens of roses, hundreds of leaves.

"Nice," I said.

Elmo grinned like a kid on Christmas. "She's nearly done."

I nodded. Elmo was an ink junkie. He'd be back. Not just to elaborate on the tattoo, but because it was Patty sinking the ink. People come from all over just for her. I do. Like me, she has her gifts. Or maybe it's that she has her mission, too. But that's her story, and this isn't that.

Patty sat back and studied her work. "Okay, Elmo, that's it for now. Let it set. Go home and take care of it, okay?"

"Okay."

"Give Steve a kiss for me."

"Sure." He got up, stood in front of the floor-length mirror for a minute, grinning at the work. His eyes were a little glazed. He walked out wearing only a beater and jeans, his leather jacket forgotten on a chair. I knew he'd be back for it tomorrow. They always come back to Patty Cakes.

She got up and locked the door, flipped the sign to CLOSED and turned out the front lights. I stripped off my coat and shirt, caught sight of myself in the mirror. An unenamored lady once told me I look like a shaved ape. Fair enough. I'm bigger than most people, wider than most, deeper than most. A lot of me is covered in ink. None of it's really pretty. Not like those roses. It's all faces. Dozens of them. Small, about the size of a half-dollar. Very detailed. Photo-real, almost. Men and women. Kids. All ages and races. Faces.

"Let me have it," she said, holding out a hand. I hadn't even told her why I was there. She knew me, though. Knew my moods. So, I dug the vial out of my pocket and handed it to her. She took it, held it up to the light, sighed, nodded. "Gimme a sec. Have a beer."

I found two bottles of Fat Pauly's, a craft lager from Iligan City in the Philippines, cracked them open, set one down on her worktable, lowered myself into her chair and sipped the other. Good beer. Ice cold. I watched her work.

She removed the rubber stopper from the vial and used a sterile syringe to suck up every last drop, then she injected the mixture into a jar of ink. It didn't matter that the ink was black. All of my tats are black. The white is my skin. Any color that shows up is from scars that still had some pink in them, but that would fade away after a while.

I drank my beer as Patty worked. Her eyes were open, but I knew that she wasn't seeing anything in that room. Her pupils were pinpoints and there was sweat on her forehead and upper lip. She began chanting something in Tagalog that I couldn't follow. Not one of my languages. When she was done mixing, she stopped chanting and cut me a look.

"You want the strap?"

"No," I said.

She held out a thick piece of leather. "Take the strap."

"No."

"Why do we go through this every time?"

"I don't need it," I told her.

"*I* do. Goddamn it, Monk, I can't work with you screaming in my ear. Take the fucking strap."

9

I sighed. "Okay. Give me the fucking strap."

She slapped it into my palm and I put it between my teeth. She got out a clean needle and set the bottle of ink close at hand. She didn't ask me what I wanted her to draw. She knew.

I didn't start screaming right away. Not until she began putting the features on the little girl's face

We were both glad I had the fucking strap.

—5—

It took her an hour to get it right, and I could feel when it was right. We both could.

I spat the strap onto my lap and sat there, gasping, out of breath, fucked up. I could see the pity in Patty's eyes. She was crying a little, like she always does. The light in the room had changed. Become brighter, and the edges of everything were so sharp I could cut myself on their reality. All the colors bled away. Except for red, white, black, and all those shades of gray. That's what I saw. It's all I'd see until I was done with what I had to do.

Sometimes it was like that for days. Other times it was fast. Depends on how good a look the girl got, and what I'd be able to tell from that look.

Patty helped me up, grunting with the effort. I was two-fifty and change. None of it blubber. A lot of it was scar tissue. The room did an Irish céilí dance around me, and my brain kept trying to flip the circuit breakers off.

"If you're going to throw up, use the bathroom."

"Not this time," I managed to wheeze, then I grabbed my stuff, clumsied my way into my shirt and jacket, and stumbled out into the night, mumbling something to her that was supposed to be thanks but might have been fuck you.

Patty wouldn't take offense. She understood.

Like I said, one of *my* people.

The night was hung wrong. The buildings leaned like drunks and the moon hid a guilty smile behind torn streamers of cloud. It took me half an hour to find my way back to where the girl was killed. My eyes weren't seeing where my feet were walking, and sometimes I crashed into things, tripped over lines in the pavement, tried to walk down an alley that wasn't there. It's like that for a bit, but it settles down.

Once I was on that street, it settled down a lot.

I stood by the step where I'd found her blood.

This is where it gets difficult for me. Victims don't usually know enough to really help, not even when I can see what they saw when they died. Like I was doing now. Half the time they didn't see it coming. A drive-by or a hazy image of a tire iron. The feel of hands grabbing them from behind.

It was kind of like that with the girl.

Olivia.

I realized I knew her name now.

Olivia Searcy.

Fifteen. Even younger than I thought, but I was right about the clothes. They were her sister's. Shoes and push-up bra, too. She wanted to look older. No, she wanted to be older. But that was as old as she'd ever get.

I knew why she was there, and it was a bad episode of a teen romance flick. She was a sophomore in high school, he was a senior. Good looking, smart, from a family with some bucks. Good grades. A real find, and maybe in time he'd grow up and be a good man. But he was eighteen and all he wanted was pussy, and a lot of guys know that young pussy is often dumb pussy, which makes it easy pussy. So, they come onto them, making them feel cool, feel special, feel loved. And they get some ass, maybe pop a cherry, and move on the instant the girl gets clingy. Fifteen-year-olds always get clingy, but there are always more of them. The boy, Drake, hadn't yet plundered Olivia. It was part of the plan for tonight.

They went to a party at some other guy's house a long way from here, in a part of town where stuff like this isn't supposed to happen, which is a stupid thought because stuff like this happens everywhere. The party was fun, and it was loud. They got high. Got smashed. He got grabby and she freaked. Maybe a moment of clarity, maybe she saw the satyr's face behind the nice boy mask. Whatever. She bolted and ran.

She didn't know if Drake tried to find her because she tried real hard not to be found.

She *was* found, though.

Just not by Drake.

For a little bit there I thought I was going to have to break some parents' hearts by fucking up their pretty boy son, but that wasn't in tonight's playbook. Drake hadn't done anything worse than be a high school dickhead. He got her drunk, but he hadn't forced her, hadn't slipped her a roofie. And, who knows, maybe if he'd found her in time he'd have become Galahad and fought for her honor. Might have saved her life.

Probably would have died with her.

Or maybe the killer would have opted out and gone looking for someone else. A lot of serial killers and opportunistic killers are like that. They're not Hannibal Lecter. They're not tough, smart, and dangerous. Most of them are cowards. They feel totally disempowered by whatever's happened to them—abusive parents, bad genes, who the fuck cares? They hurt and terrify and mutilate and kill because it makes them feel powerful, but it's a lie. It's no more real than feeling powerful by wearing a Batman costume at Halloween. You may look the part, but you're a long way from saving Gotham City.

All of that flooded through my brain while I stood there and looked at the street through the eyes of a dead girl. Seeing it the way Olivia saw it right as hands grabbed her from behind. Right as someone pulled her back against his body so she could feel his size, his strength, the hard press of his cock against her back. Right as he destroyed her. Right as the cold edge of the knife was pressed into the soft flesh under her left ear.

I felt all of that. Everything. Her nerve endings were mine. Her pain exploded through me. The desperate flutter of her heart changed the rhythm of mine into a panic, like the beating of a hummingbird's wings against a closed window. I felt her break inside as he ruined her. I heard the prayers she prayed, and they echoed in my head like they'd echoed in hers. She hadn't been able to scream them aloud because first there was a hand over her mouth, and then there was the knife against her throat and those threats in her ear.

And when he was done, I felt the burn.

That line, like someone moving an acetylene torch along a bead of lead. Moving from under my left ear to under my right.

I felt her die because I died, too. Olivia drowned in her own blood.

Then there was a strange time, an oddly quiet time, because I was with her when she was dead, too. When he wrapped her in a plastic tarp and put her in the trunk. It was so weird because while he did that, he was almost gentle. As if afraid of hurting her.

Fucking psychopath.

While the car drove from where she'd died to where he'd dumped her, Olivia slipped into that special part of the universe where the dead see each other. Certain kinds of dead. The dead who were part of a family. Victims of the same knife.

His people.

Olivia discovered that she was not the only one. Not the first, not the tenth.

She wasn't sure how many because he moved around so much. *Had* moved around. Not so much anymore. Not since he moved to this town. The victims she met were the ones who'd died here.

Twenty-six of them.

The youngest was eight.

I met those victims, too, because I was inside the memory. Like I'd actually been there. That's how it worked. I talked to them, and most of them already knew who and what I was. The first time I'd encountered that it shocked the shit out of me. But now I understood. Not to say I'm used to it, because I'd have to be a special kind of fucked up to be used to something like that. No, it was more like I knew how to deal. How to use it.

Some of them had died just like Olivia. An attack from

behind. Everything from behind. No chance of an identification. He varied it a little. One of those nearly patternless killers that the FBI have no idea how to profile. A knife across the throat, an icepick between the right ribs, a garrote made from a guitar string, a broken neck.

Most were like that.

Most. Not all.

There was one who fought. She'd had a little judo and some taekwondo. Not enough, but enough to make him work for it. It was one of the early ones, after he'd moved here. The one that made him want to never bring them home again. She'd gotten out and he'd chased her into the front yard and caught her before she could wake the neighbors. Single homes, lots of yards on all sides. Cul-de-sac. When he caught up to her, she spun around and tried to make a fight of it.

I saw every second of it.

The yard. The house.

Him.

I saw him.

I saw him block her punch, and then a big fist floated toward her face and she was gone. He was a big guy and he knew how to hit. The punch broke the girl's neck, which made it easier on her, if easy is a word that even applies.

I stood there and watched all of it play out inside my head. No idea how long I was there. Time doesn't matter much when I'm in that space. I was there for every second of every minute of every attack. Beginning to end. All the way to when he dumped them, or buried them, or dropped them off a bridge.

Stack it all up and it was days.

Days.

Shotgunned into my head.

I wish I'd had the leather strap. Instead, I had to bite down on nothing, clamp my jaws, ball my fists, clench my gut and eat the fucking pain.

It wouldn't save any of those girls. Not one. And maybe it

wouldn't matter that I felt it all but didn't have to live it. Or die from it. I know that.

I couldn't help a single one of them. I couldn't help Olivia.

But as my skin screamed from the phantom touches and the blades and everything else, I swore that I'd help the next girl.

Goddamn son of a bitch, I'd help the next girl.

Because, you see, I saw the house.

I saw the number beside the door.

I saw the tags on the car parked in the drive.

And I saw the motherfucker's face.

I went and sat down on the step next to the blood. Waited. I knew she'd be there eventually. It was how it worked.

Still surprised me when I looked up and there she was. Pale, thin, young, her face as bright as a candle. Eyes filled with forever.

"You can still opt out," I told her. "I can turn this over to the cops. Let them handle it."

She said nothing, but she gave me a look. We both knew that this guy was too careful. There would be no evidence of any kind. He'd been doing this for years and he knew his tradecraft. No semen, no hairs, nothing left for them to trace. The knife was gone where no one would ever find it. And he wasn't a souvenir collector. The smarter ones aren't. They could turn his house inside out and the only things they'd find would be jack and shit.

Even if they watched him, he'd turn it off for a while. For long enough. Police can't afford to run surveillance for very long. They'd lose interest, even if they thought the guy was good for Olivia's murder.

I sighed. Actually, I wanted to cry. What she was asking was big and ugly and it was going to hurt both of us.

She stood there with a necklace of bright red and those bottomless eyes.

She didn't say a word. She didn't have to.

The price was the price. She was willing to pay it because she was a decent kid who would probably have grown up to be someone of note. Someone with power. Someone who cared. Those eyes told me that this wasn't about her.

It was all about the next girl.

And the one after that.

And the one after that.

I buried my face in my hands and wept.

—6—

It took me two days to run it all down. The girl misremembered the license number, so that killed half a day.

Then I put the pieces together. Bang, bang, bang.

Once that happens, everything moves quickly.

I ran the guy through the databases we PIs use, and after an hour I knew everything about him. I had his school records and his service record—one tour in Afghanistan, one in Iraq. Made me hate him even more. He was divorced, no kids. Parents dead, his only living relative was a brother in Des Moines. I figured there were bodies buried in Des Moines, too, but I'd never know about them. He owned three Jack in the Box franchise stores and had half-interest in a fourth. Drove a hybrid, recycled, and had solar panels on his house. I almost found that funny.

I was in his Netflix and Hulu accounts, his bank account, and everything else he had. If there was a pattern there, or a clue as to what he was, it wasn't there. He was very smart and very careful.

No cops were ever going to catch him.

I parked my car on the route he took to work and waited until I saw him drive past on his way home. Gave him an hour while I watched the sun go down. Twilight dragged some clouds across the sky, and the news guy said it was going to rain again. Fine. Rain was good. It was loud and it chased people off the streets.

Lightning forked the sky and thunder was right behind it. Big, booming. The rains started as a deluge. No pussy light drizzle first. One second nothing, then it was raining alley cats and junkyard dogs.

I got out of my car and opened an umbrella. I really don't give a shit about getting wet, but umbrellas block line-of-sight. They make you invisible. I walked through the rain to his yard, went in through the gate, up along the flagstone path, and knocked on the door.

Had to knock twice.

He had half a confused smile on his face when he opened the door, the way people do when they aren't expecting anyone. Especially during a storm.

Big guy, an inch taller than me, maybe only ten pounds lighter. His debit card record says that he keeps his gym membership up to date. I knew from my research that he'd boxed in college. Wrestled, too. And he had Army training.

Whatever.

I said, "Mr. Gardner?"

"What do you want?"

I hit him.

Real fucking hard.

A two-knuckle punch to the face, right beside the nose. Cracks the infraorbital foramen. Mashes the sinus. Feels a lot like getting shot in the face, except you don't die.

He went back and down, falling inside his house, and I swarmed in after him, letting the umbrella go. The wind whipped it away and took it somewhere. Maybe Oz for all I know. I never saw it again.

Gardner fell hard, but he fell the right way, like he knew what he was doing. Twisting to take the fall on his palms, letting his arm muscles soak up the shock. His head had to be ringing like Quasimodo's bells, but he wasn't going out easy.

He kicked at me as I came for him. Tricky bastard. A good kick, too, flat of the heel going for the front of my knee. If he'd connected, I'd have gone down with a busted leg and he'd have had all the time in the world to do whatever he wanted.

If he'd connected.

I was born at night, but it wasn't last night. I bent my knee into the kick and bent over to punch the side of his foot. I knew some tricks, too.

In the movies there's a brawl. A long fight with all sorts of fancy moves, deadly holds, exciting escapes, a real gladiatorial match.

That's the movies.

In the real world, fights are, to paraphrase Hobbs, nasty, brutal, and short.

He had that one kick, that one chance. I didn't give him a second one. I gave him nothing.

I took everything.

When I was done, I was covered in blood, my chest heaving, staring at what was left of him there in the living room. I'd closed the door. The curtains were closed over drawn shades. The TV was on. Some kind of CSI show with the volume cranked up. Outside the storm was shaking the world.

He wasn't dead.

Mostly, but not entirely.

That would come a little later.

He wasn't going anywhere, though. That would have been structurally impossible.

I went into the kitchen and found a basting brush. Slapped it back and forth over his face to get it wet, then I wrote on the wall. It took a while. I made sure he was watching. I wrote the names of every girl he had killed.

Every one that I'd met there in the darkness of Olivia's hell.

Gardner was whimpering. Crying. Begging.

When I was done, I unzipped my pants, pulled out my dick, and pissed on him.

He was sobbing now. Maybe he was that broken or that scared. Maybe it was his last play, trying to hold a match to the candle of my compassion.

Maybe.

But he was praying in the wrong church.

While I worked, I kept praying that Olivia wouldn't show up

to see this. Most of them do. None of them should. I didn't want her here.

I looked around for her.

She didn't come.

It helped a little, but not a lot. I knew I'd see her again.

Gardner managed to force one word out. It took a lot of effort because I'd ruined him.

"P-please ..." he said.

He wanted me to end it. By then, I think that's what he wanted.

I smiled.

"Fuck you," I said.

The storm was raging, and I stood there for nearly an hour. Watching Gardner suffer. Watching him die.

Judge me if you want. If so, feel free to go fuck yourself.

When I left, I stole one of his umbrellas.

I'd worn gloves and a ski mask. Everything I had on was disposable. It all got burned. I'm smart about that shit, too.

—7—

That night I got drunk. Because it's the only reasonable thing to do.

Me and Patty, Lefty Wright, and a couple of the others. Ten of us huddled around a couple of tables in a black-as-pockets corner of Pornstash. Me and my people. No one had to ask what happened. Patty knew, some of the others maybe. Mostly not. But they all knew something had happened. We were those kinds of people, and this was that kind of town.

We drank and told lies, and if the laughter sounded fake at times and forced at others, then so what?

—8—

It was nearly dawn when I stumbled up the stairs, showered for the third time that day, and fell into bed.

19

I said some prayers to a God I knew was there but was pretty sure was insane. Or indifferent. Or both.

My windows are painted black because I sleep during the day. Mostly, anyway. I had a playlist running. John Lee Hooker and Son House. Old blues like that. Some Tom Waits and Leonard Cohen in there, too. Grumpy, cynical stuff. Broken hearts and spent shell casings and bars on the wrong side of the tracks. Like that.

Stuff I can sleep to.

When I can sleep.

Mostly, I can't sleep.

My room's always too crowded.

They are always there. It's usually when I'm alone that I see them. Pale faces standing in silence. Or screaming. Some of them scream.

I wear long sleeve shirts to bed because they scream the loudest when they see their own faces. It's like that. It's how it all works.

When I'm at the edge of sleep, leaning over that big black drop, I can feel the faces on my skin move. I can feel their mouths open to scream, too. Sometimes the sheet gets soaked with tears that aren't mine.

But which are mine now.

Olivia was there for the first time that night.

Standing in the corner, pale as a candle, looking far too young to be out this late. Thank god she wasn't one of the screamers. She was a silent one. She with her red necklace that went from ear to ear.

My name is Gerald Addison. Most people call me Monk.

I drink too much, and I hardly ever sleep.

And I do what I do.

INK

—1—

"What's this shit?" he said as he held the vial up to the light. "Looks like blood."

"Ink," I said.

He uncapped it and took a sniff. Winced. Gave me the stink-eye. "Fucking *smells* like blood."

I leaned against the doorframe and didn't say a word. This wasn't my usual tattoo parlor. I usually go to see my friend Patty Cakes who has a little skin art place just south of Boundary Street. It's a gritty little storefront tucked in between a leather bar called Pornstash and a deli called Open All Night, which, as far as anyone I know can tell you, has never been open. Patty never asks questions about where my ink comes from. She probably knows.

This guy, though ...? He doesn't know me all that well and I'm not a Chatty Cathy even when I'm in a good mood. Which I wasn't that night. There was a cold late September drizzle falling from a bruise-colored sky. Not actually night but dark enough for the shadow crowd to be out. The neon and back-alley types. The cruisers who want to hit every game in town in the hopes that they can find the luck they misplaced five or ten or twenty years ago.

Like me, I guess.

This parlor was called Switchblade Charlie's, but the guy holding my ink wasn't Charlie. His name was Cajun Joe. Probably had a switchblade, though. He looked the type. And there are types, even when it comes to knives. If he was bigger, I'd have figured him for a combat vet and that meant he might have a Ka-Bar or bayonet in a sheath tucked on the inside of his denim vest. If he was a little guy, he'd have a throwdown. Maybe a .22 or a .25. Something he could palm, something with all the serial numbers filed off. But this guy was medium height, medium weight, medium build, and medium aged. Call it forty and change. Younger than me, but only two-thirds as heavy. He had a nervous tic to his left eye and there was gristle around the eye and a cauliflower ear, so he probably picked that up from the ring. Could not have been very good because the good ones can afford the surgery to fix the cartilage damage, and they also don't work in shitholes like this one. His hands were steady, though, and his arms weren't overly developed. A guy who likes his speed and doesn't want to get slowed down by bulk. And he had a lot of skin art. Full sleeves, a collar rising to his ears, a burning cross on the back of his neck, and 88 in burning red on the inside of his left wrist. The two eights stand for the eighth letter of the alphabet—H and H. *Heil Hitler.* Cute. He also had "14" on his other wrist, on the arm of the hand holding the vial. That's shorthand for the fourteen-word credo of the white supremacy movement. The whole phrase is "We must secure the existence of our people and a future for white children."

So, yeah, a dickhead like Cajun Joe would probably carry a switchblade because those knives make a guy like him think he has a big dick and it makes other people scared. Too many 1950s gang flicks, too many movies since. People see a switchblade and they know they're going to bleed. You don't carry one to help you open packages or cut zip ties. You carry one when you want to cut someone and you like seeing them get terrified as they realize what's going to happen.

The tattoo artist stared at me, waiting for me to say something. I didn't.

"How do I know this stuff is safe?" he asked.

I shrugged. "The fuck is it to you?"

Cajun Joe thought about that, gave a shrug of his own. "Okay," he said.

"Okay."

"What kind of art you want?"

I was wearing a black hoodie with the sleeves pulled down, the hood pulled up, the zipper halfway to my throat. That hid most of the art I already had.

"Need you to finish a piece," I said. "Someone else started it but I need you to finish it."

"Like doing my own stuff," he said.

"You like getting paid?"

"Well ... yeah."

"That mean you'll finish the tat?"

He considered me for a moment, nodded. "What's the art?"

"A girl's face," I said and shoved up my left sleeve. My forearm is covered with faces. Girls and women, but also boys and men. So are my upper arms, chest, thighs, back. A lot of them. Nearly a hundred now, and plenty of room for more.

He grunted and gestured with the vial. "They're all black and white. You thinking about adding color? If so, then I got to use something else than what you brought or they're going to turn out like Indians."

"It's just the outline."

I turned my arm to show him the face. It was three-quarters done but there were bits missing. Part of the nose, some of the brow-shape, the corners of the mouth. Enough so that the face as it was looked generic. A woman. Not especially pretty, but female.

"It's all in black," he said. "It'll wind up two-toned."

I smiled. "That ink'll dry dark."

"It won't," he advised.

"It will."

Cajun Joe frowned at the vial, then cocked an eye at me. "You sure about that?"

"Dead certain."

"Okay," he said, giving me another and much more elaborate shrug. "It's your skin, brother."

I came real close to killing him right there and then. Some people can call me brother. Some can't. He shouldn't have.

—2—

When I took my hoodie off his eyes bugged at the faces already inked into my skin.

"That's some collection," he said.

"Yeah."

"They all friends of yours?"

"Not really."

"Movie stars ... 'cause some of them look familiar."

"Do they?" I asked as I hung my hoodie over the back of an empty chair.

"A little familiar. Is that one that chick from the Mad Max film? Charlie Theory?"

"Charlize Theron?"

"Yeah."

"No."

"Oh," he said. "She was hot in that flick, even if she had a robot arm."

"It's not Charlize Theron."

"Looks like her."

"Not really." I touched the tattoo. The woman whose face was inked into the inside curve of my deltoid was named Molly Flanders. A great Irish name for a great Irish American woman. Mother of two. RN at the ER over on the other side of Boundary Street. Dead now. Beaten to death by her husband because he wasn't man enough to face losing his job and because Molly got between him and the kids every time he was drunk. Molly died and so did her husband. Two separate but related incidents. Both very violent. I was involved in one of them. I put the husband in the ground and made it hurt all the way.

So, Molly was one of my people. One of the pale and quiet ones who come to see if they can hire me. I remember the first time I saw her, standing next to me at my corner booth at Dollar Bill's Tavern. Standing there with her swollen face, smashed lips, broken teeth, and broken neck. I'd tried to talk her out of hiring me. Tried to explain how expensive it was. Not in dollars. In other ways. But … after he'd killed her, Molly's rat-fuck husband had started in on the kids. One was in rehab now, learning to walk all over again. That was Kenny, ten years old, and he'd never walk without leg braces. The little one, Lindsay, two, would have to figure out how to make the world work without being able to see it. Doesn't take more than a drunk's fist to do unfixable damage to a kid's face.

Molly didn't want to go into the dark without knowing her husband had paid and paid hard. Going to jail wasn't enough. Not after what he'd done to the kids.

You see, that's how it usually works. The kind of clients who come looking for me don't want revenge for themselves. The price is way too high for that. Way too fucking high. No, they want me to step in when their killer is hurting—or in Molly's case, *has* hurt—others. Sometimes they want me to stop the bad guy before he does something else to someone else. They want me to do what the cops, with all of their limited resources and rules, can't. Or won't.

When a client wants to hire me on those terms, it means that they are willing to pay the price. Not my day-rate, which is what I get paid to find bail skips or take photos of philandering spouses. No, that kind of work is what I do for greasy lawyers and greasier bail bondsmen. Like J. Heron Scarebaby and Iver Twitch—real names of a couple of lowlifes who hire me out for conventional gigs.

No, clients like Molly and a hundred others have to pay a

higher price, but it's not to me. Not sure who they're paying. Who *we're* paying, because I owe something on that tab, too. Each time.

The price is a total bitch.

It's an absolute monster. I'm not sure I'd have the courage to pay it myself if I was in their shoes. And I didn't know about my debt until I took my first client. A village girl in Tibet who'd been gang-raped by Chinese soldiers. The same soldiers who'd raped seventeen other girls and killed six of them. The same soldiers who were garrisoned outside of her village. The village where the murdered girl had four sisters.

You see how it works?

I took that gig and hers was the first face inked onto my flesh. She's there, a few inches from my heart. Half an inch from a bullet wound I got in Iraq.

The girl and I both paid the price. And every single goddamn night we pay a little more of it.

Now I was here at Switchblade Charlie's. I watched Cajun Joe's eyes as he studied the faces on my skin. I usually keep covered up, but enough people have seen me without a shirt for me to have a good read on how they react. Cajun Joe was surprised at the number of tats, confused at the theme, and disapproving of the skill. Patty Cakes is a great tattoo artist, but I can't always provide a photo to work from. Sometimes Patty doesn't need one, not when she's totally in the zone. Sometimes she does. The tattoo artist in Tibet didn't. That girl had been his niece. We both wept and we both screamed at different times as he sank the ink onto my chest.

Cajun Joe told me to sit and when I did he moved a light on a flexible arm so that it bathed my arm. He bent and studied the partial tattoo.

"All you want is the lines connected?"

"Pretty much," I said.

"This is nothing. Anyone could have done this shit. Ten, fifteen minutes."

"I know."

Without raising his head, he glanced up at me. "But you were in the waiting room for two hours until I was free."

"Sure."

"Why me?"

"I heard you were the man for the job."

He sat back and studied me for a moment, suspicion flickering in his eyes. "Says who?"

I shrugged. "People. I asked around. Your name came up."

"Which people?"

"Hey, I came here for some ink, not to marry you," I said. "I'll pay the rate for a full tat."

The suspicion lingered and he shook his head. "You running a game on me or something?"

"No games," I said, and that was true enough. I wasn't there to play. "Word is that you're good and I don't use second string artists."

He glanced at the simplicity of the faces and maybe that's when he took a longer, better look. They looked simple, but they weren't. Not if you really looked at them. Patty Cakes did a lot of them, and she has the touch. So did that guy at the Tibetan village. And Mama Jewel in New Orleans. And each of the artists who have left their mark on me. Maybe not the best fine-artists in the world, but when you look into the eyes of each of those faces and you pay attention, you understand why people say the eyes are the window of the soul.

He made a sound. Not quite a word, not quite a grunt. More like an expression of wonder. Like when you stare at an optical illusion and you suddenly see the hidden message and realize that it was there all the time. Only now you can see it.

"So," I said, "are we good?"

He began nodding while still staring into the eyes of the dead faces on my skin. "Yeah," he said, then he looked up at me. "Yeah, we're good."

—3—

I unwrapped a piece of Juicy Fruit gum as I watched him pour some of the red juice in the vial into a little pot. He asked if it was okay for him to add some of his own ink and I said sure. The color of the mixture remained dark red, though, even after he mixed it fifty-fifty with black. That surprised him and he commented on it, asking again what was in that vial.

"It's special sauce," I told him as I put the stick of gum into my mouth. "What's it matter?"

It was clear he wanted to object, but in the end the matter was decided by the money he'd make doing half a quick job.

"You paying in cash?" he asked.

And I knew I had him.

"Yeah. Small unmarked bills."

We both had a chuckle over that. But he didn't reach for the tools until I pulled out my wallet and counted out a stack of twenties thick enough to look interesting.

Only then did he set to work.

Most tattoo artists ask to see your ID State laws about verifying age and all, but I have a face like an eroded wall, and I've been street legal for a lot of years. I look it. Besides, we both knew he was going to pocket whatever I paid him. That's why he didn't have me sign a waiver or provide my address and phone number. He could read enough about me to know that he shouldn't bother.

I settled into the tattoo chair. His workspace was shared but right now we were alone. The place used to be an old-fashioned barbershop and they still had four chairs. Someone had hung tracks for partition curtains, but they were all pulled back. The lights were low except around Cajun Joe's station, and the walls were covered with hundreds of designs. Books with thousands more. Devils and unicorns, pirate chicks and panthers, skulls and snakes. The usual shit. The stuff pinned to the wall behind Cajun Joe tended to have a rougher edge. Zombies with storm trooper helmets—and I'm not talking *Star Wars*. Swastikas and Confederate flags. And all kinds of crosses, some of them on fire.

He swabbed my arm with alcohol and then ran a disposable razor over it to remove any hair stubble. I didn't have much left on my arms.

A lot of studios use a thermal fax to make their stencils. This saves the artist the time he'd normally spend tracing a piece of art you bring in. Patty uses one for goofy shit like when people want a celebrity's signature or one of their own drawings. She never used one for the art she did for me, and since Cajun Jack was only finishing a face, he didn't have to. That allowed us to skip the step of having the scanned art transferred onto my skin.

Instead, he began prepping his tattoo machine. He took the mixed ink and poured it into one of those tiny cups they call an ink cap. He selected his needles and tubes from their sterile pouches and placed them into their slots in the machine. Then he added clean, distilled water into a cup for cleaning the needles during the tattoo process.

Some people pass out during a tattoo job. Not from the pain but from panic. The sight of the needles freaks them out. Not me, though. But I could feel my heartbeat quicken. Soon, I knew, it would begin to race. I could almost feel the sweat lurking inside my pores, ready to pop.

For me it's the actual pain. Not of the needle. Hell, no, that's just skin pain. What the fuck's that to someone like me? Who gives a small, cold shit about that?

No, it was part of the price I had to pay when I took a job that, as the face stopped being a collection of lines and became a person, something in that person woke up. And it woke inside of me. It started like a fever and then it turned into a scream.

Hard to explain.

Hard to sit through.

Patty Cakes usually insists I put a leather strap between my teeth. Helps to keep me from screaming. Makes it easier for her to work, though … she's very sensitive, you dig? Sometimes we both end up screaming.

Maybe Cajun Joe would end up screaming, too. Maybe we both would.

"How you want me to do this?" he asked. "You don't have a picture of this broad. How am I supposed to know what she's supposed to look like?"

"Connect the lines."

"Not as easy as that," he protested.

I had to work at it to keep the smile off my face. Not a happy smile. Not a friendly one, either. "I'm sure you'll make it right," I told him.

Cajun Joe took in a deep breath and exhaled through his nose. I was being weird and elusive, and it was trying his patience. I saw his eyes click over to the money on the side table and then back to the half-finished face.

He held up the needle and gave me an inquiring uptick of his chin. I gave him a nod.

He began to work.

—4—

The face looked like nobody for a while.

But I could feel her waiting to be seen.

Cajun Joe started with the jaw because that was the easiest to figure out. Most of the lines were done and it was simply a matter of connecting the chin to the jaw. It hurt, but it was still skin pain. I chewed my gum. Salt helps with nausea, but for me sugar helps with pain. This kind of pain. I sometimes went through a whole bag of M&M's or a big box of Dots when Patty was doing a face. That sanded maybe ten percent off the top of what I felt. Small mercies, but in this world you got to take what you can get.

"Who is she?" he asked as he connected the jaw to the cheek.

"A woman."

"I know that, but can you tell me something about her? Help me see her?"

Christ, I wanted to grab the needle out of his hand and stab him with it. The only reason I didn't is that I was not one hundred percent sure it was Cajun Joe I was looking for. After looking for two weeks he was at the top of my short list. Switchblade Charlie was on the list, too. And Bugsy the Mummy, another skin-jockey over on Shade Street, near that big club, Unlovely's. I had to be sure because otherwise I'm as bad as them. I'm really cool with righteous rage and harsh justice and all that movie vengeance shit, but collateral damage isn't in the game plan. Nor is an unfortunate accident. Making sure, being certain, makes this harder. It increases the risks, it ups the pain, and—for me and my client—it edges us closer to having to pay the whole ticket. If there was any way I could be certain without having the tattoo completed, then it would be a better end to the day. Not for Cajun Joe, mind you. But for my client. And for me.

Life is always a complicated motherfucker. Always, always, always.

So, sure, I decided to tell him something about her. Some of what I knew. But here's the thing ... I didn't actually know everything. I wouldn't ever get a full picture until there was ... well ... a full picture, you dig? All I had to work with was bits of memory. Tastes of it.

"She worked over on the west side," I said. "In one of the clubs."

"Waitress? Some of those bitches over there are hot. And I mean smokin'."

He worked on her eyebrow, matching the missing one to the other.

"Bartender?" he speculated. "She looks a little like this Italian girl works at Sparky's—"

"She's not Italian."

"Oh."

"Not a bartender."

"Oh."

"Prep cook. Worked in the kitchen," I said.

He finished the eyebrow. It was starting to hurt. A lot. I

waited for my comment to catch up with him. "Worked? She's not there anymore?"

"She moved on."

He cut me a quick look. "Ran out on you?"

"She's still around."

He laughed. "Yeah, I guess so. I mean, why else would you ink her onto your arm if she's gone, right?"

I said nothing. All of those faces, female and male, seemed to be looking at him. No, let me change that, they *were* looking at him. I could feel it. Feel them. In a strange way they were all there with me. Like they always are. I'm never really alone except when I go into my special quiet place inside. Meditation is the only thing that works better than sugar. It doesn't stop the pain, but it lets me be alone with my own thoughts. Right now, though, we were all watching Cajun Joe work.

He finished the eyebrow, paused, pursed his lips like a jeweler contemplating a cut, then thickened the line a little. He was good, he had moves, at least when it came to ink. He probably thought that he had all sorts of moves.

"What about her cheeks?" he asked. "They as high as they look, or do you want me to flatten them down?"

"Cheekbones are fine. Work on the hair."

He nodded. The hair was short and kinky. There was enough there for him to continue the shape and style. With every sting of the needle, I felt a knife turn in my heart. There was a big bell ringing, deep and slow, in the back of my head. The echoes hurt like punches. I was sweating now, and it took everything I had to keep it off my face and out of my voice.

"So, this chick," he said, "she your sweetheart or what?"

He was maybe trying to make conversation, maybe fishing for information.

"Never actually met her," I said.

The needle paused, hovering like a hornet above my skin. "What?"

Instead of answering I said, "Do the lips."

He studied me for a moment, his eyes coming in and out of

focus. "Um ..." he said, but left it there. Cajun Joe did a last touch on the hair, wiped the blood, and shifted to focus on the mouth. It was almost the last part of the image that would really matter. He started to work, stopped, bent to peer closer.

"Can't tell how they're supposed to be," he said.

"Full."

"What?"

"She had very full lips."

Something about that troubled him, I could see it on his face. But he said nothing as he dipped into the cup for more ink and started to shape the lips.

I wondered if she would scream when they were done. I might.

But I decided, no. The nose was the last thing. After that ... well, all bets were off after that.

The lips changed the whole picture, though.

"She looks ..." he began, but didn't finish it. His eyes were locked on the image. It was more than a picture. It was becoming the portrait it was meant to be. Dark eyes, short hair, good lines. Not beautiful by Hollywood standards. Beautiful by human being standards, but I doubted Cajun Joe was capable of grasping that.

Something was getting through to him, though.

I smiled through the pain. "Be careful, man, your hands are shaking."

He stopped abruptly, loaded more ink, but was looking at me. Hard. "You fucking with me, man?"

"No," I lied. "Just want to get this done and get on my way."

So many expressions came and went on his face. Doubt, anger, fear, confusion. Mixtures and combinations of those and more. He absolutely knew something was hinky about all this. Knew it. And he knew that I knew he knew it. It was like that, but we hadn't broken through the fourth wall yet. We were still actors playing out the roles assigned us by our shared participation in the drama of daily, ordinary life.

That wall was crumbling, though. With every drop of ink he

drilled into my skin, it was crumbling. And with every drop I was getting closer to the truth. Soon I was going to know. Soon it was going to be certain. Either he was the guy, or he wasn't.

Right now, though, his doubt was holding that wall in place. He hadn't flipped into an open and obvious knowing. There was no guilt in his eyes. Not yet.

That needed more ink.

So, I waited while he thought about it, waited while he decided to go back to the job. Watched and waited while he finished the lips.

"The nose," I said. "That's the last part."

There was very little to the nose. I'd left that part intentionally vague. Patty had understood when she did her part. The nose would clinch it, even in a black and white tat.

"What kind of nose does she have?" he asked. Was there a crack in his voice? Was it a little hoarse?

I couldn't tell.

Almost, but not quite.

"Short nose," I said, touching my arm to indicate where it should end. "Long philtrum. You know what a philtrum is? The gulley under the nose?"

"Yeah," he said softly. "I know."

"Long philtrum. Pretty deep, too."

He cleared his throat. "And her nose?"

"Do the other part first."

He did. It hurt. I bled. We both sweated. The room was cold but we both had lines running crookedly down our faces. He had a drop hanging from the point of his chin.

It seemed to take forever to finish the gulley above those full lips.

"Now the nose," I said, and I traced it on my skin with the tip of my index finger. "This long. Wide. Kind of flat from where she got it broken when her first husband knocked her around. Never set right."

Sweat ran like hot mercury down his face.

"The fuck is this?" he asked.

34

"It's a tattoo," I said. "Finish the nose and then I'm gone."

He began to work on it, but his hands were shaking pretty bad. It wasn't going to be his best work and I'd have to wear it for the rest of my life. Life sucks in a lot of ways and that part wasn't anything major. I could see the muscles at the corner of his jaw bunching, and I knew he was getting mad, too.

Mad was okay. We could work with it.

He worked on the nose, following my directions and suggestions. The more it took form the slower he worked. The nose made the face, you see. It pulled all of the parts together. It made it a very specific kind of face. Even in black and white. Even without the dark brown skin and the darker brown eyes that she had when she was alive. That nose and those lips turned the face from generic woman to black woman.

That's what he realized as he worked.

I watched him to see what that realization would do to him. That he was a racist dickhead was evident from the 88 and 14 tats. But being a racist dickhead isn't enough. Free country, free speech, and all that shit. I don't go hunting for everyone whose philosophy pushes my ideological buttons. I'm not a fanatic and I'm not a sociopath.

I'm something else, and that something else needed this guy to be a very specific kind of racist dickhead.

I needed him to look at that face and do more than realize he was inking the features of an African American woman on a customer's arm. Again, that was nothing. Like me, he probably inked all sorts of shit *he* didn't believe in. Nature of the game in a free country.

I'm not an artist but I've had enough tattoos to know something about it. There is a point when a collection of lines and curves stops being arranged ink and becomes an actual piece of art. I think it's when the subject matter comes into true alignment with the artist's technique. It's a kind of magic. The image becomes real, and when you look at it you're not seeing a painting or a drawing or a tattoo. You're not even seeing the stylized version of it that has been filtered through the artist's talent. You're seeing the actual thing. Look at Van Gogh's *Café Terrace at Night* and tell me you can't hear the sounds of laughter and conversation, of coffee cups clinking on saucers, of cutlery tinking against plates or scraping on teeth, of the gurgle of wine as it's poured into glasses. Tell me you can't smell that wine, and the bread, the cheese, the meats. I can look at that painting, even a copy of it, and smell cigarette smoke, perfume, and fresh-cooked fish. Same goes for when I look at Gauguin's *Tahitian Women on the Beach*. If you can't smell coconut oil on warm skin and hear the soft crash and hiss of the surf, then you have no soul.

When Cajun Joe finished the last part of the nose, joining the lines that formed the right nostril, the face on my arm became a person. A woman. Not the representation of a murdered woman, but her. Actually her. Alive. Not in the way she had been before she'd been beaten and raped and slashed to red ruin. And not a ghost version of her. When I looked down at her face I saw the essential woman. The truth of her. The reality of her.

It was so powerful because that acceptance of her kicked open a door in my head and my heart. Kicked it off the hinges and let all of her life pour into me. From the moment she woke up in her mother's womb until they zipped her into a body bag. I saw all of her life. It hit me in a rush, and it felt like having forty-eight years of joy, pain, understanding, love, passion, ennui, compassion, dislike, hatred, giddiness, pity, and ten thousand other emotions shoved into me through that five-inch tattoo. I mainlined her entire life and the inrush nearly tore me apart.

All of the seventeen thousand five hundred and twenty days of her life.

How many emotions does a person experience in an average day? How many in each hour? If it was even possible for a person to feel only two different emotions in any given hour that meant that eight hundred and forty thousand individual needles of awareness stabbed into me.

In five or ten seconds.

I threw my head back and screamed.

What else could I do?

Cajun Joe staggered backward from his chair, his needles and the pots of ink falling and tumbling, clinking and splashing. I was aware of it but didn't see it. Not really. All I could see was the woman's life. Rushing, tumbling, kicking, slashing as it whirled around in my head.

And then the images suddenly slowed, crystalized as they do every time I go through this. First, it's the tsunami of their life's emotions and then … then …

And then it's the memories of what happened in those last few moments of her life. Those last terrible moments.

The hands grabbing her as she pulled the kitchen door closed and stepped into the darkened parking lot behind the club. Her ring of keys—the bar key, her car key, her house key—tinkled to the blacktop. Hands on her. An arm around her neck to choke off her screams. Another hand reached around, clamped on her stomach to pull her backward from the security light, into the shadows. Turning her, slapping her, a fist driving into her stomach, knocking the air and the hope from her. The hands grabbing cloth, ripping, exposing.

Lips on her flesh. Lips forming words. Hateful words. Calling her a bitch, a whore, a nigger slut as he ripped her clothes and forced her down and swarmed over her like a blanket of hate.

She'd fought him.

She was a woman who worked nights and worked in a club that wasn't in the best part of town. She had pepper spray in her bag, but her bag was gone. She tried to punch, to claw, to bite. She fought to live. For her kids. For her sisters of color who had been consumed by monsters of this kind for hundreds of years. For women of every kind. For her own life.

And the man—if that word even fits—laughed at her and took her over and over again. Hitting her, breaking her. Destroying her.

What was left after the rape was unable to even move. Totally unable to fight.

The knife hadn't been necessary.

Except it had.

In that last moment, while she lay already dying, she had seen the face of the man who had done this. His face. His clothes.

And his tattoos.

HH.

14.

The world spun and spun around me, but I forced myself back into the moment. Even with her screaming in my head, I returned to who and what I was and why I was there.

Cajun Joe stared at me and at *her*. I knew he could see her face on my arm, but more importantly he could see her soul in my eyes.

He was sweating and shaking. Equal parts terror and rage. And hate. Let's not forget the hate. Lot of hate in that room.

"What the fuck are you?" he breathed.

I said, "My name is Denita King."

It was my voice, but it wasn't me speaking.

Cajun Joe had a switchblade in his hand. I hadn't even seen him pull it. Four-inch blade, glistening with oil. Sturdy, good for fighting.

I smiled at him as I got up out of the chair.

It may have been Mrs. King who'd spoken with my mouth, but that smile was all my own. My hands were my own. My fingers, my fists.

He screamed so loud, and he screamed for a long time.

—5—

Back at my place. In my room with all the windows painted black. Lying in bed, praying for sleep, knowing it wouldn't come. Not unless I drank all the lights out.

It's hard to sleep in such a crowded room.

They're always there. Always standing around my bed. Pale faces, gray faces. Most of them are silent. They stand there and stare at me, and sometimes at their own faces on my skin.

Mrs. King was there now. She wasn't silent. She was one of the screamers. She'd loved being alive. She'd loved her kids. And she'd fought so damn hard.

She screamed.

And she'd scream like that every night for as long as I lived. That was the price and we'd both been willing to pay it.

God damn it.

My name is Gerald Addison. Most people call me Monk.

Tomorrow I'll get up, get washed, and maybe I'll spend the day chasing a bail skip. Or maybe a client will find me.

I lay there at night and listened to the screams.

And the night closed around me like a fist.

GRIT

Her name was Betty.

All diners should have a waitress named Betty. Or Babs. Maybe Brenda. Something with a B.

This one was a Betty and she was a classic example of the type. You know what I mean. Lots of hair, combed and sprayed so that it wouldn't get messy in a typhoon. Frosted, too, because that hair color doesn't have a correlation in nature. Not supposed to.

Betties usually have a good rack, nice legs, but there's a little bit of middle age in the rump and the stockings maybe hide some veins. Bra's a push-up because, you know, gravity. Shoes are practical because she's on her feet all goddamn day. Must have fifty extra aprons 'cause hers is always clean. Couple of pins on her uniform. Cats, dragonflies. Like that. Once in a while it's seasonal. Christmas tree or a wreath. Wears a plastic nametag or has her name stitched across one boob. If she has glasses then she has a chain so she can dangle them, and even when she wears them it's halfway down her nose. Lipstick and a perfume that's not expensive but it's nice to smell. You remember that smell, even beneath the scent of coffee, eggs, Salisbury steak, beef stew, and regret.

Like I said, you know what I mean.

This Betty was at the diner at the corner of Boundary Street and Tenth. If the place has a name nobody ever bothered to put it up in lights. Everyone I know calls it "the diner," as if there's only one. There are other diners—in this part of town it's diners, bars, or pizza joints. Nothing else, not even fast food. Those other diners have names. Lucky Pete's, Stella's, American Dollar. But this one was just The Diner. And it had a really good Betty.

I was at the counter because I don't like booths. Counters are where the action is. Booths are where you sit when you want to talk somebody into something. The farther back the booth the less legal the conversation. I wasn't here for that sort of thing. I mean, sure, I do some pretty questionable stuff, but I skate on this line of the law because when you're a skip tracer you have special dispensations from the Constitution. I can kick doors a cop can't touch without losing a case. I can do all sorts of hinky shit, but it's legal. Kind of.

Ethical ...?

Yeah, not so much.

Mostly I work for six or seven bail bondsmen on Boundary Street, though most of my steady gigs come from Scarebaby & Twitch. I'm serious, that's their real names. J. Heron Scarebaby and Iver Twitch. Fucking Addams Family names, but I ran a background check on them and those are their hand-to-God birth names. I guess the fact that they found each other, became friends, and hung out a shingle is some kind of fate. Or maybe it's one of those jokes fate plays on the world but doesn't care whether you ever hear or understand the punch line. Whatever.

Scarebaby is a lawyer and Twitch is his investigator. They do criminal law, and talk about truth in advertising. I'm pretty sure all of their clients, even the ones they got acquitted, are actually criminals. Guilty as sin, and either too desperate or too stupid to get better representation. If Scarebaby gets you acquitted, you will owe him a lot of whatever you make for the rest of your life.

He owns you. I know for a fact that a lot of his clients do more crimes after being let out of jail because they need to pay off those legal fees. When someone's either crazy or sane enough to want to try and run farther than they can grab, I get a call. The job blows, the pay isn't bad, they give me really good bottles of bourbon for Christmas, and they don't need me to like them. The real perk of the job is the certain knowledge that no one I chase down for them is an innocent schnook being unfairly charged. So, I can do what I need to do to close the assignment out.

Today, though, I was off the clock. I wasn't here to meet them or to get a tip on a bail skip. I was here for coffee, the sports section of the paper, a grease-burger with cheese and chili, and my own thoughts. Didn't mind at all looking at Betty. She didn't mind being looked at, but I knew that was as far as it went. Little bit of banter that was on the PG-13 side of flirty and never, ever went any further.

It was a Tuesday night in that gap between Thanksgiving and Christmas. People who gave a shit were out shopping. The whole city was full of them. Walking over here from my office was like a salmon swimming upstream, except I wasn't going to get laid or, hopefully, eaten by a bear. I let the shoppers flow around me, and I guess I'm about as big, solid, ugly, and conversational as a rock, so they swirled past and let me be. Which was fine. Every once in a while, one of them would take a closer look. I'm bigger and wider than most and no one's called me handsome since a hooker in Shanghai and she pretty much had to. I don't look evil, but I do look mean. People get that and they don't stop to engage, and only the complete maniacs wish me a "Happy" anything.

The Diner was a refuge for anyone who wanted a quiet night. Sure, people sometimes found me there, but never for idle chatter. Betty could even tell when I wanted to shoot the shit and when I didn't. She always smiled, though, and on a cold night on a dark street like this one, that smile was usually the warmest part of the day.

Except today.

I was tired and didn't catch it right away, but when she refilled my cup and turned away, I saw her smile change. It slipped, like a mask that wasn't tied in place very tightly. In the act of turning away to return the coffee carafe to the heater her smile changed from Betty's normal no-problems red lips and white teeth to something unhappy and even a little unhealthy. And she was quick, because she saw me see the change and instantly upped the wattage. She could fake it the way a lot of lonely women looking close at the fine print of middle age could fake it. And maybe if I wasn't used to studying people and getting a read on them I might have bought the con.

When I continued to look at her for a few seconds too long, she realized that I wasn't going to pretend I hadn't seen something. I mean, sure, I didn't know *what* I'd seen, but it was something. There'd been some pain there. Some sadness, too. And something else. Shame? No. Fear. Sometimes they look the same. It's a wince, a flinching away from a thought.

I picked up my paper and my coffee cup and walked over to a booth. Halfway back, on the quiet side of the diner. And waited.

—2—

In a couple of minutes Betty showed up at my table and set the plate down. New burger and a side of fries. I'd left half my burger on the plate at the counter. She had a tuna melt with chips on a plate for herself.

"Join you?" she asked, as if that was a question.

Sometimes the formalities matter. I folded my paper and dropped it on the bench seat next to me and watched as she slid in. She didn't launch immediately into an unburdening of her soul. Some people will, but most have to work up to it, even when they come to me. This was me kind of letting her know that I knew something was up. Betty knew me, knew what I did for a living. Not just the gigs I did for Scarebaby and Twitch, but the other stuff. Some people know about that. They see the tattoos I have inked onto my skin, and they hear stories around this part of town. This is the part of town where stories like that get told.

We ate.

The short order cook had on a station that was playing Christmas songs. I don't do Christmas and I don't pay much attention to Christmas songs. But there was one song they kept playing at least once an hour, so now I *did* know it. Enough to be really fucking tired of Mommy kissing Santa and instilling in her child the belief that his mom was cheating on his dad with some fat fuck from the North Pole. There's a therapy bill waiting to happen.

I caught Betty's eyes flicking over to the tats visible on my forearms. I usually wear a leather jacket, but it was warm inside the diner, and I even had my sleeves rolled up. I watched her eyes move from one face to another. That's what they are. Faces. All over my body. Not every inch, though. Not yet. I knew that there would be more faces I'd need to add. It's like that, and Betty knew it. That was obvious.

"How many?" she asked. First thing she'd said in five minutes.

"I don't count them."

"A lot?"

I shrugged.

"Does it ..." she began, faltered, took a breath and tried again. "Does it hurt?"

Another shrug. What's the point of going into that part of it? The tats hurt when the ink's being drilled into me. But that wasn't what she was asking. That kind of pain doesn't mean shit. People get tattoos for fun. No, she was asking about whether having those particular tats hurt *me*. Because of what they are.

She looked away out the window. Even down here on Boundary the streets swirled with people. Stores had colored lights up, stoplights and cop car lights kept it all moving. Big Smalls was across the street dressed in a Salvation Army coat, ringing a bell. You had to be legally blind to believe he was anything but what he looked like, which was a crack head trying to work the rubes for small change. There were real people down here, but most of them had stopped being rubes after they'd already been conned. If you lived or worked on Boundary Street, you understood the game. Even so, a few of the locals tossed coins into his bucket. After all, Big Smalls was one of us.

Without turning to look at me, Betty said, "I wasn't going to bother you with it. I suppose this really isn't your kind of thing."

"I do a lot of things," I said.

"No … I mean, the kind of *special* things you do."

Special. Interesting word for it. I know people talk about me, and a few of them even know the deal. Or some of the deal. Nobody knows all of it except my tattoo artist, Patty Cakes, who has a little skin art place just off Boundary, right between a glam bar called Pornstash and a deli called Open All Night, which, to my knowledge, has never been open. Apart from Patty, the other people who know only have a bit of the story. They know I have the faces of certain clients inked onto my skin. I do that when I'm looking for a killer, and a little bit of the victim's blood is mixed in with the ink. It does something, creates a bond. I can't see everything, but I see enough. Sherlock Holmes would call them clues, but it feels more like I'm actually there with the vic, feeling the bullets or blades or beatings. Feeling and seeing the last few seconds of their lives. Dying with them. If they saw—or in some cases *knew* their killers—then that would give me a starting place. If they didn't know who killed them and never saw the perp's face, then I'd have to start from scratch. So far, I only have a few cases of that kind in my "open" file.

Some of the perps I'm able to track go to trial. Not with me on the witness stand, let's be real. But remember, I'm a bounty hunter and I know how to get the goods on people. I don't play by any rules but my own. And, sure, I've had to sometimes drop anonymous dimes on the bad guys, or blind-mail evidence, or even spook them into confessions once or twice.

Not all of the bad guys go to trial. Not even half. Sometimes there's no way the system is going to be able to touch them. I *can* touch them. So to speak.

But, like I said, those are special cases, and it's usually the victim who reaches out to me. Read that any way you want and you'll get close to how it works. Not nice, not pleasant, not fun. And once the case is over those vics are with me for the long haul. Their blood's in my skin. People talk about being haunted, but they don't know what that really means. No fucking way.

I said nothing. Ate a few fries. Waited for Betty.

"People say you know stuff. They say that you understand what people are going through."

I dipped a fry in ketchup, ate it, looked at her.

"I think you saw something just now," she said. "When you looked at me."

"Something," I said.

We sat for a bit. The other waitress was handling the few customers. New kid. Her name was Kristen. Not really a diner waitress name, so I figured she wouldn't last.

"It's my nephew," said Betty. "He died last week."

"How?"

Her eyes clicked toward mine, held for a microsecond, then fell away. "You probably heard about it. Over by the projects?"

Sure, I'd heard about it. Everyone around here had. The William Lloyd Garrison Community Housing Project was the official name, but I doubt anyone's called it that since they broke ground back in the seventies. It was "the projects." Nine five-story drab brick buildings erected around a playground and common area that was probably a needle park before the first tenants moved in. Poor white, poor black, poor Latino, and poor melting pot all shoved into cheap apartments with flimsy doors, suck-ass security, sub-standard plumbing, and no hope at all. Over the years, a few lucky souls managed to get the hell out, but you couldn't call it a majority. Not even close. A lot of people grew old and died there. Of the nine buildings, only three are in moderately decent shape, and by that I mean they aren't active crack houses or simply falling down. Two are condemned; one's a burned-out shell.

But what Betty was talking about was the kid who got so high in one of the crack pads that he thought he could fly. Or something. Witnesses say he fell right out of the fifth-floor window on one of the buildings. Did a turn and a half on the way down and landed in the pike position. Which is a smartass way of saying he took a header onto the concrete. Smashed his head, snapped his spine and probably never knew what he hit.

"He was your nephew?" I asked.

She nodded. "Jimmy. James O'Neill. He was only nineteen." Betty sniffed. "Jimmy was my little sister's only kid. Sherrie doesn't live here in the city; she's out in the suburbs. Got a nice house with her second husband. She's a teller at a Wells Fargo out there."

"Uh huh."

"Jimmy was a good kid until sophomore year. He went out drinking with some other kids—first time for him, I think—and they got really drunk. Sick drunk. One of the kids was a senior and had his parents' car. They … well, there was an accident. The papers said that the car never even tried to brake when it went through the red light over on the main drag that goes through Japantown. Their car hit an SUV." She sniffed and shook her head. "Oh, god, it was horrible. There was a woman in the other car bringing her daughter home from dance class. They were both killed. And the little girl was only nine."

"Jesus. What about the kids Jimmy was with?"

"There were two others and they … well, the boy who was driving wasn't wearing a seatbelt. He went partway through the window. They said he died on impact. The other one was Jimmy's best friend. He was on life support for seventeen months before the family had him disconnected."

I nodded. That was on the news, too. Kid was a straight-A student.

"Jimmy was the only one who survived the crash," said Betty. "And he was awake the whole time. He saw everything.

Saw all that blood. Saw his friends ... and the woman and her ..."

I touched her wrist to let her know that she didn't need to jam broken glass into her own skin by telling me the rest.

"What happened to Jimmy after that?"

"He was expelled and there were charges, but because he was the youngest and was in the backseat the judge went easy on him. The husband of the dead woman sued his family, though, and my sister had to cash in her 401(k), all of their stocks, their savings, and sell their house to pay the legal bills. They bought this little one bedroom place and Jimmy had to sleep on the couch because there was no room, you know?"

I sighed, getting the picture. Horror, followed by general guilt and survivor's guilt. That's a witches brew few adults could handle, let alone a kid.

"When did he start in on the drugs?" I asked.

She dug a tissue out of her uniform pocket and dabbed at her eyes. I have always found it interesting, and kind of sexy, that women will be careful of their eye makeup no matter how much their heart is breaking. "His folks tried to get him into other schools, but no one really wanted him. They tried homeschooling, but that was a mess. My sister and her husband had to work all the time to pay their bills, you know?"

"Sure."

"Sherrie doesn't know when Jimmy started using. Or maybe she did because she told me later that money was always missing from her purse. And some stuff around the house."

"Stuff a kid could pawn?" I suggested.

"Yes. But when Jimmy was arrested, the cops told Sherrie that he was a junkie." She picked her shoulders up and dropped them as she sighed, long and heavy. "They couldn't afford rehab or counseling. Not a good shrink, anyway. They made him go to NA meetings, but you know how that is. You have to want to work the program."

"And Jimmy didn't?"

"No," she said, "I think by then he was already lost."

I've heard a lot of sad shit in my life. More than most people. But sitting there with this woman, hearing the echoes of the deep grief in her voice, seeing the brave little smile she kept hoisting up so I didn't have to see her pain ... fuck, man. That was one of the saddest things I ever heard.

I leaned forward and took her hands. It was a liberty, a line that she hadn't invited me to cross, but I trusted her to know that it wasn't any kind of come on. She looked at my big, knuckly, scarred hands, and then she curled her fingers around mine and held on for dear life.

—3—

"So how do you think I can help?" I asked. "I don't mean to be a prick, but I've heard this story a thousand times. Kid loses his hold on the world, bottoms out, and then decides leaving is better than staying." There was a song lyric about life being bigger than the strength he had to get up off his knees. Something like that, but it wasn't the time to quote a song to her, not even a country and western song.

"The cops and the news people all said that he killed himself," said Betty.

"But—?"

She chewed her lip for a moment and then nodded as if she had come to a decision. Then she dug her cell phone out of her pocket. An Apple model that has been out of style so long I'd be surprised if they were still updating the operating system. Small, with a tiny screen. But she brought up her messages, scrolled through, sighed again, then turned the phone around and slid it across to me. I bent to read the screen display, and then used my forefinger to scroll up a bit so I could see more of the conversation. It was a short series of texts between Jimmy and his aunt. Jimmy had written to ask her for some cash, and she was pretty blunt in her response.

BETTY: U know I won't give U $ for that.

JIMMY: Not 4 that.

BETTY: ??

JIMMY: Need 2 get out. All weird here now.

BETTY: What do you mean?

BETTY: What's wrong?

The time code said that it was over ten minutes before Jimmy answered that post.

JIMMY: The stuff's all wrong.

BETTY: What stuff.

JIMMY: U know. Grit.

I glanced at Betty. Grit was one of the street names for crack cocaine. There were a lot of cute names for it. Cloud, gravel, nuggets, piece, raw, 24-7, bad-rock, scrabble, sleet. Like that. Maybe it makes it taste better. Who the fuck knows and, more to the point, who the fuck cares?

BETTY: What do U mean 'wrong'?

JIMMY: He knows I know it's bad. But he's selling it anyway. Says there's no more til this is gone.

JIMMY: A girl I knew got sick. They took her away.

JIMMY: Other kids, too.

JIMMY: Couple of kids in the project OD'd. But that's nuts. Wasn't enough to do that.

JIMMY: My friend Rix ran right into traffic. He was all wrong. I'm scared.

BETTY: U need help.

JIMMY: He's crazy. He knows it's bad. He doesn't care.

There was no more.

I looked up at Betty and there were fresh tears in her bright eyes.

"He wrote that to me at 5:21 that afternoon," she said. "The police report says he went out of the window at 5:30."

I sat back. "Who is 'he'? Who's the cat Jimmy was talking about? You know his name? Know anything about him?"

Her eyes darkened. "Jimmy talked about him a lot, but all he ever told me was his nickname. His street name, I guess. Dill."

"Ah," I said.

She frowned. "You know him?"

"*Of* him. Marcus Dillman," I corrected. "I work for bail bondsmen, and we always hear shit. What do *you* know about him?"

"I know he's a dealer."

"Yeah, he is. What else?"

"Not much, but I believe that Jimmy was telling me the truth," she said, and when I didn't comment, she added, "He never lied to me. To his folks, sure. To everyone else. Never to me."

"Okay," I said. "What else do you have other than Jimmy's word?"

"Nothing," said Betty. "I tried asking around, but nobody wants to talk about anything. They're afraid to. Somebody's always listening, you know?"

"Sure. There's no percentage in diming the bad guys when they live there, and the cops don't."

She nodded. "I was there this morning, but when I pulled up to the building where Jimmy was staying—squatting, I guess, though he called it crashing—there were two guys leaning against the wall. Like they were watching for me to come back because as soon as I parked, they pushed off the wall and started walking right toward my car."

"What'd you do?"

"What could I do? I left and I'm afraid to go back."

"Smart. Don't go back. Don't even think about it."

"But the cops aren't even looking into it. They marked Jimmy as a suicide and because of his record they don't even care that he died."

I nodded. "They *don't* care. They don't have a reason to care, and they don't have the time or manpower to care. That's how it is, especially in this part of town. Nobody much cares."

"I care," she said fiercely. She balled her fists and pounded the table. Not loud enough for anyone else to hear, but loud enough for me to see the fire inside her. "If no one else will help then I *will* go back. Jimmy knew something and he wanted out.

He was scared of this guy, Dill, and he knew something, and that got him killed."

"Killed? You're saying he didn't fall out of the window?"

"Jimmy didn't commit suicide, if that's what you're asking," she snapped.

"It's what I'm asking."

"Well … he didn't."

"Maybe he got stoned and didn't know what he was doing. Or maybe Dill was selling some bad junk and Jimmy took a bad high," I said, then before she could say anything I said, "No."

The timing was all wrong for that. He wouldn't have been firing up a crack pipe while he was texting his aunt for runaway money. I couldn't sell that to myself any more than Betty could.

How had Jimmy put it? *My friend Rix ran right into traffic. He was all wrong. I'm scared.*

Jesus.

I took a small bite of the burger, chewed it, didn't taste it at all, put it down, looked across at her. "What do you want me to do?"

It took her a moment to actually say it. If she really had known about how the tattoos worked and what it cost me to go as far as getting one inked onto my skin, then maybe she wouldn't have asked. Jimmy was her nephew, sure, and clearly she loved the kid, but he was dead long before he went out that window. He probably died in that car crash, and maybe should have. I don't know. I'm not a therapist and I'm not a saint. But I've seen people who have tried to live past their own expiration date. I saw the tortured ghosts they became, haunting their own lives. Sure, some of them can be saved, but coming back to life is a lot like working the Twelve Steps—you have to want to do the work. Some people don't. Some people want to be dead and are simply taking the long way around. And some people—and my guess is that Jimmy was one of them—needed to do some penance. Being alive was exactly the same as being in hell for their sins, and they had just enough self-respect to not want to

JONATHAN MABERRY

dodge that responsibility. It's fucked up and it's miles past sad, but there it is.

It took Betty a lot to ask. It took all of her love for her nephew, it took compassion for anyone else this Dill cocksucker might hurt, it took her personal courage, and it took every atom of her battered pride.

"Can you find out who killed Jimmy?" she asked, her voice rough with emotion. "Can you find out why?"

The clock on the wall above the door was one of those big, industrial battery-operated clunkers that ticked very loudly. The jukebox was between songs and the Christmas noise from the street seemed muted. I listened to a lot of seconds being chopped off by the sharp blade of the ticking hand of that ugly clock.

"Yeah," I said. "I'll find out."

—4—

Here's the thing.

I wasn't taking a case to do a full-blown investigation. Because I'm a skip tracer in this town it means I had to get a PI license, but Betty wasn't hiring me to collect evidence and build a case that we could take to the local police. She was too much of a decent person to ask what she really wanted.

Not sure the word "revenge" is the right word. And "justice" is too corny.

Maybe the word is "payback," but that's pretty trite, too.

Whatever it was, she asked and I said yes.

It was getting late, and if this was a normal gig I'd wait for daylight and maybe even put on a sports coat and try to look normal.

Instead, I left the Diner and walked the five blocks to the projects. The holiday shoppers were thinning out because nice people don't go out in the dark in this part of town. Not twice. Because the later it gets the more the neighborhood looks like what it is.

The streets were dry, and we hadn't had any rain in weeks.

That was good because I was able to find the spot outside of the building where Jimmy stuck the landing. In nicer neighborhoods someone—the cops or the building super—hoses down the pavement so there's nothing horrible to see. This isn't one of those neighborhoods, so the red splotch was still there. It didn't look like anything. Just a mess. A central impact point and tendrils of blood spatter going out as far as the blacktop. He'd fallen five stories, so he'd had time to build up some speed.

There were people around, but no thugs leaning on the wall, so I knelt and used the blade of a Boy Scout knife to scrape some dried flakes of blood into a little glass vial. I keep a couple of those in my jacket pocket for this kind of thing. They look like crack vials. The next step would be to take the vial over to Patty Cake and have her mix it with ink. Sometimes she'd roll a blunt and we'd both get baked before she set to work. Sometimes it was Kentucky whiskey. Sometimes we did it just on nerves. A lot of it depended on what kind of vibe we were getting from just being on the fringes of a new case. Or maybe the ghosts would be breathing cold air on the back of our necks and freaking us out. Even I don't know which.

I straightened, listening to the creak and pop of my knees, looking around at the desolation of this place. It looked like a demilitarized zone, but people lived there. Lights burned in a few of the windows of the other buildings and in one I saw the silhouette of a Christmas tree and as I stared at it the little twinkly lights came on. Nobody here had an extra dime, but there was someone who bought a tree and was willing to pay the bump in the electricity bill to let it shine. That kind of optimism made me want to cry.

As I turned to go, I saw that there was someone standing by a burned-out shell of a stripped car. A skinny young man wearing a hoodie and stained jeans. Sneakers with graffiti on them, hands jammed into his pants pockets, shoulders hunched against the cold. It wasn't actually too bad out, but he didn't have an ounce of meat on his bones.

I walked over and stopped in front of him. His face was almost invisible inside the shadows of his hood.

"Hey, Jimmy," I said.

He said nothing. Just looked at me. One eye was all red, the other was blue. He wasn't a good-looking kid, and maybe some of the guilt of what happened a few years ago was his, but not as much as I saw haunting his eyes.

"You know why I'm here?" I asked.

He nodded.

"Your Aunt Betty loves you," I said. "You know that, right?"

Another nod. His face was covered with blood and bits of brain and bone. He looked fucking awful. I saw tears rolling through all that muck.

"Tell me something straight, kid," I said. "Did you get wasted and walk out the window?"

He didn't move.

"Or did Dill do something to you?"

A fresh set of tears rolled down.

"Why?" I asked. "Was it something you saw?"

He looked at me. I knew he wanted to talk, but he couldn't. They can't until I have their faces inked onto me, and after that they were stuck with me. And me with them. This wasn't about justice, and somehow Jimmy knew it the same way they all knew it. If I inked his face onto my flesh, then sure, I'd be able to know how he died. Know it for sure, but it meant that Jimmy would join the parade of other pale ghosts that were always with me. Nobody could see them but me, but they were always there. At night, when I tried to sleep, they stood around my bed. Some of them were silent, and maybe Jimmy would be one of those. Some were screamers. They screamed and screamed and screamed. They would scream until my heart finally stopped beating. And none of us—not them or me—knew if that would put an end to it. If I died, would they move on? Or would we all be in that purgatory together forever?

Yeah. It's like that for me. Pretty sure Betty didn't know all of it. She'd never have asked me. She wasn't one of the cruel ones. If she'd known, she'd have either kept poking around until someone scraped her up off the pavement, or she'd eat her pain like a piece of poison, knowing full well that it would kill her one of these days. Sooner than her time.

I waited for something from Jimmy. A sign, a sense of what he wanted. If he needed revenge of some kind, then it would be up to me to make a call. I'd given my word to his aunt, but all I promised in words was to look into it. I hadn't promised to go any deeper than that.

No, I'd made that promise to myself.

God damn it.

Jimmy turned and looked past me, and I followed his gaze to see two figures approach a small metal utility door on the side of the building. Two girls. Maybe minors or maybe emaciated adults. Put them both together and I outweigh them by eighty pounds. As the door opened, I caught a brief image of a man's face in the doorway. Older, not wasted, shaved head, dark eyes, hard mouth. He also wore a hoodie, but he looked clean and fit.

Without turning to Jimmy, I said, "Dill?"

I didn't need him to answer. It's why Jimmy was here, right now.

We watched the two girls go inside. Dill leaned out and looked around. He saw me. I don't look like a cop. I don't even look like an undercover cop. I'm big, square, ugly, and anyone can tell there's something not right about me. People like Betty see one kind of thing. People like Dill see something else. He gave me five full seconds of a hard, flat stare, and then he closed the metal door.

"You know those girls?" I asked Jimmy.

His hood moved indecisively. Could have been a nod, could have been a shake. Not sure it mattered. He knew Dill. He knew something about Dill that made him willing to risk coming to me.

And that put us both out on the edge of the cliff.

I had three options. One was go home, watch some TV shit with the sound turned up and drink myself to sleep. Typical day for me.

Option two was go over to Patty Cake's and give her the vial. Let her do her thing. Light the fuse.

Or ...

Or maybe this wasn't that complicated. Maybe it didn't have to be.

I looked around at the buildings here in the projects. There's not a lot of life here and there's fuck-all when it comes to grace, or hope, or luck.

Except every once in a while.

I looked at the vial, held it up to so that I could see those little Christmas lights through the curved glass. They made the flakes of dried blood look like dust. Jimmy came around and stood in front of me. I could still see the lights through him. Ghosts, you know?

I held the vial out to him and he frowned at me, not getting it. Then he tentatively reached out his hand, palm upward. I dropped the vial. It fell through his hand, hit the ground, and cracked apart.

"This one's on the house," I told him as I began walking toward the building. Then I paused and turned to look at him. "Your Aunt Betty never gave up on you, kid. Never. Use that. Let it pull you in."

He said nothing.

I nodded and kept walking.

The door was metal, but the lock was Mickey Mouse. I jimmied it open, and I stepped inside. It smelled like shit and piss and bad decisions. Nothing unexpected.

I stood at the bottom of the fire stairs and listened. I could hear some voices talking. Muffled, wordless noise from several stories up. I began to climb. I'm big but I learned long ago to move quietly when getting shot wasn't on my Day-Planner. Rubber-soled shoes and some skills acquired in places that were even worse than this.

The lookout guy on the second floor didn't even know I was there. He was too busy texting on his cell. Had no clue at all I was there until I hooked an arm around his throat, braced my other hand against the back of his head and squeezed. There are two versions of that choke. With the judo version you put the guy out in about eight seconds—sixteen if you cut off only one of the carotids—and then you lower him down and let him sleep it off. The jujutsu version is a lot older and less civilized. With that version you quiet him with the choke, and then you shift your arm and use the long forearm bones like a paper cutter to crush the windpipe and the hyoid bone.

I didn't know this cat. He might have been every bit as bad as Dill or he might have been some kid who couldn't find work and this looked easy. Whatever. No reason to kill him. So, he got the judo choke.

People try to fight it, but if it's done right and you mean it, they've got to be pretty well-trained to get out. He wasn't. He was meat and muscle and then he was a slack weight. I laid him down, patted his pockets, and found a cheap nine mil and a knife. Took those. Debated stomping on his knee to make sure he wasn't going to be an issue later. Didn't.

Moved up the stairs.

The second guard was on the fifth-floor landing. He *did* hear me coming and tried real hard to do something about it. A lot of street kids are tough and experienced, but there's street tough and there's Special Forces tough. I wasn't always a big-city skip tracer, and I'd fought tougher men than these on four continents. He managed to get his gun out of his waistband, but I took it away from him and pistol-whipped him into two years'-worth of orthodontia. He spun around, spitting bloody teeth, and went right down. I caught him and gave him a little shove so he'd go all bumpity-bump down the stairs. Should not have pulled a gun on me.

Dill's voice came yelling out of one of the rooms down the hall.

"The fuck was that, Gogo?"

When Gogo didn't answer, Dill came out of the room with one arm wrapped around a girl's throat and a pistol in his other hand. She was naked from the waist up. Sixteen, seventeen, maybe. Almost no tits, ribs showing, some sores on her that let me know she'd been sucking rock for at least a couple of years. Probably came here with her friend to blow Dill and his goons in exchange for a pipe.

That's some sad, sad shit right there.

Dill had his arm resting on the girl's shoulder to steady his aim, but I was a shadow in a dark hallway.

"Gogo ...?" he called.

"Gogo's off the clock," I said and fired the gun I'd taken from the kid downstairs. The girl was a stick figure, Dill was a bull. She didn't offer protection worth a damn. My bullet caught Dill in the hip and the impact of lead hitting all that bone jerked him backward and spun him. Most shots won't do that. Most pass right through, but the hip's a nice, solid target. He screamed and the girl screamed and his gun went off. She fell into a ball, screeching, slapping at her body because she probably thought she'd been shot. The other girl, still inside the room, started screaming, too. But Dill screamed louder than both of them. He tried to shoot again, but by now I was running. I kicked his wrist and then stomped it flat onto the floor. I liked how that felt so I did it again until bones broke and the gun went flying. Then I knelt on him, my knee on his chest, my left hand braced against the wall, the barrel of the stolen gun jammed against his forehead.

"Shut. The. Fuck. Up," I said and tapped him hard with the barrel on each word. He did shut up, but the screams were boiling right behind his gritted teeth. I turned to the screaming girl. "Get dressed and get the fuck out of here."

She was hysterical and probably out of her mind even before this, but she still had her animal instincts. She was up and running in a second. Topless. Without her friend.

I bellowed for the other girl to get out, and she ran past me. A little older, but just as wasted. I saw that she had her friend's shirt clutched in one small fist. That tiny bit of courtesy, that little display of presence of mind, was somehow touching. I listened for them as they pounded down the stairs.

That left me and Dill.

"You got one chance, asshole," I said. "Tell me about the kid."

"What ... kid ...?" he gasped.

"Jimmy," I said, though I thought he already knew. "He said there was something wrong with the grit."

"No ... it's—"

I banged his forehead with the gun butt. "No, no. I'm not a cop, I'm not wearing a wire, and this isn't a time to get cute. What's wrong with the grit?"

When he didn't answer fast enough, I swung the gun back and hit him in what was left of his hip. More screaming. It took a little more effort to calm him down this time.

"What was wrong with the grit?" I asked when he was able to hear me.

He said two words. Not a real explanation, but enough of one. "Bad ... cook."

"Why'd you sell it if it was bad? Your fucking customers are dying, dumbass."

Dill looked at me as if I was an idiot. "Always more where they came from."

It was enough. It was too much, really. It showed the scope of what he was as a person, just as it told me exactly how much the penal system would ever fix him. Or rehabilitate him.

It made me feel old and tired.

It made me feel sick.

It made me wish that I could do one thing to him that would stop this kind of thing from happening everywhere. But that was just plain stupid. Who was I? God?

I felt a coldness in the hall and turned to see Jimmy standing there. Silent and bloody. He didn't say anything to me. Probably wouldn't if he could. All he did was watch me as I dragged Dill into the room where he'd been having sex with the girls. There was a soiled mattress on the floor, a chair, a gym bag open, and a pipe sitting on a folding chair.

If I was into the drama of it, I'd have made Dill smoke a whole bowl of the tainted shit he was selling. But Jimmy was watching me and somehow I don't think he was mean enough to want that. The kid had been willing to join me in purgatory to save other junkies like him from dying. Heroism comes in some funny damn shapes and sizes.

Instead, I hauled Dill to his feet and chucked the son of a bitch out the window. Five floors down. I didn't lean out to watch him hit. I'm a motherfucker but I'm not a sick motherfucker.

I walked out into the hall right behind Jimmy, but as I left the room somehow Jimmy was already down the far end and vanishing into the fire stairs. I stood for a moment and watched him go. There was no way to catch up to him. Not anymore. He was going somewhere else. In happier moments I like to think that maybe when it's Betty's time to go—decades from now, I hoped—a clean and healthy Jimmy would be waiting for her.

I'd love to sell that to myself. Booze helps.

The truth is that, aside from seeing ghosts like him and the ghosts that haunt me, I have no fucking idea what's on the other side. Maybe the only thing on the other side of that big light is a big black nothing. I've talked to a lot of strange people along the way. Mystics, you might call them. Everybody has a theory, but none of us know. Not for sure.

Not really.

I took my time getting out of there. No doubt someone had seen Dill fall, or heard him. And maybe someone would make a call, but police response in this part of town was always reluctant, always slow.

The air was colder than it had been a few minutes ago and there was a tingle to it. I felt something on my cheek and when I brushed it away, I realized it was a snowflake. I looked up to see a few flakes drifting down on the night breeze.

Corny as shit.

I shoved my hands in my pockets, took a deep breath of the night sky, turned, and headed home. The ghosts would still be there, but at least there wouldn't be a new one.

That's something, right?

FACES

I live down the hill, across Boundary Street, deep in the shadows of a part of the city you never go to unless someone steered you wrong.

It's cold down there, except on summer nights when you can feel the day still burning on your skin and there isn't enough air conditioning in the world to chill you out. The rest of the year, though, it's cold. Not icy, but damned cold, like the inside of a cellar where you know bad things took place. Walls are slick with it and when your breath plumes in the air, the color of the steam is off. A little gray, sometimes. Or a little yellow. Like that.

Those of us that live down here are okay with it. I mean, we don't *like* it, but we know it's where we're supposed to be. People like us. We're the mushrooms growing in the damned, cold shadows. Take a bite out of us and maybe you die, maybe you get visions, maybe you wince and spit us out.

I'm being poetic. Fuck it. I'm drunk and it's Tuesday and you're allowed to get drunk alone on a Tuesday down here.

—2—

For the record, I didn't plan to kill anyone.

Can't always say that. It was true enough tonight, though.

Hence the booze. And maybe the poetry.

—3—

The day started out on the rails, chugging along, making the usual stops.

I had a morning meeting with the two of the bail bondsmen I do scut work for. Scarebaby & Twitch. Real names. J. Heron Scarebaby and Iver Twitch. You can't make this shit up. Not sure if their parents hated them or they lost a bet with God, but those are the names they were born with. Scarebaby was a lawyer who'd got disbarred because he got caught sliding it to a lady foreman on a jury for a trial in which his client was facing twenty to life. Understand, Scarebaby is roughly the size of a Thanksgiving Day parade float—overinflated and ponderous. He looks like Charlie Brown, if Charlie Brown was a middle-aged, overweight, hypertensive slimeball. Exactly like that. Four hundred pounds of comprehensive disappointment to himself and, from what I've heard, his four ex-wives.

His partner, Iver Twitch, is a beanpole with narrow shoulders and oddly delicate hands. He claims to be a descendant of Hungarian minor nobility, and I think he maybe is. He didn't inherit any money, but he has that inbred look a lot of the old blueblood families seem to have. Eyes too close together, unhealthy pallor, too much nose and not enough chin. No trace of mercy or compassion for any human being he has ever met. He likes dogs, though, so I cut him some slack there.

No one wonders how Twitch and Scarebaby found each other or why they formed a partnership. You don't have to wonder; the universe loves to orchestrate that kind of thing.

They ran a storefront office on Mercy Street. I asked them if they picked that spot as some kind of statement, but neither of them got the joke. I've been running down bail skips for them ever since I got back to the world. Before that I was a monk—which is how I got the nickname—and before that I was a killer working black ops jobs for Uncle Sam. After a while I couldn't tell the difference between the red on the flag and the red on my hands, which sounds like more poetry, but it's not. So, I went looking for answers. Found a few; found more questions, though. Found out some pretty disturbing stuff about myself, and that made me walk out of the temple and come home to Boundary Street.

My friend, the tattoo artist Patty Cakes, says that I'm still a monk. Some kind of warrior monk; but she's high most of the time, so take that with a grain of salt. I'm nothing anywhere near that noble. I'm just a killer who looked inside his own head and found that being a killer was more useful to the world than sitting in a lotus position contemplating my navel or some shit.

The scut work for Scarebaby and Twitch wasn't anything noble. They paid me to find people who've decided running is better than showing up to their court dates. I did that and I was good at it and made enough bank doing it to drink as much as I wanted. I don't ever get to sleep without some help from Jack Daniels, Jim Beam, Jose Cuervo and the rest of my support group.

The case I was there to get, though, well …

Let me tell it front to back.

Scarebaby was behind his desk and Twitch was standing by the window, looking out to see if there were any good-looking women walking by. There were. There always are. I was in one of the brown leather visitor chairs with a folder open on my lap. The name on the folder was Antoine Hoops: thirty, black male with brown eyes, a shaved head, a threadbare little attempt at a goatee, and prison tattoos running up both sides of his neck. He had spent more than half of his life inside and had served max time on an eight-year bit for molesting a nine-year-old girl.

"He's a charmer," said Twitch without turning.

"Yeah," I agreed. "What was he arrested for this time?"

"Same thing," said Scarebaby. "Attempted rape of a minor."

"And he got *bail*? With his priors?"

Scarebaby spread his hands. "He has a good lawyer."

"How?" I asked. "Who'd represent a turd like him? No public defender got a repeat sex offender out on bail."

Twitch snorted. "It wasn't as hard as you think, Monk, because the victim is an illegal. Conchita Delgado, fourteen. Worked as a room maid at a hotel uptown. No green card, of course. She was picked up the same night as Hoops, and Immigration wants to ship her back to Guadalajara. This is all eleven months ago, and she has some feisty little immigration lawyer working for her, trying to keep her here at least until the trial. That trial was set for yesterday and Hoops was a no-show."

"If she's an illegal," I asked, "how'd she file charges?"

"She didn't," said Twitch. I saw his head turn and nod continuously as a pair of secretarial types walked by, laughing and oblivious of their observer. The girls were pretty, and Twitch's thoughts probably weren't. "A nurse saw the vic and Hoops struggling and rushed up to help."

"Brave woman," I said.

"Stupid," said Scarebaby. "Could have gotten herself killed."

Twitch half-turned. "Didn't though," he said with the kind of edge that let me know they'd been arguing about it. He turned all the way and looked at me. "Hoops tried to scare her off, but the nurse works over at Heaven's Gate."

Heaven's Gate was a shelter for battered women and children. Disgruntled husbands and boyfriends sometimes show up to try and force their women to come home and stop making a fuss. Sometimes that gets ugly. Or maybe I should say "uglier." Not unusual for the staff to get up in their faces, and I know that a lot of the women who work there—staff and volunteers—had first come there seeking refuge.

"Which nurse?" I asked.

"Darlene Crowther," said Scarebaby.

"Darlene?" I laughed. "How bad she hurt him?"

Twitch gave me a nasty little smile. "Hit him blindside with a taekwondo flying kick," he explained. "Knocked him over and kicked out his front teeth, broke his nose, cracked some ribs, and kicked his nutsack halfway into his chest cavity. And then she Tasered him."

"Nice," I said.

Darlene is six hundred pounds of tough crammed into a ninety-pound body. Tough in the way honey badgers, wasps, and rattlesnakes are tough. Small, but no sane person would mess with her. I wouldn't.

"Miss Crowther filed charges," said Scarebaby, his lack of sympathy clear in his voice.

"Is the victim going to testify?"

"Her lawyer says so, but it's not certain. She's very scared of Mr. Hoops, and besides, she's being deported."

"Then ..."

"A passerby caught some of the attack on his cell phone," said Twitch.

"Was the video clear enough to win a case?" I asked.

"Probably," said Scarebaby, "though frankly I don't give a cold, wet shit. My concern is—"

"*Our* concern," corrected Twitch.

"*Our* concern is the fact that we fronted fifty large for bail and after behaving himself for nearly a year, Mr. Hoops has absconded."

I smiled. He was the only person I'd ever met who wasn't trying to be cute or clever when he said "absconded."

"Not that I'm trying to say no to a bounty," I said, cutting a look at Twitch, "but how come you haven't gone out looking for him?"

Twitch used to be an investigator but lately he hasn't done any active legwork. "I've taken a more managerial position in the firm," he said.

Scarebaby looked down at his folded hands and smiled but made no comment.

"You want the job or not?" asked Twitch, his face and voice stiff.

"Sure," I said. "I'll find him."

They both smiled their approval and relief.

"For the record," said Twitch, "I personally do not care in what condition you 'find' Mr Hoops. He sticks his dick into kids."

Scarebaby nodded. "All we have to do is produce him to the courts."

"In whatever shape," added Twitch.

Another nod from Scarebaby. "In, as you say, whatever shape."

There wasn't a lot of love in the room for Antoine Hoops. I wasn't feeling a glow in my heart, either.

—4—

The folder had the usual stuff. Last verified address, list of known associates, complete physical description, and all the rest. I spent a couple of hours banging around the places he'd be most likely to hide out. Stores that I knew had back rooms with cots that the owners would rent out to whoever wanted to lie low; the row of shitty hotels on China Street; a motel by the boulevard. Came up dry. The staff don't talk to cops, but they'll talk to me, even though they know what I do. Word gets around. People know where I stand. If the guy was just wanted on a drug beef or for burglary they wouldn't be talking to me. This guy was a pedophile, though, so different rules apply. Everyone knows where I stand with stuff like that.

Understand something—I'm a big, mean, tough, violent son of a bitch and no one ever hurt me without me hurting them back. I've never been a victim of sexual or violent abuse. My old man was a drunk and an asshole, but that was between him and his PTSD. He never laid hands on me. My mom died of cancer when I was four. So, I don't know from abuse firsthand. I've seen it, though. In Iraq and Afghanistan. In Syria and India. Other places. Here in the city, too. I've seen it and I'm not the kind of cat who can look away. I can't pretend not to hear or not to know. Shit like that pushes my buttons even though I don't know why I have those buttons. Moral outrage, as a concept, sounds too grandiose, but that's pretty much what it is.

People know this about me, and they don't get in my way or in my face when I'm hunting for a sexual predator. Not that they go out of their way to help me. The street is still the street. They just know how I'll react if someone like Hoops slips away because of them. Very bad things have happened in the past.

I got my first lead just as the sun was starting to slip out of the sky and slide down behind the skyline. I was having a beer at a club on 8th. The Al Skorpion Band was playing, and it didn't sound like anyone was in the same key. Al looks like Archie from the comics and sings like Tom Waits, if Tom had spent the afternoon having the shit kicked out of him behind a dumpster. Growly and mean, but I liked his lyrics. Stuff about bad luck and poor choices.

My beer was only halfway gone when a woman slid onto the stool next to me. There were eight empty stools, so I figured this was either a pro hoping to score a quick one or someone looking to make a hundred because I'd been putting that number out there for information. She nodded to the bartender, and he put a glass of candy-colored fizz in front of her. He cut me a look and I nodded, and he took a five out of the change I had on the counter.

"Say it," I suggested when I was alone with the woman.

"You're Monk Addison," she said. "I seen you around."

"Okay."

"You're the guy with all the tattoos."

I shrugged. "Everybody's got some ink these days."

"You're the one with the faces," she said. Without asking permission she reached out and pushed up the sleeve of my hoodie. The tats start above the wrist. Small and large faces. Most of them in black and white. Nothing on my hands or face. Nothing on my dick, because that would be weird. The woman leaned in and peered at the faces she could see. I let her turn my wrist so she could see more of them. Then she sat back and drank two-thirds of her cocktail.

I looked at our reflections in the mirror behind the bar but didn't turn toward her. She was midforties, kind of nice looking, kind of used up. Maybe I'd seen her around. Hard to tell. She was a type. Aging hooker. Too much makeup because she was terrified of losing her looks. Every wrinkle, every line, every bit of sag means that she gets to charge less for doing more. It's built-in erosion. Of the body and the soul. Getting out of the life means facing up to entering the minimum wage job market with no experience and a face that tells everyone who has eyes what you've been doing for the past twenty-plus years. It's sad, and I don't judge for two reasons. First, I don't know what put her on the street. There's always a backstory and it is never pretty. Second, when I was young, I earned my pay by killing people. Sometimes I still do. I have absolutely no grounds for moral judgment.

Except for shit-eaters like Antoine Hoops.

"People talk about you," said the woman. "They tell stories. Freaky shit about why you have those tattoos."

"Who gives a shit?" I asked. "Look, can we put some top spin on this?"

She blinked, then smiled. "Sure, honey. Just making small talk."

"Never in the mood for it," I said.

"Okay."

"Okay. What's your name?" I asked.

"Bambi."

"Your real name."

"Honest to God. My folks hung that on me."

"Jesus."

"Kind of started me down a certain road, you know?" she said.

"No shit."

"Life happens," said Bambi. She sipped her drink. "This guy you're looking for …? There's a couple hundred to find him?"

"*One* hundred," I said.

She finished her drink and started to get up. I sighed.

"Okay, two. Whatever," I grumbled, "but only if I put hands on him."

She sat back down, trying not to smile too much. "I know where his sister lives."

"So do I."

"Oh yeah? Which sister?"

I turned to look at her. "He only has one. Rachelle."

The smile grew. "That's his blood sister, and they don't talk at all. She wouldn't piss on him if he was on fire."

"I like her already."

"Hoops' father was a no-show from the jump and his mom crack-whore'd herself into HIV. She died when Antoine and Rachelle were teenagers. They spent time in foster care, but Rachelle was adopted, and Antoine never was. He got really tight with another foster kid, a girl who was a couple of years younger."

The file mentioned foster care, but there was nothing about this. Bambi nodded, knowing she'd set the hook. I took out my wallet and peeled off two fifties and laid them flat on the bar between us.

"Hey," she said.

"Half up front, half when I put this asshole in a bag."

"That wasn't the deal."

I studied her. "You said you heard about me. You ever hear anyone say I don't pay my debts?"

"No."

"You ever hear that I fuck around?"

"No …"

"Then take the money and let's cut to the chase. I want to wrap this up tonight. You give me a cell phone number and when I have Hoops, I tell you where to meet me. If he's actually *at* the address you give me, then maybe I'll sweeten the pot."

She thought about it for about half a microsecond and then the fifties disappeared.

"Her name is Cheryl Carbone," she says. "She used to work out of the Velvet Motor Lodge, but she got out of the life after she had a kid. A little girl. Works at McDonald's. Lives on this little street off Boundary. The one with the worst-ever name for a street to live on."

"Misery Street," I said.

"Yeah."

Like a lot of people down here she was superstitious about even saying the name. Not sure who had the comprehensive jackassary to hang a name like that on a residential street, but it lived up to it.

Misery.

You got to be on the poor side of fucking poor to want to live there. No, check that. You have to *need* to live there. No one wants to. I know the guy who mops the floor at Powder Brothers funeral home, and he says that even *they* hate getting gigs over there. And they are frequent flyers. When the guys whose job it is to sell funerals get freaked out by your address, your karma is polluted.

"What makes you think Hoops is there?" I asked.

"I saw him go in the front door."

"When?"

"Couple hours ago. I was doing a house call at the corner. On the Boundary Street side, you know? Not on ..."

"Got it."

"Her house is two doors down from the corner and I saw Hoops get out of an Escalade and go running to the front door."

"Whose car?"

"Don't know—and don't ask if I copied down the plates. I didn't. But who drives Escalades around here?"

I nodded. The upper echelon of the three different drug gangs all drove identical black Escalades. Keeping up with the Joneses.

"How'd you know it was Hoops?" I asked.

She shrugged. "Seen him around a bunch, here and there. Got to know him a little. He was bouncer at Pornstash for a few months. Pretending to be gay so he could work there. Then he beat up a kid who was cruising the place. Young kid, maybe fifteen with a fake ID Looking for love in all the wrong places."

"Pornstash isn't a bad joint."

"Maybe not most of the time, but it wasn't the best place for a little fish like that to be. Fifteen, you know?"

"Point taken."

"Kid tried to come on to Hoops, and that asshole took him out back like maybe he was game for a blowjob, but then he stomped the shit out of the kid. Really hurt him, too. Big Larry came out to take a leak because the bathroom was full, and he saw what was going on. He tried to put Hoops down—you know how Big Larry is, he'll pick a fight with anyone, and he nearly always wins—but Hoops busted the crap out of him. Only ran off when other guys started coming out of the place. Laid low at Cheryl's. I seen him there before, because I do that gig on the corner about every other week. Sometimes more. When the cops busted him this last time, after he raped that girl he went to prison for, they bagged him at that intersection. Not sure if he was going to Cheryl's or coming from. But he's back there now, bold as brass."

"Not too bright going back there."

She signaled for another drink. "Maybe he figures it was too obvious and the cops wouldn't think he'd go anywhere near there."

"Or maybe he's an idiot," I suggested.

"Or maybe that." Her drink came and I paid for it. "Look, Monk … I know you have this reputation of being a scary SOB, and you look big and mean enough to handle yourself … but Hoops took Big Larry apart without breaking a sweat. No one's ever done that, far as I know. And don't get fooled thinking that Hoops lost his edge because that nurse Darlene kicked his ass. She suckered him. And she better watch *her* ass, too. Antoine Hoops is no joke."

I finished my beer. "Don't worry, sister. If I get my ass handed to me, I'll make sure you get the rest of your money."

She looked genuinely hurt and turned away to look at something else. Anything else that wasn't me. She fished a business card out of her purse and slid it across without meeting my eye. It had her name and cell number and nothing else. I sighed, picked it up, left mine on the deck along with my change for the bartender and stood up.

"Cheryl has a five-year-old daughter," said Bambi. "She's in that house with Antoine."

"Thanks," I said, but she didn't even nod. I went out, feeling like a dick for offending her.

—5—

I walked the nine blocks along Boundary Street. I had my earphones in and was listening to the live stream of Oswald Four deejaying from Unlovely's. He was in a mood. I was in a different mood.

Sometimes I cut looks up the side streets that ran from Boundary Street up the hill. The lights were so bright up there. That part of the city probably has an official name, but everyone calls it the Fire Zone. I've only been up there a few times, but it's not right for me. Or maybe it's that I'm not right for it. I always feel unclean up there, like I should be wearing a sign around my neck.

Up there you can hear the Music. That's how everyone thinks about it. Music, with a capital M. It's not just tunes and tracks. There's something about the Music up there. I think it's been played so long, so well, with such artistry and passion and insight that maybe it's become alive. Am I being fanciful? Maybe. Or maybe I'm underselling it.

You can't really hear the Music on Boundary Street, but everyone here knows about it. We even talk about it sometimes, but the echoes of the Music don't reach this far down the hill. Or maybe no one down there in the shadows strains hard enough to hear. If we want to hear it, we have to tune into Uncle Oswald's show. I once heard someone say that Oswald Four *was* the Music. That they were two halves of a whole. Not sure if I believe that, but I can't make a compelling case against it.

So, I listen in and imagine what it would be like to be the kind of person who belonged up in the Zone. I think about that as I walk around down here, and it's always on my mind every time I'm on Boundary Street.

You see, down here you don't get to see Oswald Four live. Down here you won't find Snakedancer leading the faithful in complex line dances under the tracking eyes of the watchful laser lights on Gotham Road or along Harlequin Street. Snakedancer's one of the people who belong up the hill. Up in the light.

Down along Boundary Street the clubs play sweaty blues and icy jazz and some soulful R&B that will rip you a new one if you open up to it. On Thursday nights at the Cavern, you can catch Elton Leonard and his five-piece working over Thelonious Monk tunes like "Straight No Chaser" and "Bright Mississippi," and even "Green Chimneys," and Elton plays it even funkier than Monk did, and he does it with nine fingers. He has all ten, but he never uses his left little finger and won't say why.

Down here you can go into the Stumble Inn for some Irish fight songs, and on any given night you can hear pretty much the entire Wolf Tones songbook, and a rousing version of the Pogues' "Young Ned of the Hill." And some newer, less violent stuff that Happy O'Hanlon's been writing since he came back from County Tyrone. Get a few drinks in him, though, and he'll be singing "The Belfast Brigade" or "Republican Guns" and cursing like a longshoreman. And if the blues is calling to you, then you can go to Blackbeard's where Crash Gordon and Nine Mile Sutton have been holding court, apparently, since just after the Lincoln–Douglas debates.

But what you won't hear is the Music. Not out loud. Maybe it's just that no one down here can hear it. For us, the darkness is way too loud.

Bad thoughts to have while walking a cold mile to find a child molester.

—6—

Misery Street.

The place had all the inviting charm of a colonoscopy.

I stopped at the corner and leaned for a few moments against the brick wall, chewing gum and watching the street. It was short and crooked, dirty and empty. Eighteen houses on each side, with as many abandoned cars as working hoopties lining one side. No pedestrians, but that didn't mean there was no one looking. Streets like this have a lot of unemployed people, a lot of elderly poor, a lot of shut-ins who have been so comprehensively detached from social contact that the entirety of their engagement is what they see out of the windows; and so they look. All the time.

The sun was gone, and the afterglow had faded to a muddy orange, darkening to a muddy nothing at the edges. Shadows owned the street and of the three streetlights on Misery, one was working, trying to combat the gloom with a piss-yellow glow. I pushed off the wall and walked away, went to the end of the next block, turned right along Beale, which paralleled Misery, and then cut into a narrow alley that ran behind the houses. No lights at all there. I debated using my cell phone light to pick my way through the trash, broken beer bottles and dog shit, but didn't. Couldn't risk being seen. If Hoops was in there with Cheryl, it meant that her kid was probably there, too. Danger, Will Robinson.

The backyard of Cheryl's house was dark except for the muted glow of the kitchen light as seen through drawn curtains. There was no security system, of course, but I saw the faint glint of light on something metal and crouched down to see what it was. Someone—almost certainly Hoops—had strung several lines of hairy twine hung with tin cans filled with pebbles.

Smart, if you're in an episode of *The Walking Dead*. Naïve otherwise. At least the way he strung it.

I took my folding knife from my pocket, flicked the blade into place, took a firm hold on one end of the top line and cut the twine. Then I lowered the cans to the crabgrass very carefully. Not a sound. I stepped over the lower two lines.

The back door was typical of this kind of neighborhood. Crap. But the lock was okay. A deadbolt of the kind guys at Ace Hardware insist are pickproof. They aren't.

I leaned close to the door and heard the sound of a TV playing too loud. Canned laughter. A sitcom. Useful. My lockpick set is top of the line and given time I can pick damn near anything up to lower-end industrial locks. There was some noise, but the fake sitcom laughter washed it out. The door clicked open.

Bounty hunters going after bail skips don't need warrants. I could have kicked that door in if I wanted to. Odd set of laws we have in this country. If it wasn't for Cheryl and her kid, I would have gone in hard and loud. A bit of urban shock and awe. Instead, I pushed the door open and slipped into the tiny kitchen, then closed the door to decrease the chance of a sudden draft of cold air whipping through the house. The kitchen light was on and there were pots on the stove. I cut a look at them and started to move deeper into the house, then I stopped. Turned. Looked again at the stove. Two pots. One of pasta and one of sauce.

The pots were cold, and maggots wriggled through the sauce.

I turned again to the sound of laughter and all at once the house felt different. Empty. A husk.

I don't like to use a gun, but I carry one, an old Navy Colt .45 loaded with hollow points. The gun was in my hand as I moved out of the kitchen, through the darkened dining room, and into the living room. The TV was on, turned to one of those vintage channels. *Friends* was on because *Friends* is always on. Every day, on one channel or another. I stood there, the gun limp in my hand. Chandler was being sarcastic. Joey was saying something stupid. Rachel's hair looked great. The audience was laughing themselves sick.

I felt sick, too.

They lay where he'd left them. Cheryl Carbone was on the floor, wrists and ankles tied with belts. The little girl was on the couch. She wasn't tied. There were flies on them. The maggots would come later.

Their eyes were open. The little girl's eyes were filled with things I can't even name. Even in death there was such an expression of horror that it was almost unbearable to look at her. I had to look, though. Someone has to because the dead deserve to be noticed, to be acknowledged. Even the poor ones. Maybe especially the poor ones. Most of the world ignores them every day. Now they were going to go into the ground and be forgotten, which was a crime nearly as great as what had been done to them. If I looked away, I'd be complicit in that crime. I would be guilty of catering to my own need *not* to see, which is a special kind of sin. A coward's sin that you never get a chance to wash away.

I sucked in a breath and then went upstairs, checking the other rooms, looking for Antoine Hoops even though I knew for sure he wasn't here. Then I came back downstairs and stood looking at the mother and child. Hoops had taken his time with them, and mostly with the little girl. The mother had been made to watch. Her body was covered with bruises in the shape of open hands and knuckles. He had forced her to keep watching.

Her throat was the wrong shape, so it was clear he'd strangled her.

How the girl died was less obvious and I didn't need to find out. She was dead. At five she was as old as she would ever be. Hoops had stolen all the rest of the years of her life. Maybe the kid would have grown up to be like her mom, a hooker and then someone working at a fast-food joint. Maybe the kid wouldn't have gone to college or made anything of herself. Maybe. But that isn't anyone's call to make, and it didn't mean that she was disposable just because she wouldn't amount to some standard of personal success. She was a whole person. A beautiful little child and she had died badly.

So, I stood there and looked at her, and at her mother. I wept for them. Not a lot. Not sobs. Just some cold tears that burned my cheeks. Their faces were turned toward me. As pale as the ghostly faces tattooed on my flesh.

When I heard the scuff of a shoe on the floor behind me, I didn't whirl around or raise my gun. I was already sure who I'd see there.

I was right.

They were both there. Cheryl and her daughter. Pale as candle wax, standing in the doorway to the dining room. I could see the shapes of the chairs and tables through them. The little girl stared at what was left of her physical body on the couch, taking it all in with the wide, wise, knowing eyes of the very young. Her mother held her hand. I saw that the marks of violence were not visible on the little girl's ghost. That nearly broke my heart because it showed that her spirit was already rising above what had been done to her.

Every single thing that had been done to Cheryl was still there. The broken teeth, the burst lips, the eyes swollen nearly shut, the cigarette burns. All of it.

Cheryl looked down at her body and then up at me.

I knew what she wanted. Dead people don't linger just to hang out with me. I'm not a place of comfort, if you can dig that. Vengeance isn't comforting. It never is.

Cheryl pointed to my chest. I sighed and unzipped my hoodie and then pulled up the T-shirt I wore underneath. I don't know if the faces on my skin look different when a dead person looks at them, but I suspect they do.

"You don't know what you're asking," I said.

Her finger was steady, pointing. Telling me she *did* know.

The tattoos that had been inked into me must have told her. Or maybe there's some asshole on the other side of life—Charon or whoever—handing out fucking pamphlets. I don't really know how the dead find out about me. All I did know was that

81

Cheryl Carbone wanted something from me that she thought would set the world back on its wheels. For her and for her daughter. That's what people think revenge will do. It doesn't. At best it stops the bad guy from doing more harm, and for a lot of the dead—for the ones whose faces are inked onto me—that's enough. I think they feel that it balances the scales and maybe gives their deaths some meaning. Maybe it does. The cost, though. That's a motherfucker.

You see, the way it works is messed up. Something I learned about while I was in Southeast Asia. There's a magic in skin art. In certain kinds of skin art. If I take some blood from the crime scene and mix it with tattoo ink, then have that used to ink the face of the victim onto my skin, it creates a bond. Temporary but intense. I relive the last few minutes of the victim's life. I see who killed them and sometimes I learn something that will help me find the killer. If I do that, and if I take the killer off the checkerboard, then, sure, all future potential victims are saved; but the ghost who "hired" me has to pay the fee. And that fee is that they have to haunt me. Haunt my life.

You wonder why I drink myself to sleep every night? You try this shit. Try drifting off to Slumberland with dozens of ghosts standing around your bed. Most of them are quiet, but that's not much comfort. Some weep all the time. A few are screamers.

There's no way out of it for me except death, and I'm not ready to punch out quite yet. So, I deal. I accept. And I drink.

But, man, I don't want to add another face. Not one more.

I said, "I'll find him without that."

Cheryl's eyes went wide, filled with tears that were as translucent as crystal. When her tears fell, they splatted on the floor and then vanished as if they'd never existed. She jabbed a finger toward her daughter's body on the couch.

"I know how she died," I said. "I know he made you watch."

The finger jabbed and jabbed.

"Don't make me live it," I begged.

Jab. Jab. Jab.

"Listen to me," I cried. "If I do this your daughter moves on and you don't."

The finger stopped, trembled.

"Is that what you want? You want to be separated from her forever?"

The temperature in the room suddenly dropped so fast and so low that I could see my breath puff out as I spoke.

"Cheryl," I said gently, "let me try to find him some other way, okay? Give me a day. One day. And if I can't, then I'll ..."

I let it hang because it didn't really need to be said.

The little girl looked up at her mother and then closed her eyes and leaned her forehead against Cheryl's hip. The young woman knelt and gathered her daughter into her arms. I could hear my heart beating. It was the only sound in the world.

The ghosts faded out and left me alone with the empty bodies.

—7—

I didn't call the cops.

The dead couldn't get any deader and I didn't want official eyes finding any leads that would have them dogging my trail. Instead, I creeped the place, going through every closet, every drawer, looking for anything. Found a stash of kiddie porn magazines hidden in the back of the bathroom closet. I burned them in the tub.

There weren't any glaring clues, but there was a story to be read in that place. A new deadbolt lock on the little girl's room and no trace of the key for it. There were scratches on the outside of the door. Fingernails. I think Hoops kept Cheryl in line by holding her daughter hostage in a locked room. And it was clear that he slept in there, too.

I can't imagine what kind of utter hell that was for the mother, and I could imagine her out in the hall, begging, pleading, tearing at the wood with her nails, while inside a big man tore the innocence out of a child. Over and over again.

Why hadn't Cheryl called the cops?

Probably afraid that Hoops would kill the girl. He must have made credible threats, and eventually he used up his options at the Carbone place. One last fling, this time with an audience, and then lights out. What triggered it? The impending court case? Maybe. With the video evidence it was likely Hoops would take another long fall. If he was locked up, then Cheryl could risk going to the cops and child protection services. With that kind of evidence Hoops would never see the outside of a super max prison. Never. So, he gave himself a going away party and then ran.

However, Bambi had said that she'd seen him get out of an Escalade a few hours ago. What did that tell me?

The gangbangers who ran drugs had their hands in all kinds of crime. Extortion, money laundering, gambling, human trafficking. Their people sometimes had to skip town. That meant each gang had to have a travel agent, which is what they call someone who makes arrangements. Fake IDs, passports, all the right papers, as well as transportation and lodging. Full service.

Three gangs with Escalades in this part of town.

Those gangs had a lot of muscle, a lot of soldiers.

I stood in the living room with the dead mother and her little girl. Not the ghosts, just the bodies.

"Trust me," I said to them, hoping the ghost of Cheryl Carbone could hear me.

—8—

You can do a lot of damage if you don't give a shit about what happens to you.

I found Luis Delgado, second in command of El Spiritos, the gang on the east side of the neighborhood. He didn't know that I knew where he lived. I do. When he went upstairs to take a shit, I was in the shower stall with the curtain down. I waited until he had his pants around his ankles and was squeezing one out, then

I reached out around the edge of a curtain and put the mouth of my .45 against the corner of his jaw.

Pretty sure it helped him evacuate his bowels.

I stepped out of the shower with the gun rock-steady and my finger over my lips. He did not make a sound. Delgado's eyes went wide with shock, fear, humiliation, and outrage in equal measures.

"I'm not here for you, Luis," I said quietly. "You tell me what I want, and I'm gone. Lie to me or fuck with me and they find you dead on the crapper. It's your call."

He started to say something, but the first syllable came out too loud, so I tapped him with the gun barrel. He stopped, took a steadying breath, and tried again.

"You out of your fucking *mind*?" he snarled.

"Seems to be the general consensus," I said. "You know who I am?"

"You're that freak. Monk."

"Good."

"The fuck you want?"

"Looking for a guy," I said. "Antoine Hoops. You know him?"

"What if I do, you stupid—"

I leaned close. "Don't get mouthy with me, Luis. I'm having a real bad day and I'm okay with spreading the bad mojo around. Like I said, this isn't about you. It's about what I need. It's about me putting Hoops in a bag. Tonight. I'd have gone through channels, but you're famous for dicking people around and I don't have time for that, so I figured this would work. You either have an answer for me or you don't. In either case you don't see me again after this. We go our separate ways, and this never happened. Make this complicated and I go ask the Esteban."

Esteban Morales was Luis' boss. He was currently out of town, or I'd have been in *his* bathroom. Besides, Luis was more middle management, which meant that he was likely involved with matters like travel arrangements.

Luis was in one of those no-win situations. Sitting on the

toilet, naked from the waist down, no weapon and a gun barrel cold against his skin. I had all the cards. His best-case scenario was posthumous revenge, which wouldn't do much for him.

"All you have to do is the smart thing, Luis," I said.

He turned his head so that the barrel rubbed its way from jaw to upper lip. It was a deliberate act, trying to make a point that he wasn't afraid. And also that he was going to tell me the truth. I moved the barrel back one inch so he wouldn't have to talk funny.

"We got nothing to do with Antoine," he said.

I looked into his eyes for a long five-count. Then I nodded.

"Anyone protecting Hoops is going to have a bad night," I said. "You and me have no beef unless you make one."

He said nothing, but he gave the tiniest of nods.

I left his bathroom.

The second name on my list was Nikolai Gorlov, a Romanian who ran guns and heroin and had forty percent of the import on unlicensed pharmaceuticals coming down from Canada. His office was in a double-wide parked at the far corner of a junkyard across the river. Lots of line-of-sight for his guards, and he has dogs, too.

He also likes to go to the movies. One of those new theaters where they have leather La-Z-Boys and the ushers come and take food and drink orders. Insanely bourgeois, with tickets priced at twenty-eight dollars per. I followed him in my beat-up old piece of crap car and wasn't seen because I know how to do this stuff. He bought a ticket for a Liam Neeson middle-aged action picture. I bought a ticket for a Pixar thing that started forty minutes later but slipped into the same house as my target. The place was two-thirds empty. Gorlov had three guys with him. Two of them positioned on aisle seats where they could watch him. The third who sat next to him and accompanied him to the bathroom.

Gorlov downed two beers during the first act and had to take a piss right about the time Neeson was threatening someone on the screen. The guard took up station just inside the washroom and as I entered he shifted to block my way. He was a big son of a bitch. Nearly my size, with a face like an eroded wall.

"Occupied," he said, although it was a four-stall men's room.

"Yeah," I said and hit him in the throat. There are ways to do that so you kill someone and ways to do it so you just fuck up their evening. The guard wasn't my target, so I let him thrash around on the floor trying to breathe. I quickly took his Glock and a .32 throwdown from him and dropped them into a toilet stall. Gorlov yelled and tried to pull his own piece. I took that away, too, and pointed it, and my own gun, at him. One barrel pressed beneath each eye.

"Shut. The. Fuck. Up," I said.

He did. It's so much easier when you choreograph this stuff so that there isn't a chance for people to do something stupid.

"Tell your boy there to guard the door," I said. "No one else gets in, and he doesn't make a fuss."

The guard was trying to get back to his feet. His face was as dark and swollen as an eggplant and he was sucking air in small, high-pitched gasps. Gorlov said something to him in Romanian. The man glared hatred at me, but he leaned against the inside of the bathroom door.

"Short and sweet," I said. "I'm looking for Antoine Hoops."

"Why?" asked Gorlov.

"For a bunch of shit you do not want to be part of."

"Is this about the little spic bitch he—?"

I used the guns to run him back against the edge of the sinks. He had to bend backward, and his shoulders and the back of his head hit the mirror. He winced and cursed and I pressed the barrels hard.

"Right now I only want him," I said very softly. "One more wrong word out of you and I'm going to add names to my list. Tell me you understand."

"I ... yes. Yes, I understand," said Gorlov. "Why do you want him?"

"He raped and murdered a woman and her five-year-old daughter. He's going to be trying to get out of town. If your people are finessing that for him, you need to tell me right now. And you need to tell me where I can find him. Otherwise, you are accessory to a crime that is going to be what everyone will be talking about at your funeral."

"Who in the fuck *are* you?"

"Monk Addison." I smiled. "Maybe you heard of me."

His eyes went wide and his face lost all color. "Like … with the tattoos …?"

"Like that."

When I drove away three minutes later, I wondered if Gorlov was enjoying the rest of the movie. I didn't have to tell him not to make a call to warn Antoine Hoops. The look on Gorlov's face told me that he'd heard a lot about my tattoos. Maybe he was superstitious or maybe he just didn't like to tempt fate. In either case he told me what I needed to know.

—9—

This time I kicked the door in.

Motel doors are tough, but outrage is tougher. The lock ripped out of the frame in a spray of splinters, and it crashed open all the way to the wall. I was through right away, stepping down from the kick into a flat-out run, seeing Hoops on the bed, meeting him as he came up, bending to drive my shoulder into him.

That was the plan.

He was fast, though. And he was good. Maybe Darlene had been able to blindside him, but I wasn't that lucky.

Hoops began turning as he rose so that when I hit him, I went over and around his hip and slammed into the wall next to the bathroom door. I fell hard and badly, pulling the lamp from the night table down on top of me. Hoops froze for a moment, caught between his desire to find out who I was and maybe beat the shit out of me, and a wanted man's need to run. If he hadn't wasted that time—however short it was—he'd have had me, because the double impact of wall and floor knocked most of the air out of my lungs.

That's why they call it fatal hesitation, I guess.

He decided to run for it and bolted for the open doorway. Hoops got halfway there before the lamp I threw hit him between the shoulder blades. It made him hit the frame rather than run through into the parking lot; he rebounded, hissing in pain. By then I was in the air at the end of a flying tackle. I wrapped my arms around his thighs and bore him down. We fell half in and half out of his room, both of us swinging punches that hit door, carpeted floor, concrete, and occasionally each other. He drove his elbow into my face, and I turned to catch most of it on my cheek, which hurt me and hurt him. I short-punched him, trying for his balls and catching his inner thigh instead. He howled and tried to head butt me, but I tucked my chin and his forehead hit mine instead of my nose. He grabbed my hair and slammed my head against the frame, which started a chorus of church bells ringing inside my skull. I stuck my thumb in his eye. He screamed and brought his knee up and used it to push me back to a better punching range and then he hit me three hard, fast shots. Right, left, right. Hard punches even though he threw them lying on his back. I used my arms to make a cage around my head and let him break his hands on my elbows and forearms. He could hit, though, god damn him.

I twisted and dropped my weight onto him, leading with a pile-driver elbow. He tried to squirm away, but there wasn't enough room in the doorway. I hit him hard in the belly. Air whooshed out of him, and that should have been it.

Antoine Hoops had a stomach like a piece of cast-iron boilerplate. The elbow blow hurt him, but it didn't stop him. In fact, it galvanized him, and he began thrashing around, punching and clawing and biting. The sheer, shocking intensity of it drove me back and suddenly he was climbing on top of me, and he did more damage to me in five seconds than anyone's ever done in any fight I've been in. He was fast as lightning, and his punches hit like cruise missiles. He wasn't trying to win a fight. He was trying to beat me to death.

He was winning, too.

I don't think I ever faced anyone as tough as him. Ever.

Then suddenly he reared back, falling off of me, flinging his hands up to shield his face. Hoops screamed.

My head felt broken, and the darkness was covering me like a layer of ash. Soft but thorough, and I felt myself falling down.

Out of the corner of my eye, though, I saw a shape come walking in through the open doorway. Small, slender, pale. I could see the streetlights outside through her body. Antoine Hoops scuttled back from her like a crab, shrieking louder than any sound in the world. High-pitched screeches that hurt my ears. His eyes were huge, unblinking. Drool sprayed from his mouth as he screamed.

The slender figure moved toward him with slow, inexorable steps. Smiling the worst smile I have ever seen. Filled with madness and malice and a cruel, dark delight that was appalling to witness.

Hoops scrambled to his feet, turned, looked for a way out. The ghost was between him and the door. He jagged right and left, again caught by that fatal hesitation, and then he dodged wide and ran around the specter. I was still sprawled on the floor, and he jumped over me.

But I caught his ankle. It was all I could manage.

His body mass kept moving until my grip jerked him up short, then he fell.

He tried to avoid the door frame.

Didn't.

The sound his head made when it struck the frame was like a melon being dropped out of a second story window. Heavy and wet.

Hoops sagged down to the floor in a twisted sprawl. I lay there and watched the light go out of his eyes.

Then the ghost came and stood over me, looking down at me with eyes that were filled with strange, swirling lights. Terrible lights filled with a terrible joy that in any other circumstance I would have labeled as malicious. Not now. Not with this ghost. So, what did I call that kind of joy? Are there even words?

I'd seen ghosts before. Sometimes they come and witness the end of the monsters who had killed them. Not sure if they need to see it for closure, or if they enjoy it. Don't know and never want to know.

I looked up into these eyes.

I guess I'd expected Cheryl Carbone to need to see this man die. It would have been appropriate somehow. But Cheryl was nowhere around.

Her little girl stood there watching me.

God. I will never forget the smile that was on her face when she came into the room. I'll never forget the savage joy on her face as Antoine Hoops fell. The gleeful hunger that twisted her mouth when he died. I could have accepted that smile on the face of her mother. I couldn't bear to see it on the face of a child.

I'll never forget.

God almighty.

I'll never forget.

She walked past me and out the door, and I fought my way onto my feet, swaying and damaged and sick at heart. I stumbled after her, but she was already at the edge of the motel parking lot. I quickened my pace, first to a sloppy loping jog and then to a full run, but no matter how fast I moved I couldn't catch up with her. She rounded a corner and by the time I reached that she was on the far side of Boundary Street, where she paused. I slowed to a limping walk.

The girl looked up the hill toward where the clean lights of the Fire Zone glimmered in the night. A fingernail moon was etched into the night sky, and someone had spilled a bag of diamonds across the heavens. She didn't look up at those lights. Then I saw Cheryl Carbone come walking up to her. Even from halfway across the street I could see that Cheryl's bruises were still there and that she was frowning in uncertainty at her daughter. The little girl held out her hand and Cheryl took it and they began walking up the hill.

"Wait," I called, though I don't know why. Maybe it was that I needed to understand what had just happened. Neither of them were clients of mine, they weren't bound to me or trapped with me, but the girl had participated in the killing of Antoine Hoops. This was all new.

My legs were rubbery and my ribs hurt, and there was something wrong with my head. Concussion or maybe even a skull fracture. I tripped, staggered, dropped to my knees.

"Wait," I said again.

The little girl turned to look back at me. The smile was gone. They kept walking. I think she waved at me. Or maybe she waved me on to follow. I don't know.

The Fire Zone isn't heaven. It's brick and asphalt, flesh and noise. Oswald Four plays the Music up there, and Snakedancer leaps and twists, and there are colors that flash in the air out of nowhere.

I knelt and watched them go. They both turned one last time. They were pretty far away by then, so I don't know how much I can trust what I saw. Maybe it was wishful thinking, but were Cheryl's bruises, cuts, and burns gone now? Was the little girl's smile different?

I don't know.

They turned away from me and the little girl led her mother up the hill, and after a long time they were gone.

I slowly got to my feet and stood on the curb there on Boundary Street. Down in the shadows. Down in the cold.

Where I belong.

JOB DESCRIPTION
A POEM

What do you do when the dead show up and want to
        talk?
You freak out.
You run away.
You check that you took the right meds.
You hope you're right with Jesus.

What do I do when the dead show up and want to talk?
I listen.
I grieve.
I feel my heart break a little more.
I know that I can't turn my back.

There are faces on my skin.
Dead people's faces.
Dead women's faces.
Dead children's faces.
All of them looking at me.

What am I supposed to do when they want to hire me?
I find some of their blood.
I mix it with Holy Water.

I give it to Patty Cakes, and she mixes it with tattoo ink.
And I scream when she inks it onto my skin.

What happens when the faces come alive?
They scream.
I scream just as loud.
I relive every moment of their deaths.
I see what they saw before their eyes went dark.

What happens when I go hunting?
I pack my gun and knife.
I leave my compassion behind.
I burn empathy like rocket fuel.
And when I find the motherfuckers, I ruin them.

It's not easy being who I am.
What I am.
What I've become.
I'm a killer working for ghosts of murder victims.
There is no part of this that sounds sane.

But it's what I do.

REFLECTED IMAGE

—1—

I hate mirrors.

Really fucking hate them.

Any kind of mirror. Any reflective surface.

Hate them.

Hate.

Hate.

Hate.

I hate the one in my bathroom. I can see it watching me. Them, really. Not the glass itself. I'm weird but I'm not actually crazy. And, yeah, side note … crazy would be useful. Being out of my goddamn mind might soften the edges. That's a big thing to say, I know that, but there are times when the real world is Olympic level bizarre, and no personal level of insanity is going to compete in that league.

So, no, it wasn't the physical mirror that tore at me.

It was the reflection.

My reflection.

And theirs.

All those faces.

Watching me constantly.

Every day. Night and day.

All those faces on my skin.

—2—

It was a Tuesday.

Tuesdays generally suck. They're like Monday hangovers but without the memories of joyful excess. A greasy, grimy, headachy Monday. That's what Tuesdays are.

I spent a lot of time in the shower that morning because the night before hadn't been a good one. Tears, blood, spilled whiskey, and pain. Sometimes there isn't enough soap, you know?

Of course you know.

I took a half bottle of breakfast beer into the shower and drank it while the water pounded me. I set the temperature to boiled shellfish, had my Echo playing Delta Blues, and leaned my forearms against the tile. Even in that position I could see the faces. There were more than eighty of them now. Faces, I mean. They started just above the wrist, spiraled around my arms and then cascaded down my chest and back. Black and white faces. The only color in any of my ink are the older tats, the ones I got back when I was a sergeant pulling triggers for one of Uncle Sam's no-name agencies. Several wars back. That was when people still called me Gerry. Or Sergeant Addison.

I started getting the faces around the time someone hung the nickname "Monk" on me. They're not random art. God damn, but that would have been fine. I had a buddy back in Iraq who had the face of every girl he'd ever dated tattooed on him. Fourteen faces, ranging in age from fifteen to thirty. It was only because of those faces that we were able to ID him after his Stryker rolled over an IED.

Mine are different.

With my buddy, the faces on his skin were of women who

were alive but now he was dead. For me it was exactly the opposite. The women who looked out from my flesh were all dead and I was alive.

I'd never met a single one of them when they were alive. That's not how this works.

Well, that's not exactly true. The first one, the little Vietnamese girl. I met her and even played Frisbee with her in the yard behind her family's tattoo shop in the village of Tuyên Quang. I was a friend of her mother's. I was in town when the little girl—Tuyet—went missing. I was there when the police found her body. What was left of her after the gang of bastards had used her up and disposed of her like garbage. Her mother, Patty, tattooed Tuyet's face on me and on the back of her own hand. For her it was the memory, to have that face since she'd lost everything else.

For me … well, that's how this all started.

Patty had mixed some of Tuyet's blood with tattoo ink and sunk it onto my skin. The process changed me. Changed my world. Stretched it into a new shape. Darker, bigger, uglier, scarier. More heartbreaking.

It also kicked open a door in my head and through that door stepped Tuyet. Or maybe it's more accurate to say that I stepped into Tuyet's life. I was in her mind and connected to all five of her senses during the last hours of her life. I felt what she felt, endured what she endured, screamed when she screamed, begged when she begged.

And I died when she died.

Then I was me again.

The tattoo was some kind of magic. Even now I can't really explain it. All I know is how it works. When a tattoo of that kind —blood and ink—is drawn onto my skin I always have that experience. I relive—right alongside the victim—their death. What she saw, I saw.

It painted the faces of the men who'd raped and murdered her into my head. It shoved me in their direction.

I was a soldier before that. Sometimes for the good guys. Sometimes for whomever signed my checks as a private military contractor. I had blood on my hands and more marks against my soul than I can count.

And then that fucking tattoo.

Her death was the start of a new war. The tattoo was the gun and I was the bullet.

I found those men.

I ruined them.

They died very, very badly. But let's face it, not badly enough. Nothing could redress what they'd done. To take a young life, a happy and innocent child, and destroy her faith in the world, tear away her hope, violate her on every level, and then to snuff her out, to erase her from the calendar of her own life.

Vengeance is not restitution.

Here's the real kicker, though. Here's the punch in the balls.

That magic is devious as hell. It's not kind. When I killed those men, it's not like Tuyet just went into the light and cue inspirational music. No. She lives with me now. I see her in my house, when I walk down the street, when I turn around.

I see her in the mirror.

Her and all of the other lost ones. Those whose spirits came to me after their own murders. The ones who were not looking necessarily for revenge. They wanted their killers stopped so no one else had to die like they did.

I was fired again and again and again at the same kind of targets.

There was so much more blood on my hands. I didn't mind that. Those men deserved everything I did to them. Every. Damn. Thing.

But the ghosts were stuck here. With me. My entourage, my family. Whatever it is.

Stuck.

And I see them. No one else can. I can see them. Hear them. Feel their pain, even after their monsters have been cleared off the board.

Some of them are screamers. That's fun. Ask the guy at the liquor store how much I enjoy that shit.

Most nights they're quiet though, and that's been the case lately. So, I've even gotten some sleep. Mind you, I wear noise canceling headphones and those blinder things. I play music, too. Distraction therapy to keep what sanity I have left.

The mirrors, though.

No hiding there.

Sure, I could take the mirrors down. Learn to shave without one. I mean it's not like I need one to put on my face or do my hair. My face looks like an eroded wall. It looks like I've been punched at least once from every possible direction, and with enthusiasm. Which isn't entirely inaccurate. And lately I've been keeping my hair buzzed down to almost nothing. Losing it anyway, so there's no loss there.

The mirrors are still up because taking them down feels cowardly. It feels disrespectful in a way I can't quite phrase in my own thoughts.

So, they watch me. And in the mirrors they see themselves. Wish I knew if they liked that, if it made them feel like they still existed. They can scream but they can't actually talk. Not to me. Maybe to each other, though that adds another layer of creepy over my life.

Why am I telling you all this?

Well, one of the faces on my skin was looking at me through the mirror's reflection.

I mean really looking. Eyebrows raised, mouth working as if she was trying to tell me something. Maybe something important. There was an urgency in her expression I hadn't seen before. It was as if more of her personality had suddenly come awake.

Alive.

The other faces seemed to go still, as if maybe *they* could hear her. Their eyes were filled with strange lights. Fear and something else I couldn't define.

You wouldn't think that sort of thing could scare me anymore.

You'd be wrong.

—3—

I leaned on the edge of the sink and stared at her.

She looked the age she'd been when she died. Twenty-seven, though if she hadn't been killed, she'd be closing in on thirty-five. Medium brown skin and pale eyes. A mixed-race art dealer from New Hope, Pennsylvania. Fifth victim of a ritualistic killer who targeted women in that world. First was an artist, then a gallery owner, an art critic, a model, and then her. Gabrielle Toussaint was number five. Born in the suburbs of New Orleans, got a BA in art history from LSU, and then an MBA from Wharton in Philly, moved to New Hope to open her gallery, and died.

Left behind a three-year-old son and a husband whose grief at her funeral was so profound that it silenced all conversation. Last I heard he was still single and looked like he was twice as old as he was. Their kid, now in junior high, was a skinny little ghost who drifted along the fringes of life. Two more casualties of the monster who'd killed her.

Yeah, I keep tabs on some of the families. Those I can. And, yes, that's probably going to put me in rehab or a twelve-step one of these days.

I stared into Gabby Toussaint's green eyes and tried to read her lips.

I'm no good at that sort of thing, but there was one word that she seemed to say over and over again. I finally said it aloud.

"More …?" I asked the face in the mirror.

Her answer was a scream.

She'd never been a screamer before.

She was now.

And the scream hit me like a punch. Like a bullet. Like a fucking freight train. I reeled back, clapping my hands to my ears, slipping on tiled floor. Falling. Slamming the middle of my upper back against the rim of the tub. Rocked my head back. Saw stars. The room spun like a drunken dervish. I screamed, too. In pain and in shock.

Then the mirror exploded.

It didn't just crack. The whole thing burst outward as if there was a hand grenade in the medicine chest. A thousand glittering splinters razored their way through the bathroom, slashing the shower curtain, scratching the tile, sticking like throwing knives into the door. Cutting me.

I barely got a hand up in time to save my eyes. Splinters lacerated my palm and inner wrist.

Then everything was absolutely silent.

I sprawled on the floor. Feeling like an accident victim. Like some kind of victim,

More.

More?

Jesus Christ.

—4—

The ER staff here in Pine Deep are probably second to none. God knows they've had enough practice. Some of it with me.

I spent five full hours there, trying to be patient while doctors used tweezers to pick glass out of me. Not sure if they believed the story about me slipping on a wet floor and bashing the mirror in an attempt to keep from falling. Best I could do at the time.

My friend, Malcolm Crow, the chief of police in that town, once told me that the ER staff approaches unusual injuries in almost the same way as doctors who patch up underworld criminals. They smiled and nodded, and either worked in silence or filled the time with meaningless chitchat. They did not ask probing questions.

After they were done, I looked like I'd been auditioning for a new sequel to *The Mummy*. It didn't spoil my looks any more than it improved them. I have that kind of face.

Afterward I went to see Crow and found him in his office, feet up on his desk, reading reports and listening to John Lee Hooker. There's something about living in Pine Deep that cultivated a love of the blues.

He waved me to the Mr. Coffee and then to a chair.

"You look like shit," he said.

"Feel like it."

He studied me. He's a little guy a bit north of fifty, and he had his own collection of scars. I knew where some of them came from, but not all. He knew some stuff about the faces on my skin, but not all. I brought a cup for him, and we sipped for a few minutes while he finished a report. Then he tossed the papers onto his desk.

"You want to tell me about it?"

I debated that, but then did. I told him all of it, including the backstory on Gabby Toussaint. He listened without comment or judgment because that's who Crow is. He's both been there and done that and after some events we went through together a few years back, we'd become family. Sort of. Not brothers. Cousins, I suppose; and with the clannish attachment and tendency toward mutual support that comes with all that.

"More," he said, making it a statement rather than a question.

"More," I said.

"Well, hell. That's unnerving."

"Yeah."

"You know what she meant?"

"Not yet."

He nodded to my shirt and raised an eyebrow. The office was empty except for the dispatcher, who was on the far side. I took a break and raised my T-shirt and touched Gabby's face. It was as still as a tattoo should be. Always was with other people.

"Beautiful woman," said Crow, his eyes sad.

I pulled my shirt down.

We drank coffee.

"What was the name of the perp?" he asked.

"Henry Sullivan. Thirty-eight at the time of his death," I said. "Architect living in French Town, New Jersey. No family."

Crow did some tappity-tappity stuff on his keyboard and pulled up a photo of Henry Sullivan. It was the only photo of him I ever saw; the one that was used by the papers when what was left of his body was found in a dumpster behind a 7-11 in New Hope. Ordinary guy, with reddish-brown hair and blue eyes. Utterly forgettable features except for a large port-wine stain birthmark covering most of the left side of his face. What my grandmother used to call a "stork bite." The eyes that looked out of that photo were flat and dead despite the smiling mouth below.

"How can I help?" he asked.

"'*More*,'" I said. "That's ringing a bell with me."

"What kind of bell?"

I said, "There was some thought by investigating officers that Sullivan wasn't working alone."

Crow pursed his lips. "I ... um ... thought you were *there* when she died. In the way you do that sort of thing, I mean. Like ... you saw it."

"I did. I saw the guy who killed her, yes."

"Then ...?"

"I saw what she saw," I said. "That's how it works. Only the vic's point of view. Nothing else."

"Okay," he said. "I mean, it's creepy as shit, but ... okay. I get it."

"So, there could have been someone else."

"Serial killers are usually solo acts," said Crow.

"And you know that it's not always the case."

"Sure, Monk, but you think that's it? Maybe she was trying to tell you that there were other victims. Women whose bodies were never found, or women whose deaths were not obviously connected to the ones they know of. A lot of killers have those kinds of kills."

I nodded. Many ritualistic killers work up to that pattern,

and when they're caught it's more often just the ones that fit the pattern who are directly connected. Exceptions are when there's DNA.

"Yeah, maybe that's it. Can you check for me?" I asked. "More DNA gets collected all the time and added to your databases. Maybe there's something else we don't know about or didn't back then."

"Sure," he said. "And if I come up dry?"

I shook my head. "I don't know," I said. "Not yet."

We sat and talked about it for a while. I went over every detail of the case that I could remember. That's always a bit of a challenge because I tend to come into it after the fact. I'm not the investigative officer. I'm not a cop and I'm not even that kind of PI. Mostly, I chase bail skips and do some personal protection work. I'm a hired thug.

Sure, I've picked up some tricks along the way, and the bondsmen I mostly work for gave me access to a bunch of databases and websites that help me find the skips, but I never did the investigator course work or logged the apprentice hours with a licensed dick.

Back when I lived in New York I had no real friends in NYPD. Rather the reverse. But here in Pine Deep, Crow was on my side for sure.

He looked at the wall clock. "Give me the rest of the afternoon. I need to make some calls and it's Sunday, so it might take time for me to catch up with folks off the clock."

I thanked him and went out.

The autumn sun was a cold yellow ball in a bright blue sky. I went to the Scarecrow Diner, stuffed myself into a booth in the back corner, ate some eggs, drank too much coffee, and made a lot of calls of my own.

First one was to one of the bondsmen I work for. J. Heron Scarebaby, and yes that is his real name. His partner is just as unfortunate—Iver Twitch. Proving that some people are really unlucky in terms of heritage, and that occasionally parents make it worse when it comes to naming their kids. Personally, I'd have changed my name to literally anything else.

"Can you do a background check for me?" I asked.

"Because why?" said Scarebaby. "Because I have nothing better to do? Because the only thing on my Day-Planner is running errands for skip tracers who don't know how to use the Internet?"

"Because I'm in a jam and I'm asking nice," I said.

He heard the tone of my voice. Scarebaby is not nearly as much of a dick as he pretends to be. He likes the drama of complaining and feels that, as a bail bondsman, he is professionally required to *act* like a dick.

His sigh was elaborate, but then he said, "Okay. Give me the details."

I gave him just a bit. Nowhere near what I shared with Crow. Different kind of relationship. Scarebaby and Twitch know some of what goes on with me, but they don't know the scope of it. Nor do they want to know, which is cool with me.

He told me to wait and rang off.

I waited. The coffee at the Scarecrow is first rate even by diner standards. There was an Eagles–Broncos game on the big screen. I watched Jalen Hurts do some real damage.

Then Scarebaby called back.

"Got something on Henry Sullivan," he said.

"Tell me."

—5—

I paid my tab and walked back to the police station. Crow saw me and waved me once more to the coffee pot. My nerves were already doing the Macarena, but I poured myself some and brought the cup to his desk.

He finished a call he was on and peered at me.

"You have a look," he said.

"A look? No, I don't. What kind of look?"

105

"Like you know more than you did when you were here before."

He was a sharp little SOB.

"I called a bondsman I work for."

"Twitch?"

"Scarebaby."

Crow chuckled. "I can't take that name seriously."

"Yeah, well," I said. "He came through. And maybe it's the same thing you got. Turns out Henry Sullivan was a foster kid. Went into the system out of an orphanage. Bounced around from one home to the next and was never adopted. Kicked loose when he hit eighteen. Dropped off the radar for a couple of years and then resurfaced in Philly. Got a degree in architecture from Drexel, then moved to Jersey and joined a firm. Background checks came up zip on his family, though. But I have the name of the orphanage and that's a start. Going to poke around there and see if I can get info on the foster homes. Maybe he made a friend there. Someone who might have shared his … *proclivities*."

"That's a nice euphemism for murderous psychopathic asshole," said Crow.

"The rest is implied," I said. "Is that what you got, too?"

"In part," said Crow. "First things first. I talked to a friend in the FBI who ran some numbers for me. It would break your heart to know how many young women go missing every year. In 2021 alone the number of missing girls and women under 21 who went missing was 209,375. Over 21 the number is 59,369. There are all sorts of statistical models postulating how many are runaways and drug addicts living homeless and how many are dead but unidentified because there's no DNA or fingerprints on file. Of the rest, it's anyone's guess what happened to them. My guy at the Bureau says the pervading theory is that only one in ten serial killers follow a pattern. It's virtually impossible to track and quantify patternless murders. Now, your boy Henry Sullivan was close to being patternless, and had it not been for your … um … *special gift* … he'd likely have never been caught."

"Yes," I said. "And, no, it's not a gift."

"Whatever it is," said Crow, "my point is that we can't look at the numbers of missing women and easily tie any of them to Sullivan's MO."

"Which means that if he had a partner," I said, "we're not likely to find him by looking for similar murders."

"Right."

"Balls."

"I know," he said. "So, I went the other direction and, yes, I hit the edges of the foster home thing, but I have something your buddy didn't get. Sullivan isn't his real name. He was a classic—dropped off in a basket outside of a fire station. Right out of every hard luck TV movie you ever saw. A note was pinned to his blanket that said, 'I'm sorry. I can't.' And a little card that read Henry Mathew."

"Mathew?" I asked. "Sullivan's middle name was Joseph. I saw his driver's license. And it was Henry J. Sullivan in the news."

"Ah," said Crow, "I noticed that, too. The firefighter who found him and contacted child protection services was Joseph Sullivan. The orphanage named the kid after him."

"Keeping on the first name and replacing the middle? That's odd."

"It is. Never heard of an orphanage changing what amounts to a known, or presumed, legal name. I can see the addition of a surname, and it was a nice nod—at least at the time—to name him after the firefighter. No idea why they tossed the kid's original middle name."

"Any chance you have the firefighter's contact info? He'd be old but maybe he remembers something."

"You'd need to hold a séance," said Crow. "Joe Sullivan is deceased. Died of smoke inhalation four years after he found the kid."

"Shit. I guess I'll have to wait until Monday and then talk to the people at the orphanage."

"Yeah, well ... that's the other thing," said Crow. "The orphanage burned down two years ago."

We looked at each other while the wall clock ticked very loudly. The skin on my chest felt crawly, as if the faces beneath my shirt were reacting. My version of spider sense, I suppose.

"Yeah," said Crow after a while, "that's one of those things that make me go *hmmmmm*. I mean, if the fire had been set *before* Henry Sullivan died, then the first thing I'd have done was look at troubled kids who came out of there."

"Because serial killers often do shit like that when they're growing up," I said, nodding. "Setting fires, killing local pets."

"Uh huh. Often enough that it's factored into the psychological profiles," agreed Crow.

"And if it burned during the years we know Sullivan to have been active as a killer," I said, "it'd be likely him scrubbing his back trail."

"Yes."

I smiled. "Now *you* have the look."

"I expect I do," he said.

"You're going to tell me the placed was torched, aren't you?"

He grinned. "Yes I am."

"Shit."

"Yeah."

"Did the arson team look at anyone in particular?"

"They did," he said, looking smug. "The guy who reported it had some moderately bad burns. He said he got them when he tried to go inside to try and rescue people. None of the staff or kids said they saw him go in while it was burning, though. There was enough reasonable doubt—dark night and lots of smoke, general confusion—that no one could either confirm or deny. No charges were filed."

"Who was this guy?"

Crow took a sheet of paper from the printer tray and handed it to me. "Kevin Lane. Currently living in Lambertville, New Jersey. Address provided by your local law public servant."

"Thank you, Officer Friendly," I said, plucking it from between his fingers.

"Keep me posted," said Crow.

—6—

The drive from Pine Deep to Lambertville is about twenty minutes. A-32 to State Route 32 and over the bridge in New Hope.

Yeah. A stone's throw from New Hope, where Gabby Toussaint lived. And where she died.

There are coincidences in life, but I tend not to believe in them.

—7—

Kevin Lane lived in an old Victorian house on a side street in Lambertville, within easy walking distance of shopping but far enough away for privacy. I parked and spent a couple of minutes walking the neighborhood. It was not the fashionable part of town, though. The houses were all old and there wasn't as much attention to yard work as elsewhere. Nothing had gone wild, but there was an unkempt feel to everything. The weeds were tall but withering now as autumn kicked in. The last of the summer grass had been allowed to go stiff and brown, and picked apples were left to rot among the fallen leaves.

Most of Lambertville was dressed for Halloween, with strings of orange lights, inflatable spiders and ghouls on the lawns, and decorative skeletons leaning out from around oak trees.

Not Lane's house, though. No decorations except for an uncarved pumpkin on the porch. Only one light and that was on the second floor. It was still technically afternoon, but the skies had darkened and there was a thin gray cloud cover, so it felt later.

The info Crow gave me was thin. Lane had six parking tickets in ten years. Nothing for speeding and no other violations of note. No criminal record. The fact that he was interviewed about the arson at the orphanage indicated that no follow-up was anticipated. There was a photo of him showing a face mostly covered by bandages, which was about as helpful as no photo at all. And it was in black and white.

I decided to give a face-to-face a try.

The chance of this guy being *the* guy was slim bordering on none. I am never that lucky.

I knocked.

It took him nearly a minute to answer the door.

The man who answered was bald as an egg and he leaned around the edge of the door to peer at me. The photo of him with a bandaged face did not do justice to the burn he'd received. His face was a distorted moonscape of lumps and bumps. He looked melted. The brow hung down over his eye and heat damage had warped the tendons around his nose and mouth, flaring the former and giving the latter an unpleasant uptilt. A bit like a mix of the Joker and Two-Face from the Batman comics.

"Yes?" he asked nervously. The fingers curled around the edge of the door were scarred, too. That news article hadn't come close to reporting how badly he'd been hurt. And from the lights in his eye and the tremolo in his voice, I wasn't getting the "bad guy serial killer" vibe. Not at all. Not even a twinge.

"Excuse me," I said, "are you Kevin Lane?"

"Yes?" he said again. The door was open only a few inches, enough for me to see a bit of an old-fashioned entrance foyer. Wainscoting with molded plaster images of flowers, faded floral wallpaper, a bit of a mirror in a heavy cherrywood frame, and one corner of an unlighted lamp in a wall sconce. It looked like my grandmother's house. Old, worn out, and sad.

"My name's Gerald Addison," I said. "I'm an investigator and wondered if I could ask a few questions."

"About what? Is this more about the fire? I answered everyone's questions a hundred times."

"No," I said. "It's about Henry Sullivan. Does that name ring a bell at all?"

He stared at me. "Who?"

"Henry Joseph Sullivan," I said, watching the one eye I could see. "He had been at that orphanage as a child."

"They never said anything about any kid dying in that fire," said Lane.

"No, sir. He died a few years before that. Nothing to do with the fire. Would you mind if I came in? It won't take much of your time."

"No," he said. "No more questions. I'm not feeling very well, and I don't know you."

The door closed.

I heard the lock click.

I stood on the porch for a full five seconds, feeling very acutely that I had mishandled things. Which is a fair assessment because I really had no actual plan. As I said, I'm not a private investigator in the classic sense. I chase people who skip out on court appearances, and I look for murderers I see in the shared visions of the dead. This was outside of my skill set, and on first pitch it showed.

So, I turned and walked down the steps and down the street to my car.

And then stopped halfway there.

I turned slowly and looked at the house again. I saw a curtain fall into place as I turned and knew that Lane had been watching me go. Nothing unusual about that.

Something was bugging me, though.

As the autumn wind blew past my face, I went through everything that had happened in those few moments on his porch. The timbre of his voice told me nothing. As for the burned face, well … it's impossible to read the expression in melted meat. He had been brusque, but not actually rude. I had, after all, knocked on his door at nightfall on a Sunday. And I hadn't had the sense or forethought to flash an ID at him.

So, what was it?

I closed my eyes and replayed the moment.

The door opened. Just a little. He looked out, but all I saw was the burned side of his face.

That was a bit odd right there. Was it common for someone with extreme facial disfigurement to only show that side of his face? Wasn't it more common for said person to show the other side? Maybe. I don't know enough about the psychological of physical trauma to make an assessment.

But there was something

The bit of hallway I saw. Wainscoting, wallpaper, mirror, light fixture …

And then something in my mind went *clunk*.

At the same moment the face on my skin seemed to writhe. I could almost hear her yell at me. And I knew that if the tattoo had a voice, then I was certain which word she would be yelling. Earlier she'd told me that there were more. More victims, of that I was certain. And maybe a double meaning, more killers.

But the feeling of her trying to speak on my skin—as awful and nightmarish as that is—seemed to shape a different word. And I spoke it aloud.

"Mirror."

In that edge of the old dusty mirror, I had seen the other half of his face. A shadowy ghost of an image in the unlighted foyer

I went to my car and drove away. As I did, I called Malcolm Crow and asked some fresh questions.

—8—

He woke when I spoke his name.

"Mathew," I said.

Not Kevin.

Mathew.

His eyes snapped open, and he nearly screamed.

I stood beside the bed. The room was dark, with only a little light from the outside streetlamp to separate me from the shadows.

"What the fuck," he snarled.

His voice was no longer timid. Now there was steel in it.

I stood there, naked to the waist. All those faces looking at him.

Her face looking at him.

I saw his eyes go wide. I saw the horror and confusion turn to recognition and understanding.

"I killed Henry," I said. "I killed your brother."

He stared at me.

"That was what the note meant. Henry Mathew. Henry and Mathew. The firefighters found two kids on their doorstep. Joseph Sullivan turned them both over to child protection services. You burned down the orphanage because that's where the records would be of what happened to both. What happened to you. Maybe there were fingerprints or footprints on cards, like they do with kids. Maybe there were records of a Mathew Sullivan. How did it work? Did the Lane family adopt you and not Henry? Or did you both cycle out and start doing what you did? Yeah, I know I'm missing a lot of pieces of the puzzle, but I also know I'm right. And I have a police buddy who'll be calling Philadelphia child protection services first thing Monday morning to verify what I already know. You and Henry. Twins. Cut from the same cloth. Twin brothers, twin killers. Rare, but not unique. Sad, too. I mean, I can grieve for the babies you were, but … damn … I hate everything about the men you became. Tell me … why the women?"

He said nothing.

"How many are there we don't know about?"

"No idea. I'd like to say 'none,' but …"

I looked at him. "You know how this ends, right? You know this is all over."

He whipped back the covers and came up off the bed. The poor light flashed dully on something metallic he'd snatched from under the pillow.

A knife.

Six-inch serrated blade.

He moved with cat quickness—fast and precise and deadly,

going from dead sleep to instant action. The blade moved so fast it blurred.

Had I been someone else, maybe a cop come to arrest him, I'd have likely died right there. He was that fast and he moved with absolutely no hesitation. A rare and deadly quality. The very best Spec Ops soldiers move like that.

So do I.

He moved fast, but I moved just as fast. And I moved first.

He went for my throat; I went for his arm. My blade sliced through the muscle and tendon of his knife-arm, cutting the biceps to the bone. My other hand clamped over his mouth. Screams were inconvenient. I bet he already knew that. Was he the one who kept the women silent while his brother ruined them? Or did they take turns?

Doesn't matter.

He never got his screams out.

Not then.

Later, in the quiet of his soundproofed basement, I let him scream all he wanted to. All he needed to. And in that ugly darkness he told me about the other women. Where they were buried. Where I could find his trophies. God damn, but he really didn't want to tell me. He wanted to keep those secrets with him even knowing he was going to die. He tried, too. He so wanted to have the last win here because it would mean all those families would never know where their daughters and mothers, sisters and wives were buried. That would have put a grin on his face all the way down to hell because he would have carved off a piece of every survivor, every grieving loved one, and taken those as trophies with him to the pit.

He would have gotten that, too, if I'd been a cop or a real PI or any kind of decent human being.

I'm cursed with what I do because of what I've done. Fate or the universe, whoever, could have picked millions of nice guys.

They picked me.

For a reason.

And, yeah, Mathew fought me there in his bedroom. Before I took him downstairs.

He fought real damn hard while the face of Gabby Toussaint watched. While all the faces watched. Watched me. Watched what I did.

And at one point, I caught sight of my reflection in the bedroom mirror. All of the faces on my back were watching. Their eyes were alight. There was a kind of crimson joy in their smiles. I saw them reflected. Saw the awful delight.

I hate mirrors.

Hate them.

Most of the time.

COLLECTOR

—1—

"You're a weirdo," the cop said. "You'll dig this."

We were at the Scarecrow Diner in Pine Deep. I was halfway through a mushroom omelet and five cups of coffee in. The cat across from me was Malcolm Crow, the chief of the local PD. Fifty-something, small, limps a bit, makes a lot of jokes, fools people by looking like someone they can fuck with. But there is a very short list of people who have successfully fucked with Crow. Pretty much a blank page.

"You say the kindest things," I said. "Oh, and kiss my ass."

He grinned through a mouthful of toast.

"Tell me," I said.

He swallowed, washed it down with coffee, waggled fingers at the waitress who was already on her way as if there was a Bluetooth connection between Crow's coffee cup and a buzzer in her brain. I kind of admired that. She filled both cups, even though mine was still more than half full. Waitresses like that are a national treasure.

"In tattoo parlance," began Crow, "you know what a collector is?"

"Sure."

"Tell me what you know."

I shrugged. "Ink collectors are no different than anyone else who has an eye for quality … except they get it drilled into them instead of hanging it on a wall."

"Explain that motivation," prompted Crow, adding way too much sugar and about a gallon of half-and-half to his coffee. Polluting coffee like that is the only thing I don't like about him.

"Tattoos are art," I said. "There are shitty artists, wannabes, so-so's, good, really good, great, and masterful. A real collector goes after the best of the best and gets something really fine."

"You know any?"

"A few," I said, "but I don't cruise the tattoo conventions. I'm not as much into the culture as people think."

That was true enough, even though I had about a hundred tattoos: arms, legs, torso; front and back. Except for a couple left over from my days humping battle-rattle for Uncle Sam or pulling triggers as a PMC, the rest aren't decorative. Nor are they sentimental reminders of old girlfriends. There are no smiling devils, lucky charms, chicks with improbably large bustlines, gang signs, prison ink, or any of that. Everything else inked on me is one face or another. And, except for the face of one little Vietnamese girl, they were of people I'd never met. Or ever could. They were the faces of dead people. Mostly women. All murdered. Crow is one of a handful of people who know and understand the *why* of it.

"But you *know* about the culture," Crow prompted. "You understand it."

I shrugged. "I guess. Patty knows more."

Patty Cakes was the mother of that little girl. I'd met her in 'Nam some years back. I'd burned out on the kind of shit I was doing for governments and corporations who didn't give one cold fuck about the human cost. I met her family, who'd been doing tattoos for a couple of centuries. Talk about artists? Shit, that times ten. When a gang of local thugs kidnapped Patty's daughter Tuyet, I went looking for her. But the cops found her first. What was left of her.

Patty took some of Tuyet's blood, mixed it with ink, and put her face on my chest. What happened then was weird as fuck. I was suddenly *in* Tuyet's head during the last few minutes of her life as the gang ruined and then ended that child. I felt everything they did to her.

Every. Goddamned. Thing.

But I also saw the faces of the gang members. Heard them talking. Caught some names. It wasn't much, but it gave me some leads. I've found people with less to go on. I found the gang. When the cops arrived at their shack—based on an anonymous phone tip—what they found made two hardened officers throw up. A third rediscovered the religion he'd left behind. Thing is, if I could have done worse to them, I would have.

Now Tuyet haunts me. Her ghost is with me. Always.

Always.

Patty and I cried on each other's shoulders. Sometimes we cried in bed together. Pain like that never really goes away.

She moved to the States, to New York because that's where I settled, leaving gunplay behind but not the hunger for the hunt. I became a PI and skip tracer working for various bail bondsmen in NY and Philly. When Patty burned out of the big city, she moved to the creepy little town of Pine Deep in Eastern Pennsylvania. Even though she and I aren't lovers anymore, she's the closest thing to family I have, so I moved here, too.

Crow snapped his fingers a couple of times, pulling me back to the moment.

"You still with me, son?"

"Yeah," I said. He didn't ask where I'd gone in my thoughts. He's too sharp for that. He has his own ghosts. And we have some shared history from shit that happened shortly after I moved to town.

"You sure?"

"Yeah, yeah. Collectors and shit. You going somewhere with that?"

He fiddled with his phone but then placed it screen-down on

the table. "You know anyone who's really aggressive about high-quality ink?"

"How aggressive we talking?" I asked. "Like intimidating other collectors …?"

"Like stealing tattoos."

That dropped a big ugly tent of silence around us.

"Owen Minor is dead," I said.

The thing that happened in Pine Deep I mentioned? There was a freaky-ass motherfucker who stole tattoos. He did it by touch. The ink would disappear from the victim's skin and manifest on his own. He'd then feed on the memories associated with the art, and when he was done the victim lost those memories forever. Patty Cakes was one of his victims, and damn near lost all memories of her murdered daughter. Crow and I, along with some friends, managed to stop the sick little bastard. And he was very damn dead.

"Not what I'm talking about," said Crow.

"Then what?"

He turned his phone over and slid it across to me. I picked it up and immediately lost all interest in the rest of my breakfast. Hard to eat when you were looking at something like this.

It was a man slumped on the floor by an expensive-looking couch. His shirt was torn open to reveal a space that was maybe six inches by four. There was no tattoo there. What there was … was a hole. It had been cut with great precision and it was all the way to the bone. The poor bastard sat on the floor in a pool of dark red blood, head thrown back, mouth wide where it had frozen when he died.

"This is the fifth vic like this," said Crow. "In each case the killer took more than just the art."

I stared at the image.

"There's a tattoo collector out there," said Crow.

—2—

I spent the rest of the morning at Crow's office, where—in relative privacy—he laid the whole thing out.

The first victim, Harold "Nucks" Nelson, was in Doylestown, not far from Pine Deep, found in his own garage with half his back missing. The stolen tattoo in that case was not what anyone would call a masterpiece of art. It was a demon face with outstretched bat wings. Above and below it were words in fancy font:

The Cyke-Lones Motorcycle Club
Live Fast—Die Hard—Own It

Second guy, Andrew Hobson, was a retired Army first sergeant in northeast Philly who lost all the meat on his left pectoral and a tattoo that was a superior attempt at photo-real art. The image had been that of a human-shaped gun-range target with a bunch of holes grouped precisely in the heart and brain. The guy had been one of the top instructors at the US Army Sniper School, and he had a personal record of sixty-two confirmed kills in various Middle East wars.

Third, Jillian Kang, was a woman who had no military or criminal record and was a forty-something florist in Quakertown. The tat stolen from her was on her upper left thigh … a ring of fire. It took the local cops a while to make sense of that, but when they ran her prints—which had never been done by any official agency prior to the autopsy—they matched prints from a string of arsons in which nine people had died over a span of seventeen years.

Number four, David M. Bernstein, was even scarier. All along one muscular arm had been a string of symbols related to medicine and specifically infectious diseases. Turned out he was a bug hunter for the CDC who had worked on the Zika, Ebola, and Covid outbreaks. In that case, the killer had left a nearly skeletal arm from bicep to wrist.

I looked at Crow. "And the latest vic?"

"Paul Williams, 55, industrial security specialist," he said. "Freelance troubleshooter for companies requiring special levels of protection. Works with a lot of corporations that own hospitals, some military contractors, banks. Like that. High-end electronic security like retina scanners, complex coded locks, but also software packages to oversee the function of perimeter and interior security."

"Shit."

He flipped open a folder and dealt out photos like a hand of gin rummy. The one he showed me at the diner was paired with a photo he told me was downloaded from a Facebook page. Funny thought, a biker with a Facebook page. It showed the stolen tattoo in high res, and even if the theme was nothing special for a biker, the close-up proved that the work itself was superb. The other photos were of the victims either in the morgue or at the crime scenes, along with shots of art.

He leaned back in his chair, the old wood creaking. "Thoughts?"

"On which parts?"

Crow spread his hands. "Just ramble. First impressions. Guesses. Anything."

"Before I do, what do the cops have on this?"

"They have two things so far," he said. "Jack and shit."

"Connections between victims?" I asked. "Apart from the ink?"

"Not a thing. We did some pretty deep database searches and, apart from all living within driving distance of where we're sitting right now, there are no connections. Different races and religions, they're across political party lines. Apart from the biker who was a white racist asshole with some jail time for the usual shit bikers get up to, the others are squeaky clean. On the books, at least. There was only so far we could go with the background check on the former sniper teacher. Military hates to share about their own."

"I am aware," I said dryly.

"And," added Crow, "the florist was never even on anyone's radar for the fires she set."

"Which leaves us where?"

"With me asking you to share whatever insights you might have."

I swiped a packet of gum from the top of his desk, popped some pieces out of the blister pack and chewed for a moment. Minty.

"Well ... from a distance I'd say serial killer."

"Gosh," said Crow, "talking with you is like having my very own Sherlock Holmes."

"Bite me," I said. "I guess I have two different ways of thinking about this."

"Which are ...?"

"First, he's a serial killer and these are nothing but trophies. Those photos, they're mostly high-end tattoos. Top quality, without a doubt. So, your guy is a double collector: the skin he's stealing and the art itself. I bet if you find him, he'll have the skin preserved in some creepy Frankenstein way. Somewhere only he'll ever see it."

"Yeah, that fits. What's the other option?"

"The other one is the real reason you asked me instead of every other clown you know who has ink."

He said nothing, but there was a lot going on in his eyes.

"Maybe this guy is like Owen Minor. Not the same, exactly, but someone who more than *wants* the art, but maybe needs it."

"Yeah," he said.

"Yeah," I said.

We sat with that for a bit. Then I saw his expression change. From introspection to a furrowed brow as he studied my face.

"You just thought of something," he said. "What is it?"

I shook my head. "It's foggy. Something way back in my brain but I can't quite grab it."

"What kind of a something?" asked Crow. "Have you heard of something like this?"

I held up a finger, swiveled in my chair so I could look out the window at absolutely nothing, chewed my gum, and tried to unmoor my mind so it would go drifting. Crow was the kind of person who didn't feel the need to push. He waited. I think he was playing *Ridiculous Fishing* on his cell phone, but with the sounds off. I got up and stood by the window. Not sure how long. Five minutes, maybe? Something like that.

"I need to go talk to Patty," I said, and left. I took the folder of photos with me. Crow never said a word.

—3—

Patty Cakes is about the size of a cricket. Short, skinny, all angles and sharp edges, looks emaciated but is really made of steel wire. Tough isn't measured in height, bulk, or biceps inches. She's been through the shit and is still on her feet. One of the reasons that I'll always love her and always respect her.

Also, she has an encyclopedic brain when it comes it tattoo lore.

We sat in two of the three barber chairs in her studio. The walls were covered with her designs and photos of top customers, the best of which were framed. I was not on any of those pics because my tattoos are not art and they are not fun.

She went through the stuff in Crow's folder carefully and silently and I drank two Bia Hoi, a Vietnamese beer that is low sugar and, sadly, low ABV. But it was what she had cold in the fridge.

Patty looked up from the pictures, eyebrows raised. "And ...?"

"And ... tell me what you think."

"Someone's a sick fuck." Her accent was Vietnamese with a veneer of Brooklyn.

"Apart from that," I said.

She considered, shuffling through the photos of the actual tattoos. "Top quality."

"Uh huh."

"Different artists." It wasn't a question. "I can guess who did most of these."

"People you actually know?"

"Know, yes," she said. "Just not in my circle."

Her circle was a group of mostly Asian tattoo artists. All women. All top of the line. All with history. Not sure where they met, but it was likely some kind of support group.

I said, "You ever hear about anything like this?"

Patty went and took two more beers from the fridge, gave me one. She sat on her chair, legs straddling the footrest so she could dangle her feet.

"Yes-s-s-s," she said, drawing it out but with some doubt.

"Tell me."

"Three things," said Patty. "The first is that this man is a hunter."

"Wait," I said, "you're sure this is a man?"

She looked at me with her dark eyes. "It's not the way women kill."

"At the risk of mansplaining here," I said, "isn't that a bit sexist?"

"No," she said, and her expression dared me to contradict.

"Okay, it's a man. What else are you thinking?"

"He's a collector," said Patty. "A true connoisseur. Taking only the best pieces. To frame them, of course."

"Why 'of course'?"

"Because of the sizes, you mean?" she asked.

I said, "What?"

"The pieces he cut out," said Patty. She laid the autopsy photos out on the counter. Each one showed the body on a stainless-steel table with the stark lighting pathologist's use. "Take your time with it. You'll see it."

There was a long, narrow ruler laid along each incision. I'd noticed, but I have to admit I hadn't focused on the measurements. But as I bent to pore over the pictures, I saw they ranged from four-by-six inches for the smallest ones and eleven-by-fourteen for the big one taken from the bug hunter's arm.

"Frame sizes," I said.

"*Standard* frame sizes." She looked at me. "Everyone sells them. Nothing custom, unless he makes them himself. You'll never find him that way."

"What's the third thing?"

It took Patty a long time to answer that. She looked at the photos. I watched the side of her face and listened to the *tick-tick-tick* of a clock on the wall that had miniature tarot cards instead of numbers. It was a quarter past the Broken Tower.

"I think I've *heard* about something like this before," she said.

I sat up straight. "Tell me."

—4—

Chief Crow looked at me. Any other law enforcement officer in the country would be breathalyzing me. Or talking to me about the benefits of therapy.

He sat and listened. His poker face is legendary, but he has a tell. There's a certain quality that his eyes take on. They are dark blue, like blueberries, and mostly they're cheery and affable. But when there's the right note in the air you can see other doors opening in his mind. He *knows* about a lot of this shit, and by shit I mean *weird* shit. He knows who and what I am, and I'm not joking when I say he's met weirder motherfuckers than me. Met, fought, killed. And also adopted. The sergeant of the Pine Deep police force is his adopted son, and *he* is weird on a whole different level.

My point is that Crow didn't freak out. He didn't laugh me out of the office. He didn't tell me that Patty Cakes is out of her mind. I mean, sure, she *is* but not in the usual way.

When I was done—and I rambled a bit—Crow summarized. His mind is orderly like that. Makes him a good cop.

"Patty said she'd heard about a series of murders similar to this—"

"—nearly identical—" I interjected.

"—but in Camden, New Jersey?"

126

"Yes."

"In the Filipino community there," said Crow. "And she thinks this might be the same guy?"

"Same or a copycat."

Crow nodded and swiveled toward his computer. I sat like a schoolboy in my chair while he accessed the kinds of databases available only to law enforcement. I have access to some of the same sites because I work for bail bondsmen, and there are weird rules for fugitive recovery agents like me. I watched his face. Watching faces when people aren't watching you do it is very instructive. I saw his focus and curiosity melt into interest, then deep interest, and then cloud as the details began to trouble him.

"Well ... shit," he said.

"What'd you find?"

"Patty's right."

"She usually is," I said.

He turned the monitor to show me the screen. There were three murders in Camden twenty months ago. All three had been mutilated in the same way. Pieces of flesh cut away. Other trauma had been inflicted on the bodies, but the coroner noted an unusual factor, and added some notes that were intended to explain. Crow and I brailled our way through it:

The primary unifying factor in these patients is a significantly elevated level of prolactin (PRL) in the postmortem venous blood samples. Analysis showed PRL levels consistently over 2000 mU/l. Hyperprolactinaemia is an indicator of tremendous antemortem stress and or pain, however these levels are double that which would be expected postoperative or traumatic deaths. Levels this high are sometimes seen in suicides but this is not consistent with the other evidence surrounding the terminal events. As increased levels of prolactin are associated with increased arterial blood pressure, it is probable that this was the proximate cause of the fatal cerebrovascular accidents in these patients.

"The fuck does all that mean?" I asked.

"I've read a lot of autopsy reports," said Crow thoughtfully, "and I'm moderately familiar with pathologist doublespeak. They all died of strokes induced by some kind of extreme emotional trauma."

"Well, having their tattoos carved out—" I began, but Crow shook his head. He read another section of the report, one that discussed the location and concentration of blood.

"Bottom line," said Crow, "is that the tattoos were excised postmortem. There was not enough blood on or around the actual wounds to indicate they were still alive."

"Which means they died ... how?"

He just looked at me, daring me to read his thoughts, or at least infer them from his expression.

"Oh, come *on*," I protested. "Are you trying to say they were scared to death?"

Crow handed the report to me. "You read this any other way?"

—5—

We sat with that for a long minute.

"How?" I asked.

"I have no freaking clue," said Crow.

"Also, why isn't this a bigger thing?" I said. "These killings are in different towns and two different states. Hasn't that made it an FBI case?"

"I thought about that, too," he said. "And the answer is 'no,' which opens up a whole bunch of new questions."

"As in 'why not'?" I suggested.

"As in who shut that investigation down," said Crow. "And there is no chance at all that this didn't ping real loud in a Bureau database. They have all those pattern-recognition software packages."

"Maybe there's something classified. One of the vics in Camden was a retired lieutenant colonel and one of the new batch is a retired first sergeant. And then there's the CDC guy."

"Sure, but if a case is sealed for whatever reason, there'd be a note in the system that it's restricted, with info on where people like me should address inquiries. But I'm not seeing that. And I should."

"Well … shit."

"This makes it spooky in a whole different way," said Crow. "Pushing back on something that's maybe CIA or DHS or some other alphabet group funded by black budgets is a good way for me to get my wrist slapped."

"Do you care?"

"A little," he said, then gave me a boyish grin. "Not as much as I probably should."

"Look," I said, "I'm not a cop but can you let me use one of the workstations here? I want to log onto some of *my* databases. If it comes back to bite us, then it'll be me misusing your computers. You can throw me in jail overnight or whatever."

The office was empty except for the dispatcher in her little cubicle in the far corner. Crow waved me to a desk near his and logged me in.

"What are you looking for?" he asked.

"Connections," I said.

"Ah." He went back to his desk and for the next few hours we both tapped away at keys and tried to make sense of things.

—6—

Weird shit can always get weirder.

Trust me. I know this firsthand.

Case in point:

I logged into one of my favorite sites that allowed me to access police crime statistics and information in all fifty states. First time through I ran the names of the victims to see if there was any connection now that we had a larger group of names. No joy. But then I ran with a hunch and entered a whole bunch of keyword search arguments based on their professions.

And the computer began lighting up like a pinball machine.

"Crow, you better take a look at this," I called, and he came and leaned over my shoulder.

"Okay," I said, "follow me on this. The Camden victims were all part of the Filipino community. There was the lieutenant colonel, who worked in 'logistics' at Fort Dix in Jersey. There was a YouTube influencer and extreme sports athlete. There was a top-quality private sector security specialist. And there was a retired stunt driver, a guy who'd spent thirty years doing car chases for TV and movies. No immediate connection, right?"

"Go on."

"I searched on their professions and professional connections. Lots of combinations of keywords, then I cross-referenced that with other crimes."

"Looking for what, exactly?"

"*Any* connection, really," I said. "But there's something that's been niggling at me. It bothered Patty, too. And maybe if we hadn't had that thing with Owen Minor stealing tattoos it would never even have occurred to me, but … then something came up. It wasn't something that ever made the papers. It was a report made by local police in Burlington, New Jersey, where Fort Dix is located. They responded to a break-in at the base. Normally they wouldn't because that would be handled by military police, but there was a high-speed chase through some back woods, which brought local PD into play."

"What was stolen?"

"That's restricted, but I can make some guesses," I said. And despite our being the only people within earshot, I lowered my voice. "When I was still in the military, I spent some time at Dix. The 'logistics' unit there is bogus as shit. It's a cover for a rapid-response Spec Ops team. Delta, sometimes, but also some other units with no names."

"And you know this how?"

"I was in one of those teams," I said. "So, you have a logistics officer who knew that base. You have a security specialist who could maybe bypass locks and evade cameras and other systems. And the driver. That high-speed chase went nowhere because the suspect they were chasing eluded everyone. No one could catch him or box him."

"What about the YouTuber?" he asked.

"Forget the YouTube part and focus on the content of his videos. Parkour, acrobatics, mountain climbing, caving. The guy was half circus-daredevil and half ninja."

"So, what are you saying?" asked Crow. "That our perp put together a team and then killed them afterward to keep them quiet?"

"No," I said firmly. "That's not it at all. The base was hit two weeks after the last kill."

"Then …?"

"I think we're seeing something way weirder than someone running and eliminating teams, Crow. The police reports about the chase all indicated that there was a single occupant of the vehicle they were chasing. And there's nothing to suggest that anyone else was apprehended or killed. No list of suspects anywhere I can find."

"I'm not following. How does this line up with those four murders?"

"Because," I said, "I think this guy is doing more than collecting art. They're not really trophies. Not entirely. I think he's collecting *skills*."

He pulled a chair over and sat down on it very carefully.

"Collecting skills," he echoed.

"Yes. Like Owen Minor collected memories."

"Well, fuck me blind and move the furniture," he breathed.

"I know," I said. "Look, he used those skills to break into Fort Dix, probably into whatever the Spec Ops team was there to guard or transport. Maybe a person, maybe files, or whatever. I don't know. But he somehow turned himself into a super soldier. Super villain. Whatever."

Crow stared at the ceiling for a five-count. "Even if this is true—and I more than half think you're out of your mind—why would he steal a completely different set of, um … *skills* … since then. He pretty much made himself Bullseye from *Daredevil*."

"Who?"

"Don't you ever watch superhero movies or TV?"

"Not much, no. I'm a grownup."

"Two things," said Crow. "First, blow me. Second, there's a character in the *Daredevil* comics and film adaptations. A guy who's an acrobat, unparalleled marksman, master level hand-to-hand, and master strategist."

"Does he steal other people's abilities?"

"No, that's more like the Super Adaptoid or—"

"Crow," I said, "shut the fuck up."

He laughed. "Okay. So, this perp is ... something else. But what? A vampire who steals abilities? Again, why take new ones?"

"Maybe they wear off," I said. "Minor's faded after he fed on the memories. Maybe he needs to keep feeding. Or maybe he needed to refine his skill set for a specific mission."

We sat with that for a very long time.

Then Crow said, "I'm going to make a shit-ton of calls about this. Not actually telling anyone I think there's some kind of vampire feeding on skills and knowledge, because even *I* think that's freaky, but on crimes where the perp demonstrated an unusual number of over-the-top skills."

"You know people to ask about that?" I said, smiling.

"You know people, and so do I, son."

"Fair enough," I said. "While you're doing that, I'm going to call a mutual friend."

"Let me guess," said Crow. "Jonatha?"

"Jonatha," I agreed.

—7—

Jonatha Corbiel-Newton is this millennium's Van Helsing. She's a professor of folklore at the University of Pennsylvania and the author of more than two dozen books on supernatural predators in world beliefs. She was in Pine Deep sixteen or so years ago when The Trouble happened. That's when Crow, his wife, and the guy who's now the sergeant discovered that the world was bigger, darker, and more terrifying than they had any right to expect.

I've known Jonatha for a while now, too. We have our own shared history. There are organizations, tribes, departments, clubs where like-minded people gather; and then there are connections forged by blood and shadows and shared experiences. I call that The Family, and Jonatha, Patty, Crow, and I are all charter members.

Jonatha tries to live the quiet life of a scholar, but there are a handful of us who call her and make her step over the line from antiseptic research to the real world.

"Monk," she said when she answered the phone. "I'm by the pool. Tell me this isn't one of *those* calls."

My silence was her answer.

"Sigh," she said. I heard the tinkle of ice cubes in a glass and guessed she wasn't drinking iced tea. "Go ahead," she said, "spoil my day."

I told her everything. Every detail and every suspicion. When I was done, I gave her some time to process before I asked, "Does any of this ring any kind of bell?"

"You said the first victims were all Filipino?"

"Yes."

"But not the recent group?"

"No."

"Well," she said, "I guess that doesn't really matter. The second group, I mean."

"How so? What have you got? I need something, anything, to go on. Make a wild guess if you have to. If you can—"

"*Bebarlang*," she said.

I said, "What?"

"I can't say for sure, of course," said Jonatha, "but if you need me to pull something out of my ass, then I'm going with bebarlang."

"You keep saying that word as if it should make some kind of sense."

"Listen and try not to zone out on me," she said. "In the rural jungles of the Philippines there is a tribe of what can best be described as essential vampires. And before you ask, let me remind you that less than a third of the species of vampires in world folklore were hematophagous, blood drinkers. Some were necrophagous, which are—"

"Flesh eaters," I said. "Yeah."

"And the rest," she continued, "the largest percentage of them, are essential vampires. They feed on life force, breath, hope, sexual essence, memories, faith, and who knows what else. If this murderer you're hunting is what you think it is—and I tend to agree—then there are some creatures in world folklore that might fit."

"Like your boomslangs?"

"Bebarlang," Jonatha corrected.

"Whatever. What are they?"

"Well, as my understanding comes from literature and anecdotal accounts," she said in that professorial voice, "what we know is that the *bebarlangs* are humans who have developed astral projection to such a high degree that they can send their astral bodies to neighboring villages to feed on the life essence of sleeping victims. These invisible predators sometimes attack in packs and can wipe out a family or a whole village in a single night."

"That doesn't sound at all like—"

"Do you want to interrupt or do you want to shush and let a grownup talk?" she asked sharply.

"Shushing, ma'am."

"More *advanced* bebarlangs," she continued, leaning on that one word, "can also intrude into a sleeping person's mind and steal his secrets as well as his life force. The secrets they steal can be anything from where valuables are stored, the plans of rivals, or the victim's ability to know or do certain things."

"Skills," I said.

"Skills," she agreed.

"And ... how does one identify who this thing is and how do I find this berber-whatever?"

"Bebarlang," she corrected with diminishing patience. I think she knew I was fucking with her but chose to be peeved with me. It's not an uncommon reaction. "All forms of aswangs are capable of theriomorphy—shapeshifting—but there is supposed to be a 'tell.' If you look into an aswang's eyes, even if they are in human form, and you see yourself inverted, then you've found your monster. Of course, they can shapeshift very quickly, so it's likely to be the last thing you see."

"Well ... shit."

She laughed. "Don't worry. I've never once heard a credible account of a real bebarlang ... or any aswang, for that matter. And certainly not here in the States."

"Mmm," I said.

"Tell you the truth, Monk, this isn't really my area. I can tell you a lot more about European vampires and werewolves than I can about the creatures from the Philippines. However, I know someone in the Filipino community in Philadelphia who might be able to help, Juan Garcia. My husband did a feature on him sometime back."

Her husband was Willard Fowler Newton, a Pulitzer-winning journalist.

"Is this Garcia guy in the *know*?" I asked, referring to the kind of frank conversation she and I were having.

"Not really. He's an amateur folklorist. Nice guy, but he's had some hard times. Was in a really bad car accident a few years ago. Broke his back, so he's in a wheelchair. Spends a lot of his time at a Filipino community center. Mostly buried deep in some net research for a nonfiction book on monsters he keeps threatening to write. He knows that I have a very open mind for a folklorist—which, sadly, is not as common as it could be—but doesn't know what you know about me."

"Fair enough. Where can I find this Garcia? Do you have an address and phone number?"

She provided them.

"And ... million-dollar question," I asked. "If I find this bebarlang thing ... how do I stop it?"

"From what little I know," she said, "they are vulnerable to knives. The bolo is mentioned in the literature, but possibly because it's a common knife used in farming. But just as most werewolves can be killed in exactly the same way as ordinary wolves—silver bullets are from fiction—a lot of shapeshifters can be killed just as easily."

"That's a relief."

"Not really," she said. "Bebarlangs are incredibly strong, fast, and vicious. And they can transform from their human aspect to their monster selves in the blink of an eye."

"Well ... fuck."

"Go talk with Juan. If anyone knows how to deal with these things, it's him."

—8—

Jonatha called ahead to Garcia and said that a friend of hers wanted to tap him for information about Filipino folklore. She didn't mention what kind, leaving that to me. Instead of having me meet him at the community center, he said he was working from home all day and provided an address.

I drove to Camden and found his place easily enough. A ranch house away from the urban sprawl, with a wide walkway and a wheelchair ramp to the front door. When I pressed the intercom by the door, he buzzed me in and told me where to find him then directed me to a study off the modest living room.

The house was a scholar's den for sure. Overcrowded bookshelves, lots of brooding and grotesque figures on every flat surface, side tables stacked with journals, and curios on the walls. The curtains were open but the shades down, casting the whole place in a somber and contemplative burnt orange glow. I noticed that, despite the clutter, the place was neat as a pin.

I knocked on the study door and he told me to enter.

Juan Garcia sat in a wheelchair tucked into a desk. The

surface of the desk was covered with books and papers, printouts of weird-looking creatures, and transcripts of interviews. It was clear I'd caught him in the middle of working on that folklore book.

"Mr. Garcia," I said, offering my hand, "Jonatha Corbiel-Newton recommended I come and see you."

Garcia shook my hand. Despite the damage to his lower body, his handshake was hard and strong. His face and throat were covered in healed scars and there was a haunted look in his eyes. I'd looked him up before driving down, and the accident he'd been in had been a bad one. His wife had died and Garcia had to be cut out of what was left of their Honda Accord. Around his mouth hard lines were etched: the kind that hard use, great loss, and comprehensive disappointment in life can carve. He was about my age and had been in that chair for six years, and that made him look twenty years older than me. Poor bastard.

He asked about Jonatha while I made myself comfortable.

Then he leaned back in his chair and said, "So ... how can I be of help? You're not an academic," he said, his eyes searching mine.

"I—" But he cut me off.

"Academics always lead with credentials," said Garcia. "It's a dick-measuring thing. We all do it, even those of us who are mostly amateurs."

I grinned, liking him. "And I guess I don't look the part."

I was wearing a very, very old 1973 The Who T-shirt from their *Quadrophenia* appearance at San Francisco's Cow Palace, jeans that had seen better decades, equally disreputable Tims, and a leather motorcycle jacket. I felt like a reject from a Tom Waits song. My head was currently shaved, and my chin needed to be.

"What is your interest, Mr. Addison?"

"Call me Monk," I said, and he was too polite to ask why. Most people think it's either the face—and there's an argument to be made—or that I seem to be constructed of mostly chest and

137

shoulders. I said, "I'm doing some consulting work with the Pine Deep Police Department."

"Consulting on ... Filipino folklore?" He looked amused.

"Nah, not exactly," I said. "There's an ongoing homicide case that *may* involve an element of folklore. Jonatha thought you could help shed some light on it."

His smile clouded a bit. "I'm not sure I'm following this. How could anything from folklore factor into an active murder case?"

"Maybe it doesn't," I said. "Though, for the moment, I'd like to keep the details out of play because I don't want to influence what you might tell me, if you get me."

He spread his hands. "That's an odd request, but since Jonatha sent you, I'll do my best."

I said, "What can you tell me about bebarlangs?"

He blinked at me. It was owlish, slow, and curious.

"That's not the kind of question I'd expect from someone investigating a real-world murder," said Garcia. "But ... very well. First, let's take a step back and talk about aswangs."

"Which are ...?"

"It's a bit of an umbrella name for a large number of malevolent monsters in Filipino folklore," he said. "These aswang legends are particularly common in southern parts of Luzon, and some parts of Mindanao and Visayas, especially the Visayan province of Capiz. They take a startling variety of aspects. Some are physical monsters, many are still human, a few are revenants—reanimated corpses. Some attack directly while others use astral projection to locate and attack their prey. The vampire aswang subtype isn't a typical Hollywood vampire. It uses a proboscis-like tongue rather than sharpened teeth to drain its victims. They don't live in tombs, either. They can blend into ordinary society and even take spouses and raise families. They often feed on their own family members, which can sometimes give them away. The Tagalog *mandurugo*, from the region of Capiz, is an example. But there are also viscera-sucking aswang, such as the *manananggal*, which feeds on internal organs, the contents of the stomach, or even vomit from the sick. Like the vampire aswang, it uses a long tongue. What's fascinating is that by day it often takes the aspect of a beautiful woman, but at night it sprouts wings and the upper torso tears from of the rest of its body and flies off in search of victims."

"That's charming," I said. "Some Vietnamese vampires do that, too. And Malaysian."

His eyes sharpened. "Then you *are* a folklorist."

"Me? Nah. I just picked up some tidbits here and there."

Garcia considered that and nodded. After a moment he continued. "As far as the shapeshifters—the theriomorphs—Europe has its werewolves, Brazil has its werejaguars, India has weretigers, and the Philippines has weredogs, werecats, and werepigs. The canine versions are quite fierce and feed on human flesh."

"Right, and there are witches and ghouls, too," I said, trying to gently goose him along. "What category does the bebarlang fall under?"

"That's harder to answer than you might think," said Garcia. "As Jonatha may have told you, every culture around the world and throughout history has monster legends. My country has been invaded, conquered, and flooded with immigrants from countless nations. Those immigrants and, let's face it, *invaders*, brought their own bloodlines with them. Who knows what kind of hybridized monsters are out there."

"That's disturbing as hell," I conceded. "How are these monsters handled?"

"Depends on what you mean," said Garcia. "In most cases the creature is deterred by charms and other kinds of prophylactic measures. Holy objects, spices, salt, ash, the tail of a stingray, large crustaceans, vinegar, betel nuts, and urine are just some of the things that can keep them from entering a house."

"And each item has to be prepared a special way, I assume?"

"Of course. It's not the like the movies where someone can splash holy water or wave a cross about."

"And to kill one?"

"This is a strange conversation, Mr. Addison."

"More normal than you might think."

He digested that. "To kill a witch aswang, for example, a bolo knife can be used to strike the middle of the witch's back; if that area is not struck with sufficient lethal skill, the witch can lick its wounds to heal its injuries."

"Note to self," I said.

He smiled faintly. "After slaying an aswang with a bolo, the bolo must be planted under the ground. Firearms are not advised for killing aswang, and it is useless to stab and slash at an aswang while it is in the form of an animal. Magic prayers can be used to make the aswang vulnerable; while it is in this helpless state, its body must be cut into pieces. If the aswang is cut into two pieces, each piece must be separated and taken to opposite riverbanks."

"Well, we are speaking hypothetically," I said. "Or ... do you believe in things that go bump in the night?"

He gave me a long and very curious look. "I thought you said you were a friend of Jonatha's."

"I am. Why?"

"She doesn't dismiss cultural beliefs as mere superstition."

"Hey, I meant no offense," I said. "Personally, I keep quite an open mind about things."

Again, he studied me for a long three-count. "Do you indeed?"

"Yes," I said.

"Have you had any experiences with what some people call the 'larger world'?"

"Maybe."

"Maybe," he echoed. "And you're working with the police on a murder case?"

"Multiple murders," I said.

"And you think ... what?" he asked, smiling and shaking his head. "That a bebarlang is involved?"

"Keeping all possibilities on the table."

"And what makes you even think this is a possibility?"

140

I figured it was safe to tell him some of the details and laid it out for him. I even showed him the autopsy photos which I now had on my phone. He leaned close and studied the pictures with great interest, saying nothing until I was done. Then he glanced up at me.

"Just to make sure I grasp this," he said, "you think a bebarlang is killing people in order to take their physical or mental skills and to transform itself into a kind of super-ninja?"

I studied his expression. There was a lot of amusement in his dark eyes.

"Sounds stupid when you put it that way," I said.

"No," he said. "It really doesn't."

He looked me straight in the eyes.

I looked back.

I saw him. And I saw my own face reflected in his eyes.

I was upside down.

I said, "Oh fuck."

Juan Garcia pushed back from his desk. The wheelchair rolled easily on the polished hardwood.

Then he stood.

Easily.

The muscular upper torso was matched by a pair of legs that were not at all wasted. He kicked the wheelchair backward with such force that it slammed into a bookcase, toppling books and small, odd figurines.

"I have been very careful about things," he said. And there was suddenly a bizarre quality to his voice. It was octaves deeper. Maybe too deep. Almost a growl. "How did someone like *you* figure it out?"

I got up, too, knocking my chair over as I backpedaled.

"You shouldn't have gone hunting in Pine Deep," I said.

His eyes narrowed.

"Now I understand ..." he said in that bass rumble. "The police you're working with are from that piece of shit little town. Malcolm Crow ..."

"He'll be happy to know he's that famous."

Juan Garcia smiled a ghastly smile. His face was already beginning to change, to melt away the humanity and take on bestial aspects. I was scared out of my fucking mind.

He said, "Chief Crow will never know how clever you are, Mr. Addison. Though … maybe I'll whisper that in his ear before I devour everything that makes him who he is."

"What's the point of this?" I demanded, backing away, stalling for time while I looked for the closest, easiest exit.

He held his arms wide. "Look at me. Look how powerful I am. Do I look like someone who was nearly cut in half in a car accident? Do I look like a helpless cripple? No. I can run, climb, fight, fuck, *take* whatever I want since everything that mattered was taken from me."

"But breaking into military bases?" I asked. "Why? I don't get it."

"You don't have to get it," he growled, then he laughed. A sneaky, nasty, mocking laugh. "Jonatha thinks she knows everything about everything. Arrogant bitch. She thinks I'm just another Filipino immigrant who came here to live the American dream and just had the bad fortune to get mangled in a car accident. She is as dimwitted as you are oblivious. I came here as an agent of my president, Rodrigo Duterte."

"That fucking psychopath …?"

"He is a visionary and a hero," snarled Garcia. "He handpicked me and my wife because we were his top agents. That accident? We were targeted by American agents. My wife died, and when they saw I was ruined, they could have killed me. They could have at least had the mercy to do that. But instead they *allowed* me to live. They condemned me to live out my years as a cripple, as a broken man."

His face was losing all traces of humanity. I'm not even sure how to describe it. I've never seen anything like it.

"But I was never just an ordinary man. My wife was like me, but that accident actually killed her. Such a loss. Such a waste of life."

I kept moving backward.

"We were patriots, Mr. Addison," said Garcia. "We were elite and respected. I am *still* one of my president's most effective agents. With my new set of skills, I will be able to infiltrate another facility. You clearly know about the last infiltration and think you are trying to stop the second ... but this will be my *ninth*. And there will be many, many more. Tomorrow night I'll enter a biological research lab and bring out weaponized anthrax spores. Aerosolized anthrax that my president will use against the enemies of our country. And you, Mr. Addison, will be found floating in the river."

He stopped talking then because his throat was no longer shaped for human speech.

Jonatha was right. He was fast.

Really damn fast.

If I'd been unarmed, he'd have had me. No doubt about that.

But Jonatha told me about knives. About how the aswang can be killed with knives.

I had knives. I had a pair of really good knives. Two Marine Corps Ka-Bar fighting knives with sharpened clips. Seven inches of carbon steel. I'd made a stop home for them before coming here ... Not that I thought in a million years that Garcia could be the monster.

I'm just a careful motherfucker.

He rushed at me.

I reached under my jacket and pulled steel.

Jonatha was right.

—9—

I was in the ER back in Pine Deep watching the doctor stitch me up.

"And this was from a *fall*?" he asked, one eyebrow raised.

"Yeah," I said. "I fell down my cellar steps into a barrel that was filled with pieces of metal. I make metal art."

"Metal," he said, looking at me.

"Sure," I said.

The doctor gave me one of those meaningless smiles that look like a grimace and let the topic lie. He left forty minutes later. Crow, who had been silent the whole time, was slouched in the guest chair in the ER bay.

"Fell into a barrel of metal," he said.

"Yeah."

"Clumsy."

"Yeah."

We smiled at each other. Not a lot of humor in those smiles. But a hell of a lot of shared understanding. Outside, the sky had grown dark under a canopy of bruise-colored clouds.

We didn't say much more.

What else needed to *be* said? There were monsters in the world. We knew it, and we were both glad most people didn't. In our own way, each of us was a kind of monster. Me maybe more than him.

Thunder growled away to the east and soon a slow, sad, cold rain began to fall.

WE WEAR THE MASKS

—1—

When I found the killer, he was sprawled on a cemetery slab reading poetry.

That kind of slab is a called a ledger. Kind of funny, kind of weird. Or maybe just a coincidence that I was reading too much into.

The killer was alone and spoke the words aloud. I paused beside a gnarled old elm tree and listened. He spoke quietly, and even though he had a low, growly voice, I could make out the words.

"We wear the mask that grins and lies, it hides our cheeks and shades our eyes. This debt we pay to human guile; with torn and bleeding hearts we smile, and mouth with myriad subtleties."

I half-assed recognized the poem. "Is that Paul Dunbar?"

The killer stopped reading, shaded his eyes with the small paperback, and peered at me with dark eyes that looked out but didn't invite me to look in.

"Sure," he said.

"Can't remember the title."

"We Wear the Mask," he supplied, his tone neutral but not hostile. A careful man.

"Right," I said.

We studied each other for a moment.

He was a big guy. Big, ropey arm muscles and mountainous shoulders, bull neck, face that looked like everyone in his hometown had hit him at least once. Lots of visible scars. Doc Martens and jeans; a leather biker jacket rolled into a pillow for his head.

And tattoos.

I'd been told about them. The black tank top he wore showed a lot of them, all over his arms and the visible part of his upper chest. They were all in black and white, and they were all faces. Mostly women's faces; a very few men. Adults and kids.

"Monk Addison," I said, not really making it a question.

"And you are?"

"Joe Ledger."

There was a small flicker in his eyes, and I guessed he was making connections.

"You're what ... a case manager for the Agency?"

"Not now or ever."

"Then what?"

I came and squatted down at the foot of the slab on which he lay.

"I work for a different kind of company," I said. "Not the CIA or FBI or any of the alphabet groups you'd know."

"Is it one of those 'so secret you'll have to kill me' teams?"

"Not really. It's just not one you'd have ever heard of."

He sat up, crossed his legs, and laid the book open and face down on one thigh.

"Rogue Team International," I said.

"Not the DMS?" he asked, and there was a flicker of a devilish smile.

I gave that a moment. "Crow tell you that?"

Malcolm Crow was the chief of police in that little town. I'd met him the first time I visited Pine Deep. Not sure if he and I were actually friends. Allies, for sure. But Crow, for all his outwardly jovial and prankish humor, had a hell of a lot of walls up. I was in his circle of trust when it came to the kinds of things I do, but that wasn't all the way in. To be fair, that went both ways.

Monk shrugged. "It came up in conversation."

"Over beers?"

He gave me a look. "Nice try."

Crow had been going to meetings for a very long time. His drink of choice was either coffee or Yoo-hoo.

Monk picked up his paperback, plucked a stem of grass to use as a bookmark, and tossed the book onto the marble.

"Are we going somewhere with this, sport?" he asked.

"Crow told me something about you," I said.

He didn't ask what. Just waited.

"You're a PI?" I asked.

"Skip tracer, mostly."

"So, you can find someone either way."

A shockingly red cardinal flew past and landed atop a nearby tombstone. We both watched it for a moment.

"You looking to hire me?" asked Monk, still watching the bird.

"I'd like to talk about it."

"Just 'cause you're a friend of Crow's don't mean I work pro bono."

I patted my shirt pocket. He heard the crinkle of paper. "Not looking for a freebie."

He held up a hand and I fished out the check with two fingers and offered it to him. He took it, glanced at the number. One eyebrow lifted and handed the check back. I took it but didn't put it back in my shirt.

"Am I supposed to be awestruck by the number of zeros?"

"What, you have something against money?"

"I like money just fine," he said. "I'm a little particular about what you think that amount will buy."

"What if I said I wanted someone dead?"

He smiled. It wasn't a very nice smile. "You can take your choice of possible replies," he said. "You could go fuck yourself. You could tell Crow that I'm not in the mood to be punked. Or you could go fuck yourself."

"You said that twice."

"That's because I mean it."

"I ran your background. You were Special Forces and then you were a PMC."

"Past tense."

We sat with that for a moment.

I reached over, took his book, opened it to glance at the Dunbar poem, nodded, then replaced his grass-stem bookmark with the folded check.

"I think we'll get along fine," I said. "You like diner food?"

—2—

We sat in a corner booth at the Scarecrow on Main Street. Pine Deep pretends to be a sleepy little arts-and-crafts tourist town, but I knew a lot about its real history. It can be summed up in three words: Very. Weird. Shit.

That wasn't why I was there, though.

Or, come to think of it, maybe it was.

I was working my way through a mushroom, onion, tomato, and cheddar omelet and a lot of very crisp bacon. Monk was doing an admirable job with today's special—an open-faced turkey sandwich with all the trimmings. No idea how many cups of coffee we'd each had. I judge diners on omelets and coffee—and the Scarecrow was way up near the top of my list. And the waitress, a big, middle-aged blonde with lots of frosted hair and a cardigan over her uniform, which was decorated with a slew of cloisonné pins of cats and small dogs. Her name, God bless her, was Betty.

Every good diner should have a Betty.

I noticed that she smiled at Monk. A lot. Understand, he is not a good-looking guy. Vin Diesel could play him in a movie, but they'd have to rough him up a bit. Hard to peg his race. Bit of this, bit of that.

But the waitress liked him and when he smiled at her there was no tough guy attitude. No flirtation, either. He was kind to her, and polite. And Betty seemed to be at ease around him. That said a lot. Sure, you probably think I'm crazy for taking character judgment cues from a diner waitress, but that's never steered me wrong. Not once.

When we were alone, Monk said, "You're taking the long way around getting to the point."

"I am," I admitted.

"Any particular reason?"

"It's a strange ask."

His eyes narrowed just a little. "Ask anyway."

I sipped my coffee and sat back, cradling the cup between my palms. "The way you find people …"

I left it open. He knew I wasn't talking about him running down bail skips.

"What about it?"

"Does the blood sample have to come from a dead person?"

Monk studied me. "That's how I work."

"Always?"

"Pretty much."

"'Much' isn't the same as always," I said.

He ate a forkful of turkey stuffing, chewing as he looked past me out the window. There was very little traffic in the middle of a sunny spring afternoon.

"It's not something I like doing if the vic is alive."

"Why not?" I asked.

"There are complications," said Monk. "It can do some damage to people who've already been hurt. And … there's the other thing. Maybe Crow told you about what happens after I wrap one of those kinds of cases up."

"The victims haunt you." It felt weird to say that out loud.

Monk sipped his coffee and looked at me over the rim. Then

he set the cup down. "Little more complicated than that," he said, "but roughly ... yeah."

I glanced around. "All the time?"

"All the time."

"Even now?"

"You can stop looking around, Ledger," he said. "*I* can see them. No one else can."

"Can you see them right now?"

"I see them all the time," he said.

"Jesus skateboarding Christ," I said.

We drank some coffee and looked at nothing at all for a bit.

"I don't get how that works," I said. "If someone is murdered and they—I mean their ..."

"Pick a word," said Monk. "Spirit. Ghost. Whatever."

I shook my head. "You do realize this is a weird conversation, right?"

"This is my life. A ghost hires me to find who killed them. Not for revenge, because I don't really do that. They want me to stop the fuckers from killing anyone else. I find the asshole who killed them and ... do whatever I have to do. When the case is closed, the ghost stays with me."

"That's ... that's so unfair."

"Oh, you think life's supposed to be fair," said Monk. "Wow. Must be fun to live inside your head. Are there Disney animals prancing around?"

"Actually," I said, meeting his eyes, "I don't think life is fair at all. When I was a teenager my girlfriend and I were jumped by a gang of older teens. They stomped me near to death and raped her. Ten years later she killed herself. I never found those guys—and believe me I looked."

"Fuck, man ..."

"A few years ago, one of the bad guys I've been chasing halfway around the world delivered a bomb to my family's house on Christmas Eve. Killed everyone, including my little niece and nephew, my dad, my brother, and my brother's pregnant wife. So ... no, I don't think life is fair."

"Jesus fuck," he said, placing his hand on my forearm. "I'm sorry, man."

"Thanks."

We looked at—and through—each other for a moment. "Guess we both have ghosts haunting us," said Monk.

"We do," I agreed.

Betty came and refilled our cups.

When she was gone, Monk said, "Tell me about the case."

—3—

I gave him the bones of it.

"In my line of work," I said. "I sometimes do joint actions with other teams. Official or unofficial because not everyone goes to war under a flag, you dig?"

"I do," he said."

"One of those teams is known as Arklight," I continued. "It's an all-female group that goes after human traffickers. And by 'goes after' I mean they play very rough."

"All women?"

"Why? You don't think women are tough enough for that kind of work?"

Monk laughed. "Fuck, man. If I was a bad guy the *last* thing I'd want hunting me was a group of well-armed and pissed-off women. Rather cover myself in steak sauce and go swimming with bull sharks."

"Lot of guys don't get that," I said.

"Lot of guys are idiots."

"Fair."

"So ... these Arklight women ... what about them?"

"They have field teams, and one of them was operating in New Jersey, down near Hammonton. You know the area?"

"Edge of the Pine Barrens, sure," he said. "Blueberry capital of the world. Lot of Philly and New York Mafia guys used to live there. That who your bad guys are?"

"Unlikely. The mobsters who live there generally don't shit

where they eat. More to the point, they don't want trouble where their families live. And, while they're into prostitution, it's not the same level of human trafficking."

"Okay," he said.

"However, someone *is* using that part of the Pine Barrens, the southwestern edge of the Wharton State Forest, to process women and children for sale to a specialty clientele."

"I'm already not liking where this is going."

"You won't," I said. "Arklight sent a five-person team in, following a tip that runaways were being picked up from all along the Jersey shore. Kids as young as eight, mostly girls. A few boys. And women no older than twenty."

"Fuck."

"The tip Arklight was following led them to a kind of processing and training facility where the abductees were cleaned up, given their shots, given dental work, and all kinds of grooming. Taught to—and I quote—'act right.'"

Monk looked at the food on his fork and then set it down. "Get to the part where these Arklight gals cut some nuts off."

"Wait, it gets worse," I said. "Usually, a lot of these kinds of victims are groomed for sale to chicken ranches, at least the young ones. And the women who cleaned up well enough went to private collectors, exclusive men's clubs or party boats. The ones who caused issues were put on the streets, with heavy-handed pimps running them."

"You said 'usually,'" he prompted.

"The last report from the Arklight team said that these victims were being prepped for film work."

"What kind?"

"Three kinds," I said, feeling my stomach turn to acid. "Videos. Specialty stuff for exclusive buyers. Rape films, with guarantees that the subjects were virgins. Torture films. And snuff films."

Monk looked as sick as I felt. But he said, "Okay, then why isn't SWAT crawling all over these assholes? There's no jury in the world who'd let any of these cocksuckers skate."

"Well ... Arklight hit the facility and hit it really hard. They weren't in the mood to take prisoners. There's not much of a chapter on 'mercy' in their playbook."

"First good news I heard," said Monk. "How does any of this involve me?"

"The assholes at that facility must have been tipped somehow," I said. "The Arklight team went dark. No communication at all. I happened to be in Baltimore—visiting my family's grave—when I got a call asking me to take a look; there was no other Arklight team available. I drove up to Jersey to the address my contact gave me. What I found was a bunch of firefighters hosing down the ashes of that facility. An old cranberry processing plant that closed down pending litigation between heirs of the owners. There were eight dead. Five men and three women. The latter of which are likely most of the Arklight team, though it'll take dental records to prove it. The men were probably part of the group of scum-suckers running the place."

"No kids? No hostages?"

"No. And whoever torched the joint used a lot of accelerant. Cops aren't likely to find evidence."

Monk paused. "Wait, back up ... you said that the three dead women were *most* of that Arklight team ..."

"Right. It was a four-person team," I said. "The fourth was found in the woods. Don't know her real name. Arklight agents use combat call-signs 24/7. Hers is Tituba. She has three bullets in her and third and fourth degree burns over eighty percent of her body. Tituba's in a coma. There's brain activity, but not much of it. Doctor I talked with said she isn't likely to survive, and if she does ... well ... there's only so much modern medicine can do."

"Fuck me."

"Yeah."

"So ... she's alive but the chances of Tituba telling us what happened and where the prisoners might have been taken are between slim and none."

Monk started to take a sip of coffee, stopped, and sighed. "Which is why you came here."

"Yes."

"How did you even know to ask Crow about me?"

I hesitated on that. "Well ... last time I saw Crow, which was at my family's funeral, he and I went out and had a lot of diner coffee. I knew that there had been some kind of weird-ass thing that went on in Pine Deep a couple of years ago. Something about a freak who stole tattoos and the memories attached to them."

"Owen Minor," said Monk. "Yeah. Past tense."

I nodded. "While Crow was telling me about it, he told me about you."

"You guys have that kind of relationship?"

"Based on the last three times I was in Pine Deep ...? Yes."

Monk chewed on that for a bit. "Okay, two things," he said. "One, I'm not happy that Crow told you about me. It's not for public broadcasting."

"I'm not the public," I said. "The group I work with—Rogue Team International—we get into some very, very weird shit."

"Not as weird as the shit I get into."

"Don't bet on it."

We looked at each other while I drank some coffee. Monk nodded.

"Okay," he said.

"What's the second thing?"

"If I do this," Monk said. "If I do the ritual with Tituba, then that isn't the end of it."

"Meaning what?"

"Meaning if you're going to go fuck these boys up then you're not doing it without me."

I smiled. "Crow said you'd say that."

"We have a deal?"

I held out my hand. "God damn right."

"Before we go," he said, "we need to make a stop. I have a friend who needs to come with us."

I nodded. "The tattoo artist?"

"Her name's Patty."

"Then let's go get her," I said.

—4—

I'd told Monk that I was familiar with "weird." But then he went and upped the game on me.

We went to the hospital where Tituba was on life support in the ICU. Hospital policy is that guests aren't allowed in ICU except in rare cases. My boss, Mr. Church, made a few calls and suddenly everyone at the hospital was tripping over themselves to accommodate us.

"Who do they think we are?" whispered Monk as we headed down the hall to Tituba's room. "I mean—you look like a baseball player and I look like a thug. Neither of us look even remotely like doctors."

"Honestly, I have no idea. But the word I got was that the staff would give us ten minutes alone with Tituba, no questions asked."

He gave me a funny look. "Your boss, this Mr. Church character ... he must have some real juice."

I grinned. "You have *no* idea."

We found Tituba's room and paused in the doorway. Hospitals always smell awful—the stink of too much antiseptic, the nasty-sweet smell of failing bodies, the olio of medicines, and a general air of sickness. However, we were both smacked in the face with another, much worse aroma. Burned meat.

It is a terrible thing to experience, especially in context. Whereas I'd never met Tituba before, she was in the extended "family" of the RTI. Violin, the senior field agent for Arklight was an ex-lover of mine and, more importantly, she was a fellow soldier fighting the good fight. Not for politics or a government, but the deeper and, to us, more real and meaningful war against true evil. Monk and I, like Violin and Mr. Church and the rest of our fellow warriors, were monsters. We had each done dreadful

155

things, but always for the right reasons. We went to war under a black flag because to stay our hands, to stand aside, would be to allow the innocent to be hurt. Folks like us, once committed to the war, have no real exit strategy, no retirement plan. I used to believe it was a kind of hubris that made me feel that it was my *place* to be in the war; but I've learned different. There are not enough people on our side. Never enough. And so, we stay in the game. We do not and cannot lay down our swords and shields.

The people who did this to Tituba were a different kind of monster. They did this because of greed, because of a total lack of empathy—or worse, a disregard for it. They have no mercy, no pity, no real kindness, no moral compass. They are worse than any storm or flood or infection because those things have no malice, no intent to harm. These people thrive on pain and humiliation, on destruction and viciousness. I'd said as much to Monk on the drive to Jersey, but I soon realized I was preaching to the choir.

We stood in the doorway and looked at what was left of a human being. Most of her was wrapped in burn dressings. Every kind of machine pinged and beeped. They fed her and breathed for her and maintained the pretense of life.

For her. For a warrior who had tried to stop them from destroying the lives of young women and children.

I'm fairly eloquent, but there were no words for what I felt. Beside me, Monk stood in a sham of nonchalance; but I could feel the outrage, the pity, the compassion. And the hate.

"Draw the curtain," he said in a voice that was tight and hoarse.

I closed the door and pulled the curtain across. He reached into his inner jacket pocket and removed some items: a small syringe, an alcohol swab in a packet, and a little glass vial with a rubber stopper.

"Can she feel pain?" he asked.

"I don't know," I said.

He moved around to her left side where there was a small,

unburned patch of skin on the inside of her forearm, just below the elbow. Looked at the syringe. "Fuck."

With more gentleness and care than I would have expected from so brutish a man, he swabbed the skin with the alcohol, then inserted the needle and drew off a few cc's of blood. He removed the stopper and carefully shot the blood into the vial. I saw that there was some clear liquid already inside.

"Saline?" I asked.

Monk looked at me for a moment. "Holy water," he said.

He packed up his stuff and stowed it all away inside his leather jacket.

Then we lingered for a few minutes, looking down at the ruin of a powerful woman. Violin had texted me a photo of Tituba so that Monk's tattoo artist friend would have a reference. She had been born in Barbados and was twenty-six years old. Very dark skin, light brown eyes, a careful smile. Violin told me that she'd been taken from the streets of Bridgetown and sold to a brothel when she was thirteen. An Arklight agent named Sycorax freed her and seventeen other girls when Tituba was fifteen, and by then the madam running the brothel had forced Tituba to have two abortions. After the second one, the madam had her pet doctor tie her tubes. No more children.

Sycorax had cut the madam's throat in front of the freed prostitutes. Tituba willingly joined Arklight, eventually leading her own team. They ran dozens of successful missions, but that story ended in the Jersey Pine Barrens.

"Let's go," said Monk.

We went.

—5—

Patty Cakes, the tattoo artist, was a short, heavily tattooed, nearly emaciated Vietnamese woman with shadows in her eyes. I did not know her story and Monk offered nothing. Nor did Patty. She seemed wary of me at first, but when we all sat down at a table in a suite we rented at a local hotel, I told her Tituba's story. While I spoke, Patty studied my eyes and the lines on my face. Something changed between us then. There was no need for us to talk about it. We all got it.

She extended her hand to Monk. "Give."

I saw that there was a tattoo of a small girl on the back of Patty's hand. A smiling little face, beautiful and innocent, and placed so that Patty would see it every time she worked on a client.

"Is that your daughter?" I asked. Patty gave me one of the coldest looks I'd ever gotten but said nothing. Monk's eyes jumped to mine and he gave the tiniest shake of his head. I did not pursue the topic.

He removed the vial from his pocket and handed it to her. Patty held it up to the light, shook it, looked at it again.

"Okay," she said. "I'll get set up."

She had a portable tattoo kit in a beat-up old brown leather suitcase. Patty opened it on the coffee table and began sorting through her stuff. There was a pen-style tattoo machine, which looked like a big magic marker. Monk took that and plugged the charging cord into the wall. There was a foot pedal attached to the power cord that she tested by stepping on it to make the needle work.

I watched as Patty laid out a plastic sleeve-cover for the machine and a vet wrap, which is like an Ace bandage that would give her better grip and more control. She pulled over a small table —the kind intended to allow you to eat while sitting in a comfy chair—and she covered that with Saran Wrap to create a sterile place for her tools. She placed a tube of A&D ointment which she used to lubricate the skin and hold the ink caps in place so that they didn't spill when she dipped into them. Then she laid out small caps for her ink—the colors were simple: white and black. Next was a Nalgene squeeze bottle of antibacterial soap mixed with distilled water, and a squeeze bottle of rubbing alcohol.

Then she pulled on a pair of black nitrile gloves and nodded to Monk. He took off his leather jacket and the black tank.

Nearly every inch of his torso was covered with tattooed faces. In any other circumstance that would have been on the weird side of cool, but I now knew the meaning behind them. Each was the face of someone who had been brutally murdered and whose ghost now haunted Monk.

I mean … I sometimes see the ghosts of my family and a few other key people in my life—Grace Courtland, Helen, a few others—but to be haunted all the time? Shit. I'm already crazy by any useful metric, but that would drive me out of what's left of my mind. And yet Monk Addison seemed to be able to deal. When this was all over, and if we were both on *this* side of the grave, I wanted to ask him how he managed it. Maybe there was something I could use.

She paused and then fished one more thing out of her bag—a thick leather strap that had visible bite marks in it. She handed this to Monk.

"I didn't think tattoos hurt that much," I said.

They both gave me identical pitying looks.

"You think this is a normal ink job?" asked Monk.

"I …"

"He doesn't know shit," said Patty. Her tone was matter-of-fact, nearly absent of inflection. Wasn't sure if that was how she always was, or because a stranger was in the room. Probably the latter.

Monk sat down in a chair and leaned back, the strap still in his hand. Patty adjusted the shades of the bedside lamps to bath him in brightness.

"Picture," said Patty, snapping her fingers in my direction.

I took out my cell, found the image, and handed it to her. She studied it for a long, silent time, then laid the phone on Monk's thigh. There was a spot on his chest, just below a picture of a young Asian girl. Then I realized with quite a harsh jolt that the girl inked on Monk's chest was the same as the one on the back of Patty's hand.

Oh fuck.

I wanted—needed—to say something, to apologize to Patty, but Monk's headshake had warned me, and I kept my peace.

"Strap," said Patty. Monk sighed reluctantly and placed it between his teeth. He nodded, and Patty went to work.

I sat on the edge of the bed and watched.

She worked fast and yet the level of detail was astounding. It was photo-real, as were all of the faces. Again, that was impressive and creepy as hell.

Years ago, before I met Mr. Church and got shanghaied into working for him, all of this would have completely freaked me out. After all, this was some kind of magic. Or sorcery. Or something. Not really sure of the difference. While working for Church I'd seen some stuff that shoved me completely out of my comfort zone. Things that challenged my accepted worldview and forced me to accept that the world was far larger, more complex, and much, much stranger than I once believed. It's fair to say that I no longer know the limits of what I do, can, and should accept as truth.

All that said, seeing Patty ink Tituba's face on Monk's chest unsettled me on a very deep level. You see, apart from being haunted by the Arklight agent's ghost, as soon as that tattoo was completed, Monk would relive everything that happened to the woman. He would, in essence, *be* her. He would see everything she saw; hear everything she heard. And, God help me, *feel* everything she felt.

I felt myself tensing, gripping the edge of the mattress as the face took on more and more form. More reality. My heart was hammering so hard it hurt. I kept realizing I was holding my breath and had to gasp out lungsful of stale, poisoned air.

"Here we go," said Patty, and this time there was emotion in her tone. Sadness and pity. It was a lot like battlefield empathy when a soldier is sitting vigil for a critically wounded comrade.

Monk nodded. His face was dripping with sweat, and his hands were closed around the arms of the chair with such force his big muscles were as rigid as stone, the veins thick as electrical cables.

Patty took a breath and inked the last little bit that completed the face.

Monk sat still for two, three seconds.

Then he threw back his head and screamed.

—6—

It was bad.

It took a long time.

Monk looked like a man strapped into the electric chair.

Patty knelt beside his chair, not touching him but clearly wanting to. Her hands kept beginning the motion of reaching for him and each time she pulled them back through sheer force of will.

I wanted to do something—*anything*—to help, but when I started to rise, Patty wheeled on me and hissed like a cat. I sat down, helpless and appalled.

Finally, the screams and the terrible physical tension slowed.

Slowed.

And stopped.

Monk caved forward, head hanging between his shoulders, chest heaving, body slick with sweat, hands twitching.

Before I could say anything there was a forceful knock on the door. I hurried over, glad to have *something* to do. I opened it a crack and saw the same guy who'd checked us in downstairs. Beyond him, peeking out through a narrowly opened door, was the face of the person in the room next to us, and I understood.

"Sorry," I said, cutting the desk clerk off at the pass. "We're watching a monster movie. Had the sound up too much. Must have sounded like bloody murder. I'll keep the volume down. I apologize. Really. Sorry."

Before he could really get in a word, I handed him a five-dollar bill and closed the door. Quietly.

When I turned around, Monk was sitting up a little straighter, but he looked like he'd been thrown down a flight of stairs after being mugged.

"Is it always this bad?" I asked.

Patty's face was unreadable. "Only except when it's worse."

Not really an answer, but still answer enough.

I walked over and squatted down in front of his chair. "How are you doing? And no, that's not the world's dumbest question. I'm serious. I've never seen this before. How *are* you?"

When he looked at me, I did not see much of Monk in his eyes. Instead, there were lights that I knew did not belong to him.

"Don't touch him," warned Patty.

I glanced at her. "Why?"

"The memories—*her* memories—are still alive. He's still living it."

"Jesus."

"Give him a few minutes."

I stood up and went back to sit on the bed and watched Patty clean her stuff and pack it all away.

"Did you do all those faces?" I asked.

She cut me a look. "Most of them."

"Why? No ... that's the wrong question. *How?* How did you know to do this? How did *he* know?"

"It's complicated," she said. And it was all she was willing to say on the subject.

Monk suddenly got up and blundered past us. He went into the bathroom, slammed the door, and I heard him retching. He was in there for a very long time. I glanced at Patty.

"It's like that sometimes," she said, then her face softened a little. "When it's really bad. When the memory is really ..."

She left the rest hang.

I sat there, feeling wretched and sad and freaked out.

—7—

When Monk came out of the bathroom he went over and hugged Patty. Not sure what the current state of their relationship was. Not lovers, but more than friends. He was twice her size, but he clung to her. I felt immensely awkward and decided that I needed to go to the bathroom. Or, at least, into the bathroom.

When I came out, Patty was gone and Monk was standing at the window looking out at the cars in the parking lot. I sat back down on the bed. After two or three minutes, he spoke.

"I told her."

"Told … who?"

"Tituba."

"Oh."

"I told her the deal. The costs."

I waited.

"The things those motherfuckers did to her sisters …" He shook his head. "It's all in my head, man."

"Jesus. I'm sorry. I should never have—"

"No," he said sharply, cutting me off. "This is what I do."

There was still a tremolo in his voice.

"What did … *she* say?"

"Exact words?"

"I guess, yeah."

Monk turned and his face was a mask of pain and hatred. "She told me to ruin them. That was her word. Ruin."

"Christ."

"She knew what they had been doing. What they will keep *on* doing. What they were doing to the women they kidnapped was beyond awful. What they do to the kids …?"

He shook his head, not willing to put it into words, and I sure as hell did not need to hear it. I understood.

After a long moment he said, "Funny thing is that when I pulled triggers for Uncle Sam, and even when I was a PMC, I saw things as black and white. Good guys and bad guys. One set of political exigencies versus another. Maybe cultural or ideological clashes, you dig?"

"Sure."

"But all that time I never really believed in good and evil. Not as existential concepts. Nobody had a really white hat or a really black hat." He shook his head. "Hard to believe I was ever that naïve, but I never truly believed that *evil* was a thing. Evil for its own sake, above and beyond politics or greed. Actual evil."

"And now …?"

He shook his head. "Now I know that it exists."

I said, "A buddy of mine put it this way once—nature versus nurture versus choice. Evil is a choice. It's a line drawn by ethics and civilization and religion and all accepted ideological excuses. But evil? That's a deliberate choice."

Monk nodded. "Yes, it is."

We stood with that hanging in the air for quite a while. Then I said, "Big question is, did Tituba know enough to give us a lead?"

It was weird to say it, and Monk's answer was a smile.

Trust me when I say that you do not *ever* want anyone to smile at you like that.

And, God help me, I think I smiled the same way.

—8—

The location Tituba had provided was a commercial graphics company in Mullica River Beach near Batsto, tucked into a corner between arms of the Wharton State Forest. It was a sprawling one-story structure made from cinderblock. Front door, back door, and a small loading bay. No windows at all.

We drove by the building twice. Each time from a different direction. We didn't pause. One time I was behind the wheel and Monk was looking, matching it to the borrowed memories in his head. Second time he drove and I scoped out the surrounding landscape.

We pulled into the parking lot of a paint and tile store that was closed for the day. Monk pulled us into a spot where overhanging tree branches cast a pool of dense shadows.

"You're the super-secret agent," he said. "You have a plan in mind?"

"If I was even half sure there weren't hostages in there," I said, "I'd be leaning toward epoxying all the doors shut and torching the place."

"And I'd be okay with that."

"But we can't take the risk."

"No," he agreed.

We looked out the window at the empty lot.

"You've done this sort of thing before, right?" I asked.

"Once or twice," he said casually, meaning a lot more than that.

"You remember your ABCs or are you rusty?"

It was too dark in the car to see his face, but I could feel him looking at me. And I could tell the wattage of that look.

"Question withdrawn."

"Thing is," he said, "I got a Glock nine with a single mag, a knife in a shoe holster, and that's it. No body armor."

"Son," I said, "I didn't come all this way to fuck around."

I popped the trunk. We got out and stood in the pale glow of the trunk light. He watched as I opened two metal cases.

"Fucking hell," he said. "You planning on storming the gates of hell?"

"Boy Scout motto," I said.

He nodded.

Be Prepared.

We suited up.

We each put on body armor—my stuff is a blend of Kevlar, spider-silk, and graphene. It'll stop anything just shy of an armor-piercing rifle bullet fired by a sniper. It'll even turn a blade, which Kevlar alone will not. Limb pads and groin protectors. Multi-purpose chest harnesses and equipment belts on which were plenty of ammunition pouches, pouches for flash-bangs and other things that went *boom*. I had an Emerson CQC-7BW folding tactical knife. Similar in weight and length to the Wilson Rapid Response I used to carry. It's eight inches overall, with a 3.3-inch blade. Weighs 5.2 ounces, so it puts virtually no drag on a fast hand. I have very fast hands.

I didn't have magazines for the model of Glock Monk had, but he was fine with a SIG Sauer P226, which is the same one I carried. That way, in a pinch, we could share magazines. The mags were chambered for the .357 SIG, a high-velocity, high-penetration round that had all the stopping power a couple of maniacs like us needed. I'd brought shotguns, too, but we left them. Can't trust a scatter gun when there was likely to be a lot of friendlies in the area.

"What are those?" Monk asked, pointing to a pair of odd-looking handguns. "They some kind of Taser?"

"No," I said. "Snellig A22XPs. High-velocity gas dart guns. Loaded with Sandman, a ketamine-based immediate-onset knockout cocktail. Lightweight, high-capacity magazine firing collagen darts. Trust me when I say you do not want to take an accidental shot. Instant knockdown and you spend the next five to eight hours having the worst nightmares of your life."

"Damn."

I took one and showed him how to use it, which was very simple.

Monk turned to me. "You planning on taking prisoners?"

"No," I said. "But if the hostages panic during the fight ... we can't wrangle them and deal with the bad guys."

"You'd use that Sandman shit on kids?"

"Only if it was the only way to keep them safe."

"You ever done that?"

"Yes."

"They had nightmares?"

"So did I."

He nodded. We both strapped the Snelligs to our thighs.

Last thing I took was a two-pocket pouch. One side had some gadgets I've found useful in the past, like breaching plasters, tripwires, and that sort of thing. The other pouch had a bunch of what looked like dead sparrows and mice.

"The fuck's that shit?"

"Drones," I said.

"Well … hell. And you just happen to have stuff like this in your trunk?"

"Better to have and not need than need and not have."

"I saw that embroidered on a decorative pillow once," he said.

I closed the trunk, and we walked very quietly to the row of pine trees that separated the paint store parking lot from the graphics lot. Monk watched as I took three bird drones, switched them on and threw them, one by one, into the air. The wings deployed and they flapped off like real birds. The AI and guidance software was next gen … by like a mile.

I pushed up my sleeve and punched a few keys on the small tactical computer wrapped around my forearm. It was lightweight and constructed on flexible plastic, so it fit to my arm without bulk.

"You cats have some nifty toys," said Monk.

"Our science team are overachieving super nerds," I said. "Okay, I'm engaging thermal scans. Let's see who's in there."

"Thermal scans? Okay, James Bond."

"The better pop culture reference is Ethan Hunt."

"Who?"

"Character Tom Cruise plays in the *Mission: Impossible* films. Don't you ever go to the movies?"

"Don't you ever even visit the real world?" he countered.

"Touché."

The thermal signal from the drones showed up as a collection of red dots on a black approximation of the building floorplan. We bent close and studied it. I used the sizing function to highlight clusters of the red dots here and there.

"Lot of people in there," said Monk. "But how can we tell who's who?"

"Size. Look, see there? Those thermal signatures are smaller than the others. That's a kid or small woman."

"If that's the case, then look at that," he said, pointing to a cluster of about fifteen small dots in a corner of the building and one larger dot outside. "Hostages and a guard?" he suggested.

"That'd be my guess."

We continued scanning. There was one room, a bit larger than the others, where there were at least a dozen larger dots in various places, and then a small dot and a large one central to all of them. Various other heat flares were visible.

"Lots of machinery," I said. "Probably cameras and recording equipment, lights, and all that."

Monk pointed to the big and little dot in the middle. "That's a kid and adult," he said with a growl in his voice. "Those pricks are making a movie right now."

I pushed my sleeve down and we looked through the trees at the building. I oriented myself.

"That's our way in," I said.

"Let's haul ass," said Monk.

But I touched his arm. "I know you've been in combat, man," I said. "So, you know to pick your targets and conserve ammo. That's not the O.K. Corral in there."

Monk gave me a hard look. "I know what that place is, Joe."

We nodded to one another.

And then we were moving.

—9—

The drones told us there were no motion sensors, so we ran like hell, taking advantage of the many cars and pickup trucks parked in the lot. Once we reached the door farthest from where the filming was being done, we crouched and listened for any noise that would indicate we had been spotted. But there was nothing.

I removed an Anteater from my pouch and very quietly explained to Monk that it was a device for detecting surveillance electronics. As expected, the door was wired with an alarm. Beside the door was a good quality card reader.

"How we going to get past that without tripping the alarm?" he asked.

"Watch and learn, Grasshopper."

I took a device from my pouch that was roughly the size of a quarter. After peeling plastic from one side, I pressed it to the underside of the card reader and gave it a few seconds for the software to uplink to MindReader, the scary-as-balls supercomputer my team uses. After counting Mississippis, I took a blank keycard from my pouch and slowly swiped it. Counted again, then swiped it a second time. This time the red light over the door turned to a comforting green.

"Can I get one of those?" he asked. "It'd make my life a shit-lot easier."

"Let's wrap this and then we'll talk," I said.

We drew our weapons. Both of us had high-end sound suppressors on our handguns. They are not actually silent, but they're usefully quiet. Monk opened the door and covered me as I moved inside and faded left. He came in and eased the door shut.

We were in a loading bay. There were two panel trucks inside, and I could guess that's how they transported the prisoners and equipment from Hammonton. We moved down the gap between the trucks and paused when we heard a sound. A moment later a guard came into view. He wore the kind of generic security uniform you'd expect for companies of this kind and had a Bluetooth earpiece in his left ear. He spoke in a low voice as he strolled.

"... yeah, we'll be done in a couple hours," he said. "That works for me, 'cause I'm beat. Been a long day. What? Nah ... everything's good. Not even a peep from the cops. Huh? Sure, sure. What do you want on it? Don't give me any of that pineapple bullshit. Pep? 'Shrooms? That works. Peppers on your half. Okay. I'll call you when I'm done and pick it all up on my way. Nice. Later."

He ended the call and then Monk ended him. Two shots center mass. The asshole was dead before he knew he was in trouble. He crumpled in place.

I took his phone and pocketed it. MindReader can crack cell phone encryption, and even if the other people here were using burners—and the guard was not—we'd be able to get all calls to and from, text messages, images, and even grab stuff from the GPS.

We moved to the exit door. It was closed but not wired. I opened it a quarter inch so we could listen. Nothing immediately outside but deeper into the building I heard a sound that drove nails into me. A kid, a little boy, was crying. Begging. Pleading. And a man's voice telling him what was about to happen. The kid screamed.

And then we were in motion. Monk ranged ahead, taking a lot of quick, small steps so as not to spoil his aim. I was a half-step behind him and on his five o'clock. We followed the cries, which were escalating from fear to terror.

A woman came out of a side room, looking down at a clipboard as she flipped a page over. Her head jerked up and she was just beginning to open her mouth for a scream when I shot her in the head, painting the doorway with blood and brains.

We ran past her corpse, drawn by those screams.

The hall ended in double doors on swing hinges. We paused for a moment only, peering through a gap. There were thirteen adults in a large room. Lots of lights with umbrellas to bounce the glow; sophisticated digital recording equipment on wheeled carts; boom mics. All of it clustered around a queen-sized bed. The boy was on the bed, and the rumpled sheets showed how he had crabbed backward away from a man who wore a zippered leather mask, leather wrist bands, and an array of belts and straps all over his body in some kind of grotesque S&M design. His cock was out; huge and erect, and he was stroking it.

I could feel Monk tense beside me, and I wondered how much of his bottled-up rage was his own and how much was Tituba's still boiling inside his head. Equal parts, no doubt. And that fury was palpable.

My own was dialed to eleven, too.

I touched Monk's shoulder. "We need the cell phones and the recording equipment intact if possible. Primary goal is that kid and the others in the room back there."

"And those sons of bitches?" he asked.

"All I see are targets, brother," I said. He gave me a single, sharp, savage nod.

We raised our guns and entered the room.

—10—

In bad movies the good guys entering a scene like this make some kind of announcement. Sure, cops need to do that when making arrests. Neither of us was a cop. Yelling a war cry is downright stupid because it gives them a moment to react.

Instead, we came in quick and quiet and the first clue they had that we were there was when Monk shot the guy who was clearly the director. Two shots literally dead center.

I fired at the guards first. There were four men with slung automatic rifles. I am not the world's greatest shot, but it was an enclosed space and a target-rich environment. Missing would have been harder than hitting people. *Killing* them was what took the skill, because wounded people can still shoot.

I emptied most of my magazine into the guards, using eleven shots out of the 15-round mag. I pivoted and shot two people closer to me, then the slide locked back. I dropped-and-swapped and kept firing with the fresh mag.

Monk was like a storm—unleashing his fury as he surged through the crowd.

Seven people were down in the first five seconds. The rest scrambled for cover and drew weapons.

Monk hooked an arm around the kid and pulled him down behind the bed. The boy was shrieking, but Monk pressed him down, pinning his squirming body with a knee while firing over the thick mattress. The big asshole in the bondage gear dove down behind a wheeled toolchest.

The bad guys were hiding behind the machinery that I really wanted to preserve for my team—and Arklight—to take apart in hopes of finding more about their whole network. So, I dodged behind a stack of metal equipment boxes.

"Frag out," I yelled, then plucked a flash-bang from the pouch and hurled it high so that it would drop behind the precious electronics. Monk curled down over the kid, wrapping him in his brawny arms and using his bulk to shield him.

The flash-bang flashed and banged. The effect is huge and ugly. The blast is so bright that it burns the retinas, and the bang is deafening and debilitating. I was up and running while the echo was still banging off the walls and the camera crew were screaming.

Two of them were curled up on the floor, hands clamped to their ears. They had been the closest and no doubt their eardrums had ruptured. Not that it mattered because I shot them where they lay.

Suddenly there were bullets burning through the air all around me. I dove and rolled, coming up behind a cart stacked with more gear boxes. The incoming fire came from two directions, and when I peered under the cart, I saw two men with rifles hurrying toward me from different corners of the room. One, I guessed, had been the one standing sentry outside of the hostage room. The other came from god knows where.

Their rounds tore into the cases, showering me with metal splinters. I flattened out, aimed under the cart, and fired half a dozen rounds at the foot-level. The work shoes of one guard exploded into messy clouds of red. He fell screaming, and I put two more rounds into the top of his head.

The other took that moment to rush me. He rounded the cart so fast that I didn't have time to pull my arm out from under. So, I kicked him in the shin. Real damn hard. Something cracked, loud and wet, and he fell almost on top of me. I twisted and raised a knee to take his weight and lever him sideways. He tried to use the rifle as a club as he landed, but I used my free hand to bash the barrel aside and then chop him across the throat. He began twitching and kicking and gagging, but the sound was muffled by the wreckage of his throat. I tore the rifle away and sent it skittering along the floor and let him choke to death. He wasn't worth the extra bullet.

As I got to one knee, I saw that Monk had somehow lost his pistol and was engaged in a brutal fight with the S&M freak. The guy had to be six-five and had more muscles than anyone really needs. He also knew how to brawl.

But so did Monk.

The guy kicked the bedframe and it slewed sideways toward where the dead director lay. He came at Monk with a maniacal flurry of big punches and short kicks. Monk seemed to be composed of nothing but elbows, shoulders, and hip bones, though. The attacks had to hurt but the big man wasn't doing a lot of actual damage. And an assault like that is immensely draining. You could manage it if you know how to breathe right during maximum exertion. The big guy may have known that, but he was likely freaked out and scared because people were dying all around him. He was wheezing a bit, and that's when Monk schooled him on how to do it the right way.

Monk timed his move so that when the big guy threw a horse-killer of an overhand right, instead of blocking, Monk slipped it, nimble as a dancer. As the fist passed within an inch of his jaw, Monk hammered him with three very fast, very hard short hooks to the guy's right kidney. Then he straightened and pivoted, his feet screwing his weight into the ground, his bent knees and supple waist packing one hell of a lot of PSI into a sweeping elbow smash to the guy's temple. That spun him, straightening his body and knocking a lot of lights from his eyes.

Then Monk grabbed the guy's balls with one hand and threw his own overhand right down into his own palm. There was every bit of Monk's anger and whatever Tituba loaned him in terms of rage and hate. They call that punch an apple smasher for all the reasons you'd expect.

The big man uttered a shriek so high, so piercing that it tore the air worse than the flash-bang. Maybe he was dead right then. Maybe he only wished he was, but Monk leapt at him, hooking his arm around the man's bull neck as he bent the guy backward. Monk landed in a deep crouch, torquing his waist radically to one side. There was a huge *crack* and the big man went utterly slack. Monk let him fall and the rapist's head lolled on a rubbery neck.

Gruesome? Sure. The alternative was ten thousand times worse.

The kid was still in a fetal ball on the far side of the bed. In that moment I wasn't sure if I was glad or not that he hadn't seen what Monk did to the man who wanted to destroy him. Either way, a really good therapist was going to have to throw that boy a lifeline.

As I spun away from that, swapping in a fresh magazine, I very nearly shot a teenage girl. She'd come out of nowhere. And then all of the hostages were running through the room in a blind panic. They did not know where to go or who was the good guy or bad guy. There was no chance of using the gun, so I shoved it into my holster and whipped out the lock-knife. The blade snapped into place while I was running.

I'd lost count of how many of these bastards were left because more seemed to have come from other rooms. The closest was a fat man wearing a T-shirt with the American flag on it. Talk about mixed messages. He was no fighter and tried to raise his hands and surrender. I slapped the hands down and slashed him across the throat as I ran past.

I sensed more than saw Monk chasing some of the guards. Despite the catastrophe unfolding, those guards seemed as reluctant as we were to risk shooting the equipment or the hostages. Maybe it was a perceived value thing. Or maybe they thought they were going to win.

Monk and I disabused them of that notion.

In very, very bad ways.

—11—

When it was all over, rounding up the hostages and convincing them we were the good guys took some doing.

It wasn't easy. Not the physical logistics.

Not the emotional part.

Once they understood—and it was the older ones who caught on first—then they swarmed us. We were two big men, armed to the teeth and spattered with blood, but they clung to us. Weeping. Screaming. Clinging so tightly it was hard to breathe.

Or maybe it was the tears that choked Monk and I that made breathing so hard.

Can't say.

Won't try.

—12—

We took the kids into the loading bay, though Monk went in first and hid the guard he'd killed there.

We got them to sit down. Monk stayed with them while I stepped outside to make a call. Mr. Church was waiting on the other end of the line even though it was the middle of the night in Greece, where he was. I told him the status and he said he would take care of everything. I didn't need to ask for details. If he said it would be handled, it would be.

Within forty minutes there were ambulances outside. No cops, though.

The EMTs were all women, and that mattered. They were professional and knew how to deal with victims of sexual abuse. They smiled and spoke in soothing tones. But when they glanced at us, we could see the ice and the steel. We let them do their job.

When the last of the ambulances vanished into the night, another group showed up. One of them was someone I knew. A friend who had once been the sniper on my team when I worked for the Department of Military Sciences. Now he owned his own company of private military contractors. Sam Imura.

He came in and had clearly been brought up to date. He had a face like you see in photos of old Samurai. Hard, emotionless.

"You could have called me, Joe," he said.

"When this started breaking it happened fast, Sam," I said. "There was no time to call for the cavalry."

He nodded. Not liking it but accepting. "Church said that an Arklight team will be wheels-down in Atlantic City within the hour. He asked me to secure the scene until they arrive."

"Thanks."

Sam glanced past me to where Monk was sitting on an equipment case, staring down at the floor. God only knows what he was seeing.

"Church told me about him," said Sam.

"Yeah."

"Is that all real?"

"Yeah."

"Christ."

"Yeah."

"Joe ...?" he said after a few moments.

"What?"

"That woman in the hospital ... Tituba?"

"What about her?"

"She ... died three hours ago."

I closed my eyes. Three hours ago was right about the same time Monk and I were fighting everyone in the main room. Around the time he was fighting the man in the S&M gear.

That answered one of the questions in my head. It had been Tituba and Monk. Both of them.

I said nothing. Sam went off to oversee the packing of the film equipment and to collect all cell phones and tablets. That left me alone in the loading bay with Monk.

I went over and sat down next to him.

He was slowly rubbing the new tattoo on his chest. Tears broke and rolled down his craggy face. I wrapped one arm around his shoulders, and I wept, too.

DEAD TO ME

—1—

I died twice.
   Didn't take.

—2—

I was halfway through the crossword puzzle, doing it in pencil because I'm not an officious dick. God only knows how many cups of coffee—my eyes were jumpy and I think I was hearing colors. They had some goofy-ass Christmas radio station playing. I was trying to shut out any reference to Mommy kissing Santa, for fuck's sake. And I was in no mood to rock around anyone's Christmas tree.

Last two weeks were ass-kickers. Three bail skips in three different towns across two counties. One was a biker—one of the Cyke-Lones who spend so much of their free time being world-class dicks, and all of their work time running fentanyl from Miami to Philly along I-95. Local cop nabbed him for running a red light and doing sixty-five in a thirty-five residential zone. If he'd kept his mouth shut and just took the ticket, he'd still be a free man. Instead, he mouthed off to the cop, who was a woman. When she pushed back, he shoved her. All 275 pounds of him. Downside of that story was she wasn't taking shit that day and showed him how a Taser works. He skipped his court date, and when I found him he wanted to try me, too.

I'm 240, none of it fat. One of my exes told me I look like a cranky silverback. She isn't wrong. So no, I wouldn't mess with me either. He did, and now he's in northeastern hospital waiting for his release so he can start physical therapy.

Second guy was less violent, but thought he was smart. Crooks are seldom smart, and those who skip out on a court bond are demonstrably stupid. He started crying as soon as he opened his front door and saw me.

The third guy was a wife beater, and when he went missing I knew where to find him. Sitting in his wife's car, hoping to continue the conversation that local PD had interrupted. The wife's bruises were nearly healed, but she was doing therapy three times a week and looked like she hadn't slept all year.

Only thing is, it wasn't her who opened her car door. Nice, remote parking lot. No witnesses, which was his pick. Worked for me, too. I think it's fucking hilarious that he's in the room next to biker guy. Maybe they'll have wheelchair races.

So, I was beat and not looking for work or fishing for trouble.

The chief of police there in Pine Deep, Pennsylvania, slid into my booth. He wasn't smiling, which is not a good thing because he's one of those happy guys who laughs at everything. Wasn't laughing now, though.

"No," I said.

"Hello to you, too, Monk."

"Look, Crow," I said, "I am off the clock. I am so off the clock that I wouldn't trace a bail skip if he was sitting at the next table."

We were in the back corner of the Scarecrow Diner.

Crow placed a folder on the table and slid it across to me.

"No," I said.

"Just take a look."

"Not a chance."

"Monk, this is a bad one. Just take a look."

"No," I insisted.

He reached across and flipped it open. The top picture was the kind you never want to see. Ever. And I have seen some shit.

Seeing that photo meant that he wasn't here about a bail skip. This was him asking me to do my *other* job. The one I do well but don't like doing. No, scratch that. It's the job I absolutely hate. He took a small glass vial from his pocket and stood it next to the folder. There was a dark reddish sludge in it. Flakes of dried blood floating in holy water.

"No," I said.

But we both knew I meant yes.

—3—

"What's her name?" asked Patty.

She's a little Vietnamese woman who weighs about as much as my shadow. Her eyes are about a thousand frigging years older than the face they're in. Hard grief lines cut around her mouth and between her brows. She had a little girl's face tattooed on the back of her left hand. She drilled that ink after some bad men in 'Nam took her child away and ruined her in every bad way you can imagine. Left her dead in the dirt like trash. I found them and did what I do, but it didn't—couldn't— bring her back.

We bonded over the whole long, sad, awful time. Sometimes we go to bed together; mostly we don't. We drink, we get high, we cry a bit. There's no definition for what Patty Cakes and I have. Friendship doesn't say it right, and family isn't it, either. Crow calls it being Children of the Storm Lands. People who are connected by the intensity of what they've suffered and who somehow manage to keep hold of their empathy. He's weirdly sentimental and philosophical for a small-town police chief, but he's not wrong.

I was in the middle chair in Patty's tattoo parlor, watching as she mixed the blood with black ink.

"Kristin Howell," I said. "Eleven going on never grow up."

"It was bad?"

"Worse than bad."

She turned and gave me a long, flat stare that was as hard, as uncompromising—and as fragile—as ice.

"You'll find him," she said.

"Yes, I will."

The reference photo I gave her wasn't the one Crow first showed me. This one was of her smiling. Taken last Christmas. When she thought monsters were something in the movies.

"Take your shirt off," she said as she finished her alchemy with the ink.

To this day I still don't understand how it works. Neither does Patty. We've figured it all out over the years. The process sounds simple—blood from a crime scene where someone died mixed with ink Patty has imported from back home in Tuyên Quang. She does the faces in black and white. Her style is photo-real. She leaves one section, maybe a line, unfinished until she's satisfied with the face. Then she does that last bit.

Then it hits me.

Hard.

Like a cruise missile directly to the brainpan. As soon as the art is done, I feel it and see it and *am* it. I relive the last few minutes of the victim's death. I see what they saw and hear what they heard. I feel the things done to them. And when they die, I *feel* that, too. Every last goddamn moment of it, all the way to the point where something like a black veil drops over my eyes. The vision ends with the last beat of the vic's heart.

No, it's not a superpower. Not sure it's a curse, either. It is what it is, and I live with it.

The worst part for Patty is when the vision kicks in. Apparently, it's not much fun to watch. Plus, there's all the screaming, if I don't bite down on a leather strap.

The worst part for me is the fact that the dead are usually the ones who contact me to do this sort of thing. Tell you all about that next time we have a bottle of really good bourbon on the table. Short version is that the dead—those who contact me, which is about half or a little more of these kinds of clients—take a big damn risk, because if I do catch the bad guy and cash him out, they don't just go into the light. Their faces are tattooed on my skin, so as long as I'm alive they're stuck with me. No one else can see them except the other ghosts. And me.

Some of them are quiet.

Some are screamers.

Nights for me are long.

What makes it all worth it is taking someone off the board who won't go on to kill again and again and again.

Oh, yeah, and about the two times I died ... one was in Afghanistan. I was on a night op and we walked into some fancy shit. Russian-made fragmentation mine. The two guys in front of me got all of it and we buried them in bags. I got hit in the throat and nearly bled out. Went flatline in the evac chopper and some young medic brought me back.

That was before the tattoos.

Second time I was careless and walked into a different kind of ambush. Thought I was chasing a regular off-the-rack bail skip and instead got in the middle of a Thai gang war. Took two 9mm in the chest. Circled the drain and tried to ride it all the way down. When I woke up eleven days later, some of the tattoos had faded out and about a third of the ghosts with them. I don't understand it. Not then, not now.

For the record, not looking for a hat trick. Two's fine, thank you. Three would be playing Truth or Dare with the Grim Reaper. Hard pass.

"How'd it happen?" asked Patty as she bent over her gear and made a thoughtful selection as to which needle to use.

"That's just it," I said. "Crow doesn't know. They found her body in a vacant lot on the west side of town, two doors down from the yarn shop. Nobody saw nothing. No stores in the area with surveillance cameras. No passersby, nobody walking their dog. Couple of teenage kids found her while they were cutting school. They lost their shit, seeing something like that. Crow said one of the EMTs spewed chunks, too. There's dead and there's *dead*, and this is the other kind."

She nodded. She grew up in Vietnam. And even though she missed the big celebration of bloody pointlessness that we called a Police Action, she still saw her share. The regime there loves tourists but seems to hate its own people.

Plus, she saw her little daughter.

"What do the police know?"

"Forensics got jack and shit," I said. "No hairs or fibers, no footprints—ground was frozen solid. No semen. Just the girl, her blood, and the worst day everyone who knew her will ever have."

Patty came around and stood right in front of me, the needle in her hand. She wore a mask with most people but not with me. I saw her eyes, the set of her mouth, the scream of a mother's grief implied in the way she looked at me.

"You'll find him," she said. Not a question. A command.

"Yes," I said again. "I will."

She nodded once and then began to sink the ink.

—4—

The first thing that made me realize something was wrong was the fact that it didn't hurt.

I mean, sure the needle stings, but there wasn't any of that *other* pain. I didn't need the strap.

You'd think that would be some kind of relief. But it wasn't.

Any change in the process took me immediately into unknown territory, and I am not a fan of that zip code. I don't *like* doing this kind of thing in the first place, but I've gotten used to the process. In the few times that there have been variations, it hasn't been something good. No hugs and puppies.

The second thing that made me realize this was off the rails was a weird, deep, twisted feeling that I *liked* it.

That scared the piss out of me.

And I don't scare easy.

—5—

The room went away. Patty Cakes, her studio, the ink and equipment, the artwork on the walls, the Tom Waits music on the box, and everything else.

Gone.

I felt myself change. That part, at least, was familiar. It meant that I was stepping into someone else's body, connecting to their nerve endings, aligning with all five of their senses.

It's as strange as it sounds, and since the people whose lives I briefly inhabit are in the process of being brutalized, hunted, tortured, and murdered, it's also pretty fucking awful.

This had a different quality entirely.

There was a kind of joy.

A sense of freedom.

A wild surge of personal power.

Things that you cannot even remotely imagine are the feelings of someone being destroyed by a psychopath.

I looked down at my hands and felt both surprised and disappointed that they were not covered with blood.

I wanted them to be.

I needed them to be.

I could actually *feel* the warmth of blood spilling over my fingers and knuckles and the palms of my hand. My left hand. I could smell the blood ... a very distinctive scent, like freshly sheared copper.

That smell usually turns my stomach because of its association with so many dreadful things I've seen. It's the most powerful mnemonic for pain and suffering, misery and degradation. It calls to mind vile treatment of the innocent.

And yet ... in that moment, as those experiences became *my* experiences, there was an entirely different set of emotions flooding like a burst soil pipe through my mind, filling my senses.

This was beautiful.

This was powerful.

This made me feel like a god.

I tried to get up from the chair and blundered into something. Warm, yielding. Frightened. I made a grab for it, stabbed at it.

Stabbed.

That's what I tried to do. Yes. Stab.

Cut.

Slice.

Open.

Reveal.

God help me.

There were sounds. Two voices raised in screams of different intensity, the timbre carrying different meanings. One was younger, weaker, more acutely terrified; and that one was filled with that special kind of revelation that bursts upon the mind when the very worst thing that could ever happen *was* happening. With no way to stop it. There was a helplessness, and a kind of acceptance.

Half of me hated that. I wanted to recoil from even the thought of it. Turn, stagger away to safe distance, to remove myself from the experience.

The other voice was older. Wiser, but in sad ways. I could feel that depth of awareness, of understanding. I felt the resignation that such things happened because the world was wired that way. That voice spoke from a cynical and yet objective understanding that despite the Christmas decorations and fairy lights twinkling all along the streets, there was no Santa Claus, and maybe no Jesus, either. That bad things happen because God doesn't really give a cold shit. Read the Old Testament, you'll see.

I saw.

I know she was right. But in that moment, I didn't know *who* she was.

I did know the younger voice. I had watched her every day. She walked past the cellar window of my house. Her and a whole pack like her. Taunting me. Daring me.

Asking for it.

Asking for what I was giving her now.

For …

What.

I …?

Wait.

I fell onto hands and knees. There was something wrong. The ground beneath my feet wasn't cold concrete. There was no snow or ice left. How? That made no sense. I'd stepped out of my van not two minutes ago. It was seventeen degrees. Last night's snow hadn't melted.

What I felt was … tile?

I looked around, but what I felt did not match what I saw. The floor—and it was floor, not pavement—was cool but not cold. There was warmth around me. And music playing. Some guy with a growly voice. No idea who it was, but I thought I *should* know.

What I saw was the girl.

The one I wanted.

Eleven. I wanted to stop her, save her, protect her from—

From what? Not from me. No … from growing up. From becoming one of those *older* girls. The ones who flaunt everything that I can't have. The ones who make me feel stupid and impotent. The ones who laugh at me. Or, worse, don't even look at me.

I wanted this girl to die pure. Untainted by *needs*, to stop her from learning how to hate and ignore and …

Stop!

Fucking stop.

Just fucking stop.

I pushed myself up off the floor and turned toward my car. I could see it, but it looked strange. Like I was seeing it through the smudged lens of a broken camera. I hurried over to it but stopped immediately. Where was my knife? Shit—did I leave it in the …

The girl?

Did I leave the damn knife in the girl? That was stupid. They'd know. The only thing I touched with my bare hands was the knife. I needed to feel her. Skin. Hair. Teeth.

Blood.

God, how I needed to feel it. Warm. Hot and salty, too, when I tasted it. Feeling how quickly it cooled on my skin. Delightful. Made me have other thoughts. Hungry thoughts.

But this wasn't about that.

Not really. Not entirely.

It was all about setting her free before she became one of *them.*

I looked at her, lying there in the snow. Old, withered weeds, frozen at angles like people leaning in to watch and to share. She was there. Opened up so God could see her. Opened wide so the angels could find her innocent heart and take it to heaven.

Like the others.

How many now? Eight, was it? Nine?

That made her number ten. Sweet and pure, and she'll be that way forever.

Where was the knife, though?

I'd taken it to church with me two days ago. Dipped the blade in the font of holy water. Prayed over it. God spoke to me from the patterns in the oak paneling in my bedroom. Telling me great secrets. Telling me what to do. What I *had* to do. Calling me to my good work for the Lord.

God, you see, doesn't want girls like that to grow up and become vile and hateful and …

The knife. Focus. Where's the knife?

Is it under her?

I bend and turn her, and there it is. I have to work fast because the devil has people, too. They pretend to be nice and decent and all that bullshit. But they're not. They're evil. They're dead inside. There are no hearts in them for the angels to find. I know. I've opened them to look. Before.

Before I found God's work.

The knife is stuck. Damn. Damn. Damn. Stuck hard.

Shit, I cut myself with it.

Then I stop, watching my blood drip down, chilling as it fell. Joining hers. Caressing her skin. My blood.

Her blood.

Our blood.

God must have wanted this to happen. A sacrament. I'll have to remember that.

For next time.

And the time after. And all the times after that.

The ritual changes, evolves. And I must be dutiful to my purpose. I look at the blood. It's there. It's part of this. Part of her.

They'll never know, though, will they? Blood mixed with blood. Only a little of mine mixed in with all of hers. They'll never know.

No one will ever know.

I put my gloves on. That makes the cut hurt, but it makes the blood warmer.

No one will ever know that it's my blood.

No one. Ever.

I mean, how could they?

I get in my car and drive home. Inside the garage. In my house. Up in the bathroom. I don't wash off yet. Not yet. I need to do the dirty thing first. I always have to. Better to do it when I'm alone and no one's looking.

Then bed.

Then sleep.

Then dreams.

—6—

She slapped me awake.

Patty.

Not being nice about it.

Slapping my face one way and backhanding it the other.

It hurt, and I growled at her, pawed at her, trying to block. She slapped my hands away and hit me again. And again.

"Wake up," she snarled, then yelled it louder in Vietnamese. *"Thức dậy!"*

I covered my face with crossed arms.

"Stop it, Pats, for Christ's sake. Stop."

She did.

My brain came back into my own head. I was on the floor of her tattoo parlor. She was straddling me, clamping my floating ribs and belly with her weirdly strong skinny thighs. As I slowly —carefully—uncovered my face, I saw that her face was red with stress and anger and a hell of a lot of fear. Other emotions, too. Private ones.

"Are you *you*?" she demanded.

I had to give that some real thought. *Was* I me?

"Yes?" I said and I heard the rising inflection, making it a question. Patty balled a hand into a knotty little fist and punched me in the chest. She is remarkably strong, and it hurt.

"Are you *you*?" she roared.

"Yes, yes, for fuck's sake, it's me."

"Mẹ đồ ngu."

Motherfucker.

Then she got off me and stood up, panting, sweating, fists still balled. There were tears in her eyes. *"Mẹ đồ ngu,"* she said again.

I pulled myself up and leaned my back against the wall. I was as out of breath as if I'd climbed a mountain carrying a bag of rocks.

"What happened?" demanded Patty. "Why'd you go nuts like that?"

"Like what?" I asked.

Her eyes narrowed and she gave me a long, cold, appraising stare. "Tell me about her."

She pointed at the tattoo of the eleven-year-old girl.

It took me a very long time to make sure my head was my own. Though, I could still remember it all. Could still feel it all. I have been inside the heads of murder victims, victims of torture, of rape, of nearly every kind of violent madness. This was different. This was a different kind of violation. The stink of it was on me. My hands tingled with someone else's touch. It was disgusting. It was terrible beyond any words I know. Even my blood felt polluted.

"It ... it wasn't her," I said, tripping over it.

"What do you mean? It was her blood, her face." She jabbed me on the forehead of the face she'd just inked. "I didn't do it wrong."

I felt a shame that ran deeper than anything I've ever felt, and I have done some very bad things. I used to be a black-ops shooter for Uncle Sam and then a military contractor in one of those don't-ask-don't-tell kind of private companies that did wet work for multinational corporations. I have a lot of red in my personal ledger. This I know and I accept the penance and punishment that goes with it. My ghosts. The work they want me to do. It's what I deserve.

But this ...

No. This was different. This was a shame—a self-disgust that was like leprosy of the soul.

It took a lot of time, but I told Patty all of it. Everything I felt, saw, heard, knew, wanted, and did. I watched how it changed her face. Paling her skin, bruising her mouth, setting fires in her dark eyes. She took a step back from me, because what she was hearing was the kind of thing men had done to her daughter all those years ago.

And what that *felt* like was in my head. I had felt everything that *he* had felt, and there was a dark joy lingering at the edge of my mind.

Patty had taken only one step back. She hadn't fled. She didn't do that, and even with all she's done for me over the years, the fact that she did not abandon me in that moment made me love her more than I've ever loved anyone. Not talking romance, and I think you get that. This was love on a level where human beings are supposed to relate but usually don't. It was empathy in the way empathy should be—a superpower. And, on top of everything else, that was what defined Patty Cakes.

She did not help me up. That was fine. I wouldn't want to touch me, either.

I stood there, swaying, unable to look at my own face in the mirror.

"Where's my jacket?" I mumbled. She picked the leather off the floor and handed it to me. When I took it, I made sure not to touch her. Not yet.

Patty walked over and unlocked the door, but paused, her hand on the knob as she looked up at me.

"The blood," she said, "do you think they know? Crow? The cops?"

"That it's his and not hers?"

She nodded.

"No. Crow wouldn't do that to me. I don't think they know there was more than one person's blood."

"You said he only bled a little, but that was the blood Crow gave you. Are you *sure* he didn't know?"

I just shook my head.

"Do you know who he is?"

I had to think about it. I don't usually share specific thoughts. With dead people I just relive their deaths in a kind of five-dimensional Sensurround. But that's because they're dead. This man was alive, and somehow that changed things.

"No," I said.

Her eyes went wide. "Then you can't find him? You'll have to tell Crow. He has to get you *her* blood."

I put on my jacket and zipped it halfway. Then pulled my

biker gloves from the pocket. My left hand still hurt where he had cut himself. He was a lefty. He'd still have a cut.

"I don't know his name," I said. "But he took me home with him. I know where he lives."

Her eyes changed. They stopped being shocked and sad, and instead took on a reptilian coldness. There was no trace of mercy in them at all.

"Then find him," she said.

—7—

Pine Deep wasn't a big town. Covered a lot of acreage, but most of it was farmland. The center of town was just a few blocks wide. It didn't take me long at all. I went to the crime scene, started there, and I let the cocksucker guide me all the way to his front door.

He was even smiling when he answered.

Tall guy. Soft, though. Weak blue eyes, fleshy lips, rosacea on his cheeks giving them a healthier pink glow than the rest of his worm-white skin. I saw his hand. He was wearing a uniform shirt from a company that installs residential security video equipment. I saw that and understood. I saw the bandage, too.

I smiled at him.

And his smile went away.

I pushed him inside.

He tried to scream.

Tried to run.

Even tried to fight.

Fuck that, though.

I dragged him by the hair down into his basement. There were pictures on all the walls. Photos lifted from digital cameras. Bedroom and bathroom stuff. Awful. Children. Little girls.

He tried to explain. God and angels and purity. Shit like that.

I broke his jaw first, so I didn't have to listen to it.

I knew it. I was there.

The house stood alone on three-quarters of an acre. No one right next door. No one to hear.

I didn't use a knife. Didn't need a goddamn knife.

He made a lot of noise.

I let him.

It was a very long night.

But later, when I finally got home and showered for over an hour, I slept. The ghosts all around me were quiet. For once, they let me sleep.

When I dreamed, they were my own dreams again.

Thank god.

ON LONELY ROADS

A POEM

I dreamed that I was dreaming.
Or, at least, I thought I was.
Driving through Pine Deep at night.
Too many hours, too many beers past "unsafe to drive."
Coming back from a dirty bit of business out in the
 sticks.
Blood on my hands. On my clothes.
On my face.
Red in my mind's eye. Coppery in my nose.
Blood.

I don't remember stopping my car.
Driving on autopilot, I guess.
Half in the bag 'cause it had been a very bad day.
The kind where even when you win, you feel like a loser.
 You feel lost.
Nobody wins on days like that.
I mean, how could they?
And it's worse doing what I do.
Ghosts hire me.
Their faces are inked onto my skin.
They whisper ugly things to me.

Telling me how they died.
Begging for answers.

I relive their deaths. That's how it works.
Once the ink is on me, that's what happens.
Making me feel everything that was done to them.
Every.
Single.
Thing.
Some of them scream, too.
No one else can hear them, but I can.
Every single night.
Guy at the liquor store thinks I'm an alkie.
He has no idea.

Not the first time I fell asleep behind the wheel.
I have some scars from a sideswipe.
Nearly found Jesus that night.
Another time I woke up with splints and stitches and
       drains.
But this?
This was different.
Not even sure I could understand how.
Different.
For sure.

And here's the twist—I wasn't even sure I was sleeping.
Sometimes being awake is its own kind of dreaming.
I could tell you stories. But ... I expect you already know.
You get it.
You get me.

But here I was. My car in a cutout nearby the edge of
       the drop-off.
Way down below was Dark Hollow.

A moist, reeking cleft between three mountains.
Swampy down there.
Lots of flying things that buzz and bite.
Snakes and owls and roaches bigger than my thumb.
No one goes there because they want to.
Not anyone with their brains wired right.

You could say, "That place is haunted" and even the
staunchest skeptic would say, "No shit," and
without irony.
It's like that down there.
I was parked near the edge.
Either dreaming it or waking up weird.
Either way it was me stopping on the wrong road.
In the wrong part of the night.
Last I remembered I was listening to oldies.
A playlist I made forever ago.
Lonely, plaintive stuff.
Mostly Tom Waits and Leonard Cohen.
Stuff they wrote on bad nights.
After wrong turns and questionable decisions.
Like the day I had

Song that was playing now was another oldie.
Another downbeat tune
All about the comfort of darkness
Hello, old friend.
But I wasn't safe within a womb
I was in Pine Deep
On a back road I didn't know,

I don't remember coming here.
Why or when or by what route.
A carve-out on a disused forest road.
I know I sat there for a long time.

Engine on, headlights punching out through the
    shadows.
Dark as fuck.
I leaned out the window and looked up.
I remember seeing the stars.
There at the outer range of my lights.
Cut crystals on velvet
Beyond reach
That song still playing.
Or looping. Not sure.

Maybe that's why I saw it.
It.
Maybe the song summoned it.
Or woke it.
However that works.
Or ... is something in a dream.
Was I even awake?
Even now, I still don't know for sure.
I mean ... most people don't see stuff like that when
    they're awake.
But this was Pine Deep.
So "most people" don't live here.
The ones who do have their reasons.
Whether they know it or not.
I do.

At first, I didn't believe what I was seeing.
Impossible thing.
No way it was real.
Didn't want to see nothing like that.
Looked anyway.
We're all braver in our dreams.
It rose up from the ground.
I think it was part of the ground.
Or maybe it hides that way.

So you don't see it.
Until it wants you to.
Until it wants you to.

God damn it was big.
Big as fuck.
Bigger than a bear. Bigger than ten bears.
Taller than a telephone pole.
Not as tall as the trees.
Except its horns.
Big rack of horns.
God damn.
Spreading out wide.
Like an elk.
Too many points to count.
Big.

Built like paintings you see of minotaurs.
All that chest and shoulders.
I'm big, but I was a bug.
It could close its hand around me.
Crush me.
And I wouldn't be able to do shit.
Headlights and fog painted it blue.
Ghost blue.
Except for those eyes.
Those god damn eyes.
White, like the sun at noon in August.
White like the moon on bad October nights.

The worse part wasn't its eyes. Or size.
The worse part was that it saw me.
Me.
Standing there beside my car.
No idea when I got out.
Just standing there.

While it towered over me.
There's no meter to compare scale.
Or strength.
Or power.
It was it, and that was enough.

I know my folklore and I know a lot about what's in
    the dark
Behind shadows
Out of the corner of your eye
Behind you.
But I didn't know this thing.
Not Sasquatch or Shampe or Mogollon or Hodag or
    Wendigo
Not Katshituashku or Wechuge or Atakapa or Lofa
Not Shíta or Uˋtlûñ'tä or Yé'iitsoh
None of those.
Nothing, I suspected — knew, felt — that had a name
Not a name a white man would know.
Or a black man.
Maybe if the colonists hadn't killed the people who
    lived here
There'd be a name.
Not now.
Nor did it need one.
It was.
And that was all it needed or wanted to be.

I didn't even try to run.
I mean, how could I?
Didn't even think about getting in my car.
Why bother?
It was right fucking there.
Could have stomped my car flat.
So, I stood there in the swirling fog.
Looking up at it.

Seeing it.
Knowing that it saw me.
Saw. You know?

I'm not normal. We both know that.
Lot of people think I'm the scariest thing they ever saw.
Mostly that's true.
That's not about intent. It's about potential.
But this thing ...
Jesus.
It took a single step toward me.
Earthquake step.
Trees shivered.
Leaves fell.
The nightbirds took flight and circled.
But they didn't flee.
No.
That was something.
That said something.
The thing looked down at me.
I live in Pine Deep but I'm not from there.
It was.
I knew it. I could feel it.
It's lived here longer than the trees.
Maybe as long as the mountains.
I'll never know.

It looked down at me.
In me.
Through me.
It shook that rack of antlers.
I saw the muscles of its shoulders ripple.
I watched its hands open and close.
And open.
And then it paused.
For just a moment.

Considering me.
Which is scary in its own way.
To know it had that kind of awareness.
To be the focus of its thoughts.

I saw the head nod.
Not a bow.
Hell no.
Not to me. Let's be real.
A nod, though, sure enough.
And I nodded back.
Getting it.
I lived in its town.
I stood in its forest.
It saw me and knew me.
No. Maybe understood me really says it.
And I saw it.
And understood it.

Then it turned away.
Into the mist.
Bending toward the ground.
Not falling.
Becoming.
I can't explain it better.
It's not something words were built to say.
But I think you get me.
Like I got it.
I stood in the headlight's glow.
Feeling the cold and damp.
Feeling the power beneath my feet.
In the air. Everywhere.
And knew I was home.
This was Pine Deep.
My name is Monk Addison.
I live here now.

I got into my car and sat for maybe half an hour.
Tom Waits whispering secrets to me.
Then I backed up, turned.
Found the road again.
And the night closed around me.
Carrying me home.

NEEDLES

They always know how to find me. Don't ask me how it works. I keep trying to fall off their radar, but it never works.

Fucking dead people.

I was drinking Irish Car Bombs at a shithole of a beer joint off the main drag in Pine Deep, Pennsylvania.

Sign over the door said Jake's Hideaway. Pretentious name for a place this nasty, dark, dirty, and loud.

Maybe thirty people in all, broken into little gangs that clustered around different parts of the place. There is no actual "Jake," as far as any of us regulars can tell. There may have been one once, but since none of the framed photos on the walls are from later than 1977, we all figure Jake was small time mob, and either mouthed off to the wrong wiseguy, skimmed the take on whatever action he was running, or stuck his dick someplace it didn't belong. Something like that. There are five bullet holes in the wall behind the bar and nobody who works there will say a damn thing about what happened to Jake.

Over the years, and over all the drinks, we've all had our theories. Maybe one of them's actually true, but we'll never know. Which is okay. Sometimes you need to have a few mysteries. Otherwise life, the way it actually appears, is too real and has too many sharp edges.

We toast Jake now and then.

It was a Thursday and Little Jewels was in his favorite corner holding court.

Thursdays are when he gets his disability check. Little Jewels lived small but partied big. He liked buying rounds because people liked being around someone who was doing that. Everyone laughed at his jokes, slapped him on the back, fist-bumped him. He went home nearly broke, but he went home happy. If you took Tom Waits, starved him to a scarecrow, gave him yellow-gray hair and bad skin, you'd have Little Jewels. Same kind of hobo wisdom and back-alley insight, same bombastic charisma.

I liked him.

When Little Jewels wasn't as flush, sometimes one asshole or another would try to push him around. Last Tuesday it was a couple of bikers from the Cyke-Lones motorcycle club. Guys who are so far up their own asses they believe their own hype. Big hair types straight out of Central Casting—beards, bellies, biceps, but no evident brains. The kind who have to hit something that'll scream or their dicks won't get hard. You know the type.

There was no one else in the place. It was too late for the dinner crowd and Tuesdays never had much going on in the evening. Bikers were bored. I don't think there was any motive beyond that. They were bored and Little Jewels was broke and sitting in his corner nursing a beer that had gone warm and flat.

They didn't see me in the far corner by the jukebox. I was five rounds into a run on the Hideaway's supply of Brothers' Bond. One of those celebrity bourbons that was actually pretty good. A little pricey by the glass, but I had bank from taking a couple of back-to-back bail skips. Drinking alone because there's like five people I give a shit about and none of them were there. Just me and my thoughts and the ghosts on my skin.

I sat in the shadows and watched the bikers make their mistakes. First it was snide comments. Then they moved onto loud observations about Little Jewels' height. His weight. His mixed race and that skin disease—vitiligo—where the body loses patches of pigment. They thought that was funny. Or maybe an insult. They started calling him "patchwork nigger" or "jigsaw man"—leaning on "jig." Shit like that. Not clever, and not new, but Little Jewels is sensitive about how his skin looks.

I watched him dig into his pant pocket for enough bills to buy them a "go away" drink. Hoping to placate them. Thinking he could swing that.

He's too nice a guy to know evil when he sees it. Small evil. The kind of small meanness that some people think is strength but isn't.

I debated staying out of it. The barman could have said something, but Joe Tommy was working the shift and he's nobody's idea of a tough guy. No bouncer on a Tuesday 'cause it's always slow.

Joe could have called it in, maybe got Chief Crow or that giant freak of a patrol sergeant he has working for him. Mike Sweeney. Could have done that but didn't. The Cyke-Lones would figure out who dropped that dime, and Joe Tommy wasn't the type who could even endure a casual beating.

Little Jewels could because he'd been beat a lot over the years. People have told me. All before I moved to Pine Deep.

I kept hoping the bikers would step out of this cliché bullshit and go back to their end of the bar.

They didn't.

It was the shorter of the two who hit Little Jewels. An open hand slap that knocked the glass of Bud from his hand and sent it crashing and smashing to the floor. Joe Tommy started to say something, but the bigger biker just pointed a finger at him. That was all, and that was enough. Joe shrank back against the bottle racks and looked like he wanted to crawl through a hole in the dimension.

Even then I hesitated. I was tired, and it's never a good thing for me to get into a fight when I'm tired. Never. It makes me cranky and it makes me go for the ugly moves that end things quick and dirty. If you're a fighter, you'll understand that.

When the shorter biker slapped Little Jewels again and started loudly asking if his nigger dick was patchwork, too, I sighed and stood up. Didn't scrape my chair or anything dramatic like that. Didn't announce myself until I was standing four feet behind them.

"That's enough," I said.

They turned to me. They'd maybe seen me in there once or twice, but they didn't know who I was. All they saw was a guy with bigger shoulders than either of them, jeans, a leather jacket with no gang signs, no bike club art. Just a jacket over a white low-scoop tank top. They saw the tattoos. The faces inked into my skin. If they *had* heard about the ink, that would have been when they checked their watches and realized that they needed to be in some other zip code.

But they didn't know me at all.

They saw a face that no one would ever call handsome. A face that has been punched at least once really hard from every conceivable direction. A nose that was askew but didn't look like it ever belonged on a white man's face. Heavy brow. Some scars. I'm mixed race, too. Even I don't know what all's in my DNA. I can tell you this, though, I'm pretty sure none of my ethnic forebears much liked shit like what these two clowns were doing.

The little one had the mouth, and he told me to fuck off. He added some frills to it, telling me where and how to fuck off, and with which livestock. The big guy closed in on my 7 o'clock. They were both so damn sure this was going to go their way.

Like I said, I was tired. Beat. I wanted to do two, maybe three more hits on the bourbon and then go home, watch some reruns of *Justified*, and sleep until next month. My arms were heavy, and my neck hurt. I was not in the mood for this nonsense.

"Don't ..." begged Little Jewels. I could see it in his eyes. He didn't want any trouble. He didn't want me hurt. Not even sure he wanted the two bikers hurt, but we were in the dance now. Nothing was going to stop this from playing out.

I said, "This isn't a debate. Game's over. Get out."

If I was in a better mood I'd have asked for an apology. You know, to make it more theatrical. Have a little fun. But I wasn't there.

The short guy reached for Little Jewels' neck.

I caught the hand. Big hand for a small guy. Hard as rocks. Callused.

I broke it.

Real bad. There are tricks for it. When I was younger it would have been something slick, maybe a parry and backfist-jab-overhand combination. Dance him a bit. Take him to school.

That's not how tired guys fight.

I caught the hand in exactly the wrong way for him, closing my hand around his fingers like a left fielder catching a ball. With my right hand I grabbed his straightened fingers and gave them a twist. Sounds like a bunch of celery when the fingers break in multiple places. Then I gave the wrist a nice twist, too. Much louder snaps.

He began screaming as I turned to the big guy, who was goggling at me, trying to make sense of what just happened. He started to say something, but I wasn't there for that. I short-punched him in the throat. Used one way it's a killing blow. Used another is just hurts like fuck and you don't talk above a whisper for two to three weeks. Fucks your breathing up, too. He staggered back and I used the toe of my Doc Martens to kick his kneecaps loose. First one, then the other.

He went down wheezing and trying to scream.

I turned back to the short biker, grabbed him by the ears and slammed his face on the curved teak rail. Just the one time. Do it hard enough, you only need once. His head banged and rebounded, and he sat down hard on his ass at Little Jewels' feet. Then he fell backward, nose shattered, front teeth still stuck in the bar.

I sighed. "Call the cops, Joe. Two ambulances."

"Cops are going to take you in for that, Monk."

"Somehow I doubt it."

And they didn't.

—3—

That was Tuesday of last week.

Now it was Thursday of this week, and Little Jewels was holding court. I was in a better mood and was right there with the crew.

I don't usually hang with the laughing crowd, but Thursdays are different. Thursdays are usually shitty bad luck days that rarely fit right. Bills come due, leads dry up, can't-lose horses get beaten by three lengths, and the new movies aren't playing yet.

I'd burned off the first four days of that week on a bail skip job that dried up and blew away because the asshole—Ronnie "the Needle" Di Carlo, who we all thought ran to avoid his court date—was found in a dumpster with his throat slit and his tongue pulled out and hung down the front of his chest. A Colombian necktie they call it, but there were no Colombians in this town. And nothing in his file even hinted that Needle was a snitch. Might just be a trendy thing 'cause a lot of guys use the necktie thing nowadays. It's showy and dramatic and sends a message to whoever else might be on the hit list.

So, those four days were completely wasted, which means I didn't get paid. My bills still showed up in Thursday's mail, though, because bills are never late. Luckily Little Jewels was buying beers, so I had one and made myself laugh at his lame-ass jokes, and, like all the others, I pretended to have a good time.

Until Needle showed up.

Yeah, and he was dead as shit.

—4—

No one saw him but me. That's part of it.

I mean, yeah, Needle was really there, but he wasn't there to everyone. Even after all this time I'm not sure how that works. Maybe it's that I'm cursed, which sounds pretty grandiose, even to me. Or maybe it's what my friend Patty Cakes thinks that the world of the living and the world of the dead are parallel dimensions and that some people under certain circumstances can either walk back and forth between or can simultaneously live in both. Or something. Patty does a lot of magic mushrooms, so factor that into the logic.

Bottom line is that ghosts find me.

I've even tried asking some of them how it works, but they always seem as confused as I do. Weird. You'd think that they'd get some kind of insider information once they woke up dead. You'd be wrong. They don't know shit, and they stumble around scared and lost and not sure what to do next. They don't even know how they find me.

I do know *why*, though.

Because it's what I do. And how I do it.

The ghost of Ronnie "the Needle" Di Carlo came into Jake's Hideaway covered in blood that was still wet and glistening. The Needle slipped inside the bar as a woman left; she was talking on her cell and didn't see him, though she gave a small shiver as she passed. She could *feel* him, I think, at least on some level. It happens. Civilians don't see shit, but I do.

Needle looked around, spotted me, and lumbered in my direction. He was a sight. His throat was sliced neatly open, and the ragged snake of his tongue glopped down over his chest like the worst version of a novelty necktie. I was standing at the bar and saw him in the mirror as he approached.

Understand something, before that night I'd actually never met Ronnie Di Carlo. He was a face on a photo and data in a case file. I work for a bunch of different bail bondsmen, but this gig came from the guys I do the most for, J. Heron Scarebaby and

Iver Twitch. Real names. Both of them are a couple of complete brass-plated cocksuckers who have no human emotions other than greed. But the checks they write me always clear, so they're good with me. They deserve their names, though. You hear those names and you pretty much know what kind of people you're going to be dealing with. Better people would have changed their names to—well, pretty much anything else.

They offered me the gig to find Ronnie Di Carlo. Bounty was five large, which worked for me.

"Why they call him 'Needle'?" I asked.

Twitch snorted. "He started it. Thought it made him sound tough and dangerous. Though, a lot of people thought it was because he had a little needle dick."

"Did he?"

"Nah," said Scarebaby. "Truth is, he used to be a junkie who worked up to user-dealer and then dealer. But he had the nickname hung on him when he was shooting horse. And you know how nicknames stick better than dog shit."

"What was he busted for?" I asked.

Twitch snorted. "Standing too close to real crooks."

"Meaning?"

"He was scooped up in a raid on Tommy G's packaging plant."

"Ah," I said. Tommy Giancarlo, a.k.a. Tommy G, was trying really hard to be a player in the vacuum left when Philly's actual mafia got taken down in a huge RICO thing. All four of the city's dons were busted along with fifty-three of their top family members. Huge bust. They're making a movie about it for HBO.

Tommy G was one of a bunch of mid-level vermin who moved up to snatch up whatever action was safe to grab. There was New York muscle coming down and pissing on everything to stake out their territory, but that's a slow process, and there was a lot of money to be made in the interim. Of the maybe fifteen crews, Tommy G was somewhere in the middle. Couple dozen clowns all acting like they stepped out of *The Sopranos*. They were making money and, so far, there hadn't been much bloodshed between the scavengers. Once the New York boys got a better foothold, Tommy G and the others would vanish into the Jersey Pine Barrens or as chum tossed out by the bucketful somewhere east of Atlantic City. Old story, new players, and the wheel goes round and round.

"If Needle was just one of the crowd he'd be under the umbrella spread by Tommy G's lawyers. So, why'd he skip bail?"

Scarebaby spread his hands. "This we do not know."

"We'd like you to find him and ask that question," said Twitch.

"Any idea where I should start?"

"In your own backyard," said Scarebaby. "A lot of Tommy G's boys have been laying low in Pine Deep."

"Why there?"

"Far enough from Philly so they can act normal and raise families," said Scarebaby. "Close enough to be in town when they need to be."

"Needle had a little place on one of those big farms that they subdivided after that Trouble bullshit," said Twitch.

The Trouble was the nickname for that big domestic terrorism thing close to twenty years ago. Bunch of white power mouth-breathers spiked the local water supply with hallucinogens, dressed up as vampires, and killed several thousand locals and tourists. Still stands as the worst terrorist incident on US soil. They made a movie about it called *Hellnight*, but they tweaked the story so that it was real vampires, along with ghosts and werewolves. Whatever. People always want to sell their own version of what happens.

Twitch gave me a list of known associates along with addresses.

So, I took the gig and went looking. But before I could find him, someone else did and they did him ugly.

I thought this was going to be a piece of cake. From the data in the file and what I learned online, Needle was no one's idea of a genius. Low level even after he got clean. A gopher for Tommy

G. And stupid people are easy to find. Why? Because they're stupid. They're creatures of bad habit and they don't even have the survival instinct God gave a sewer rat.

But I was wrong. Ronnie the Needle was a bitch to find. I went looking all casual-like at first, then more earnestly as the days passed. Never did find him.

A couple of kids from Pine Deep middle school found him. Sprawled in a dumpster with his tongue pulled out of a slit throat. Poor kids are probably going to be in therapy for a long fucking time.

Now … Here he was, dead as shit and looking for me.

And people wonder why I drink.

—5—

Needle stood there for a few moments, looking around, maybe still trying to understand how the whole "oh, shit, I'm dead" thing is going to work out.

I wondered if he just appeared outside a second before he came in, or did he have to trudge over here from the morgue? Or did his ghost appear where he'd been killed? After all this time, I still don't know.

I watched him as he caught sight of himself in the mirror, and for a bit there I thought he was going to do something comical like straighten his tongue thinking it was his tie. That would have been how it played out in the movies. Life doesn't have the same laugh track. I saw the shock fill Needle's eyes. The realization, and all the things that came with it. The horror at how he looked. The terror of remembering how it felt to die like that. The pain of knowing he had failed his own expectations and maybe failed people who cared about him. Then the embarrassment that he was a failure even as a snitch. I saw some facial tics, maybe as he remembered the pain of being murdered.

I let my eyes drift around to watch the crowd here at the bar, looking for sensitivity or some kind of instinctive empathetic twitch. Saw it here and there, but no one actually turned his way.

They *felt* something, but they didn't *know* anything. When ghosts get emotional there's often a change in the air around them. People shiver as if there's a cold breeze, they jump at sounds that aren't part of their anticipated experience; they cry or wince or laugh for no reason, fueled by the echo of borrowed emotions. But all that passed and Needle stood for a moment, head bowed on his chest, grieving, I suppose, for every part of his life he'd managed to fail and disappoint.

I pushed off from my space at the bar, clapped Little Jewels on the shoulder, nodded to some of the others—Red Sally, Mook, Billy Spoons, Nightstick, Fat Moe, and the others—and headed over to the bathroom.

It was a one-man show in there, with a toilet that I wouldn't dare sit on if I was at gunpoint, a sink that looks like it was used for a failed science experiment, an empty paper towel dispenser, and a trash basket filled with garbage, including the torn cover of a Mormon bible, a banana skin, and a soiled disposable diaper. Maybe there's a story that covers all three items, but I didn't want to know it.

I backed into the corner, my hip against the filthy sink and waited. Needle didn't knock and he didn't phase through the wall like in horror flicks. One second he wasn't in there with me and the next he was. It happened in the space of a blink.

"Why the fuck do you guys *do* that?" I groused. "Freaks me the fuck out."

Needle seemed confused by the question. So, instead he looked around at the squalor and wrinkled his nose. When a guy who's been tortured and brutally murdered then left to bleed out in a dumpster turns up his nose at how bad the bar's bathroom is, it's time for some Scrubbing Bubbles.

It was pretty tight in the john and Needle smelled of drying blood, piss, and whatever else was in that dumpster. The bathroom fan didn't work but he didn't seem to notice his own stink. Or didn't care. I mean, let's face it, guy's tongue's hanging down the front of his chest, not sure some BO is all that much of a thing for him.

"I know you can't talk," I said, "so just listen, okay?"

Needle stared at me with eyes that were filled with every negative emotion in the bad karma catalog. Then he gave me a tiny nod.

"People like you come to me because you want me to find who killed you and then do whatever it takes to make sure they don't do the same to someone else. You do understand that, right?"

He paused for a moment, then nodded.

"If I do this," I said, "it doesn't unfuck you from the way in which you are currently fucked. You get that, right?"

Another nod.

"This isn't about closure," I continued. "I don't do closure. Not in the neat-and-tidy sense of things. I'm not a saint and you're not an angel and this is all going to end badly for everyone."

Needle did not nod, but he was listening.

"This isn't just me killing the guy who killed you, Needle," I told him. "Even if I did get that particular guy, he's probably on the payroll for someone else, and it's that person, or maybe someone that person works for, who said to do you ugly. That person owns the guilt—the real guilt—for killing you. If I go after that person, then there has to be a good reason."

He gave me a "what the fuck" look and gestured to his throat and dangling tongue.

"Do you know who did this?" I asked.

He started to nod, then shook his head. Then shrugged.

"Thanks," I said. "Very useful. Was this a mob thing?"

He shrugged again, though his lips formed the word, *Maybe.*

"Why would the mob want you dead? You rat them out to the cops?"

Needles shook his head vigorously enough to make his dangling tongue wag. The whiskey and cheesesteak in my gut thought real hard about exiting through my mouth.

"Your file says you worked for Tommy G."

A small nod.

"He have any reason to want you scratched off his list?"

Another shake. Smaller, though.

"Tell me right now and don't fucking lie," I said. "Do you have *any* idea why someone did this to you?"

Another shake. A real tongue wagger.

"Okay, I said, "but there's one more thing, and you need to pay really close attention. If you want me to go after who did this to prevent him or them from doing this to anyone else in Tommy G's crew, you can go fuck yourself. If this is a mob hit, like maybe a new crew is setting up in Philly and wants to clean house out here in the 'burbs, that's fine by me. I got no sympathy. At all. Hear me?"

A nod.

"So there has to be a better reason," I continued. "Something cleaner. If you think the clown who did this might go after someone innocent, then we can talk. Otherwise, go haunt a house somewhere."

Needle stood there and stared at me. His lips moved as if he was trying to say something, despite the two big reasons why he couldn't—the whole ghost thing and the fact that his tongue was hanging like that.

He nodded again, a bit more emphatically.

"Going to say it once more, dude. If you want me to do this, then there has to be something more at stake. *You're* not enough."

It was a nasty thing to say, as truths often are. Needle's eyes went a little damp and for a long five-count he couldn't even look at me. Then he flipped open the tail of his sport coat, dug into his back pocket and produced a wallet; sorted through some plastic sleeves until he came to a picture of a young woman with disappointment carved into her pretty Italian face. She held two little kids, one about three and the other newborn. The babies were filled with innocence and joy and life.

He met my eyes.

"Your wife?" I asked.

He drew a little X in the air between us.

"Ex-wife, okay," I amended. "Belle. Those are your kids?"

A nod from Needle. Then he touched his dangling tongue and then touched each of the two children.

I cut him a look. "Did the guy who killed you threaten your kids?"

He considered, then pointed at his family again then spread his arms as if to indicate more people. Then he touched his heart. That's when I got it.

"The killer threatened to kill everyone you know and love?" I suggested.

An emphatic nod.

"You do know bad guys say that shit all the time. It's a classic threat. If I had a dime for every TV show or movie that's used that line, I could buy Buckingham Palace."

He nodded again but shook those pictures at me. More or less saying "but what if he really means it?" I grokked that.

Which explained a lot. He was at that point in his existence where he realized that he still had something to lose. Maybe he woke up from being dead and that was the first thing on his mind. That threat. Clearly, he took it seriously.

It made me soften a bit to Needle. He was risking a kind of damnation, or maybe a purgatory, as a ghost lingering on Earth in order to save his kids. Maybe even his ex-wife. It was a *lot* to risk. A whole hell of a lot. I could feel some of the faces on my skin moving. It wasn't visible to the living, but Needle stared and he recoiled. Ghostly tears rolled down his face.

I reached out to take the photo from him, forgetting in the moment that it was a spirit, too. It turned to smoke as soon as I touched it. Needle looked alarmed, but then looked down to see that he was still holding the picture.

Then I sighed and leaned back against the closed toilet stall door.

"Fuck," I said.

He gave me a look that was equal parts hopeful and hopeless.

I gave Needle a nod and looked up at the ceiling for a moment. When I lowered my head, I was alone in there.

—6—

I went back to the bar, had one more drink, and waved goodbye to all the stiffs and goons and suckers and players grouped around Little Jewels. Got some returning waves, a few grunts, some indifference. It was all good, so I pulled my hood up over my head and went out into the cold.

Pine Deep had been hot as balls all spring and summer and all the way to trick-or-treat, but November first had come in like a bitter bitch, unpacked her bags, and turned everything into a lengthy prologue for winter. Too much northern wind during the day, too much freezing rain at twilight, black ice all night long. I wound a scarf around my face and headed into the wind.

From this point on Needle wasn't going to be much help. The dead weren't there to play Watson to my Holmes. I'd probably gotten as much from him as I needed, and the rest I'd get a different way. I used Google on my cell to search for news articles about his murder. The first thing I needed was the location of the dumpster, which was nicely provided along with a photograph of police levering a body bag out of the mouth of the big green metal bin. That was enough to help me find the spot, and it was walkable.

First, though, I decided to go and see the police chief, Malcolm Crow. He's a friend and he was here in Pine Deep during The Trouble. I've heard a dozen different rumors of what he did, and all of it sounds like tall tales. He's a little guy, maybe five-six or -seven. Close to sixty and weighs maybe eight pounds. But that's the window dressing. He's not skinny—he's all wire and steel cable, and he's been doing some nasty-ass jujutsu since he was a kid. Some of the more reliable tales say he once cleared out a whole bar full of bikers and walked away without so much of a scratch. I actually believe that one because I've been in the shit with him and saw him fight.

His patrol sergeant, Mike Sweeney, was there during The Trouble, too. Only a kid at the time, but stories say he did his part when things went south. It's easier to believe that when you see what he grew into. Six-six, better than three hundred pounds, and none of it is fat. He looks like he could deadlift North Dakota. Hardly ever smiles and always has Crow's back.

Both of them know about me. It kind of came up during our own trouble. We were up against a freak named Owen Minor who had some kind of twisted mind control mojo. He sicced the whole Cyke-Lones bike club on us, and that was a bloody shit show. Crow did his chop-socks but Sweeney … yeah, we don't need to talk about what *he* did. I'll just say this: I will never, *ever* get on his bad side. I'm scary enough in my own right, but he scares the living hell out of me.

And that's Pine Deep in a nutshell. It's Pennsylvania's version of the Hellmouth from *Buffy the Vampire Slayer*. It's like the very soil is a magnet for weirdos, killers, assholes, psychopaths, serial killers, terrorists, and all sorts of dangerous fucktards. It pretends to be an artsy tourist town that celebrates Halloween 24/7, with all the brochures happily claiming that it's the most haunted town in America.

Thing is … it is. That hasn't been so good for the locals and the tourists. Oddly, the crowds come back every year for the Haunted Hayride, the Haunted House, the Halloween parade, and the monster movie marathons at the Dead-end Drive-in.

Key takeaway here is that people are out of their goddamned minds. Me, too. I moved here knowing all that. In a damaged way, it's why I feel at home here.

I walked by the police office and saw Crow in there, feet up on his desk, reading a Joe Lansdale novel. I tapped on the glass and he waved me inside.

"Coffee's hot," he said, not rising.

I went and poured a cup, sipped. Winced. "Jesus …"

"Said it was hot," Crow murmured. "Didn't say it was good."

I hooked a chair with my foot and pulled it over. He tore the corner off a blank incident report and used it as a bookmark and set the novel aside.

"So … what brings you out on a dark and stormy night?" he asked, eyebrows raised.

"A case," I said.

"Skip or … the other kind?"

"Bit of both," I said and explained it all to Crow. He listened the way a good cop does—actually paying attention and not interrupting.

"How can I help?"

I shrugged. "You anywhere with your investigation?"

"Not really. Killer messed him up, did that necktie thing, tossed him in the trash."

"Any prints at the scene?"

He gave me a pitying look. "Son, have you ever heard of fingerprints playing a genuinely important role in any criminal investigation?"

"Only on TV."

"Not so much in the real world," he agreed. "We were able to cast shoe impressions for a size eleven work boot. Timberlands, with some unique tread wear. That said, want to know how many men in Bucks County wear Tims? And how many of those are size eleven?"

"Sigh," I said, saying the word out loud. "I read what was in the papers. Don't suppose there's anything you left out …?"

That's a cop thing, holding key details back to filter out copycats and false confessions. Crow smiled like a jack-o'-lantern, reached into a drawer for a file, opened it to the coroner's report, and tossed it down in front of me. I bent over and read through the autopsy details, which were what I expected. Then I screeched to a halt. When I glanced at Crow he nodded.

"What the actual hell?" I asked.

"Yup."

"The killer *bit* him?"

"Keep reading."

I did. When I was finished, I leaned back and rubbed my eyes. "Shit on me."

"Uh huh," said Crow. "Not exactly Hannibal Lecter. No missing organs, no chianti and fava beans. Took random bites. There was no trace of the flesh he tore out anywhere near the crime scene. So, there is a presumption of consumption." He made it sound funny, rhyming it. But his smile wasn't born from actual humor. "Welcome to Pine Deep."

I glanced over at the dispatcher who was on the far side of the office. She was knitting and listening to some old Shania Twain stuff.

So, I leaned in toward Crow. "Do you have a theory on that? I mean, given that this *is* Pine Deep."

"Don't worry," he said. "We're not in a reboot of *Night of the Living Dead*. Needles Di Carlo has not risen from the dead and begun chowing down on the locals." He paused and caught me eye. "Unless there's such a thing as a zombie ghost."

"Christ, let's hope not," I said. "Any other forensics?"

"The saliva recovered from the bites is from a living person."

"You run DNA?"

"Yes and no."

"No hits at all?"

"We ran it, but he's not in our database. We checked with the Staties and Feds. Guy's never been arrested. We are exactly nowhere."

"Well ... balls."

"Indeed." Crow paused. "You really going to do the tattoo thing for this?"

"Yeah."

"But ... Needle wasn't some innocent lamb here, Monk. He was arrested for crimes committed. Maybe small time, but hardly a pillar of the community."

"Wife and kids," I said.

Crow sipped his very bad coffee and peered at me over the rim. "For a big, spooky, nasty-looking son of a bitch, you have this soft spot."

"Yeah. But ... pot, kettle ..."

"It's going to get you hurt."

"Been there. Done that," I said. "Have the souvenir keychain."

His smile dimmed. "It's going to get you killed."

I drained my cup, winced, set the cup down, and stood. "Small loss to the world if that happens."

Crow studied me. "If you think that, brother, then you're as dumb as you are ugly."

I mumbled something and went back out into the cold wind.

—7—

I thought about dying as I walked.

Life's been weird for me for a long time. I used to be a soldier, and I liked it for a while. Liked the noise, the blood, the power. That's some addictive shit right there. That's a great way to lose yourself, and I did exactly that. For a long time. I dove into those red waters with a will. I pulled triggers for Uncle Sam, and I pulled them for companies like Blackwater and Blue Diamond. It's a better high and a worse addiction than heroin.

Then something happened. One of those bullets must have ricocheted around and hit me between the heart and mind. It bled the rage out of me. It killed the version of me that wanted to go to war and left behind something different, deader, emptier. Had me one mother of a dark night of the soul. Well, *nights*. I drank my way out of those kinds of jobs and let the random tides of life push me around for a while. Went looking for some kind of redemption but didn't find it. Not exactly. Instead, I stumbled into what one inebriated Vietnamese monk said was my destiny. Sure, whatever. What I found was what I was supposed to do from then on.

I won't go all maudlin and grandiose by saying it's my curse or that it's some sacred calling. It's a thing. I can do it and I don't know why. I don't want it, didn't ask for it, and would give it away in a New York minute if I could.

If.

That's a big, ugly, back-stabbing, nasty piece of shit of a word. *If.*

I brooded on that as I walked. The wind was trying hard to beat me up, and there was that unique smell of impending snow. Early for it in Eastern Pennsylvania, but the weather was as messed up as everything else in this town.

Needle had been killed in what amounts to Pine Deep's bad side of town. It's only a few blocks in either direction, hanging like a wart on the left ass-cheek of what was otherwise a moderately upscale arts town. It's known as the Corner. Couple of biker bars, couple of tattoo parlors that Patty wouldn't spit on, some shotgun houses that aspired to be as classy as crack houses. Some abandoned buildings left over from The Trouble. While the rest of the town built back up, the Corner turned sour. Sergeant Mike Sweeney patrols there a lot and keeps the infection from spreading further into town.

The coroner's report troubled me, and my mind kept coming back to it.

When Needle appeared to me, there were marks of violence beyond the death wound, but no bites. The dead appear to me as they were the instant they died. That meant the bites were postmortem.

I wondered if Needle had actually seen who or what killed him. If it wasn't a zombie, what did that leave? A cannibal of some kind. That stuff is creepy as hell but not necessarily supernatural. Necrophagy, I think it's called. Flesh eating. Charming.

What this brought up is whether the bites were part of whatever message the killed wanted to send, or if it was part of the psychosis of the killer. Had to be something weird because button men for the mob—and that was the presumption, given the Colombian necktie—weren't known for getting all bitey. There's nothing in the lexicon of modern crime in my head that offered any starting place.

I found the green dumpster squatting awkwardly in a slot

between a stack of rain-soaked boxes and some drainpipes crawling up the side of a greasy brick wall. There was trash everywhere, and the alley smelled worse than the bathroom at the bar, which is not a competition you ever want to win. A single tatter of yellow crime scene tape was wound around one handle of the dumpster and it fluttered in the cold breeze. I stood there for a long time and studied the place where Ronnie Di Carlo's body was found.

Had he actually died in there? Couldn't tell that yet and wished I asked Crow. He'd bled here, though, and that was all I needed at the moment. I climbed up onto the rim of the dumpster and looked down at a cleared space that had been excavated by the forensics guys. The container had been about a third filled with trash, and most of it had been pulled out and heaped against the wall. The rest was mashed down from all of the first responders who'd had to climb inside to document the scene and then haul out the body. The alley was empty and what little car traffic cut up and down the street was like part of another world; no one was looking at me or what I was doing. The Corner was a bad part of town and no one but a crazy person goes looking for trouble.

"Shit," I said, then climbed up and jumped down into the trash. There is probably some kind of existential statement in that, but I wasn't in the mood for self-exploration.

Even frozen, the trash was nasty as hell.

Crime scene cleanup is supposed to be a thing, but it varies in how that plays out. Spill blood in a high-rise on the Upper West Side and they scrub it down to the joists, but it was clear Crow and his guys didn't burn up a lot of calories prettying things up. Not on the Corner.

Needle's blood had dried to a muddy brown, but there was a lot of it. I removed a small glass vial from my pocket, pulled off the stopper, then used the blade of my spring-knife to collect some flakes of the blood. I wiped the blade on my cuff and stowed the knife, then took a bottle of holy water from my other pocket and used an eyedropper to add seven drops to the vial.

Never more, never less. Learned that trick from a priest in Ecuador. I replaced the stopper, gave it a vigorous shake to mix it, then put everything away.

I climbed out and went home to shower off the stink before heading over to Patty Cakes' place.

—8—

Patty has a tattoo joint just south of Boundary Street, sandwiched between a boutique that sold Christmas ornaments all year round and a lesbian bar called the Convent. The bouncer at the bar was a friend of mine who goes by the nickname Axiom. Every time I ask her why that name, she gives me a different and completely false answer. Patty told me that it's an in-joke, but didn't tell me what it meant. Fair enough. Everybody's got their thing, and everybody's got secrets.

Patty was in her shop working on a naked blonde girl with improbably firm boobs and no ass at all. Great legs, though, and with her spray tan you could barely see the faded needle marks behind her knees.

Patty was finishing a delicate rose on a climbing vine that trailed up from the blonde's Brazilian landing strip, around her pierced navel and up to the undersides of those plastic boobs. Patty is a true artist and when she's allowed to do things her way her ink looks photo-real. Like the faces on my skin.

The blonde stared at the ceiling, tears streaming from the corners of her eyes but a beatific smile on her lips. Her pupils were the size of dinner plates. Without looking away from her work, Patty told me to beer up and sit down. I fetched a cold Singha from the mini fridge—a Thai beer that always goes down smooth. I sat and watched Patty work. And, sure, I looked at those boobs. I'm weird but I'm human.

When the rose was finished, Patty sat back, and it was like she was disengaging from a power source. Her personal light always seemed to diminish when she wasn't actively sinking ink. She began cleaning her gear and the girl sat up, wincing but still smiling. Then the blonde stood up, seemed to notice me for the first time, and stood hipshot, pointing at the rose with both index fingers. Only thing she was wearing was sneakers.

"Pretty great, huh?"

"It's a knockout," I said. Maybe it came out a little hoarse.

"Go get dressed, Kimba," Patty said in her thick Vietnamese accent, and gave me a sour little look.

The girl went into the back and returned after a couple of minutes, dressed in ripped jeans and a midriff T-shirt. No jacket despite the cold. She waggled her fingers at Patty, tried to wink at me but used the wrong eye, and went tottering out. Patty locked the door, turned off the neon window sign and flipped a card to the CLOSED side. I had a fresh beer for her by the time she sat down, and we drank for a few minutes while she came back into her head from wherever she goes when she works.

"Kimba?" I said. "Wasn't he a boy white lion on Saturday afternoon cartoons?"

"What can I say." Patty took another pull. "Last week I had twins in here. Romulus and Remus."

"That's kind of cool—"

"They were teenage girls."

"Oh."

We drank.

I removed the vial from my pocket and set it on the table next to her pots of ink. Patty nodded, finished her beer, accepted another, and then picked up the vial and held it against the light.

"Fresh," she said. "Two days?"

"Little less." I explained about Needle, the necktie, the bites, and his kids. Patty studied me for a few moments, blowing as she does across the mouth of the bottle. The sound is like a foghorn.

"Why don't you get a regular job?" she asked, but I knew it was rhetorical. She does what she does, and I do what I do. And this part of it is something we do together, even though it hurts us both.

She poured the blood and holy water into a cup and began

225

stirring in some black ink. Always black. All of the faces on my skin are black and white. I once asked her why she doesn't use color and all she said was, "Color doesn't work."

Pretty sure she doesn't know why any more than I do.

I took off my shirt and sat at an angle so she could use a small bare spot on my right side.

"You're going to run out of skin," she said.

"Yeah. Maybe I'll retire and take up farming."

"Farming? Growing what?"

"I don't know. Pot, if they legalize it here. Or maybe tomatoes. They're easy. I think."

"You'd be a lousy farmer."

"Not sure I care all that much."

She handed me a thick leather strap and we went through the usual dance of me telling her I didn't need it and her telling me I was a liar. I always needed it. She can't work if I'm screaming.

I bit down on the strap and for a while my world was the buzz of the needle and that pain.

—9—

It happens like this …

As Patty begins shaping the face the only discomfort is the bite of the needle. It's not fun but it's not too bad. I'm a big boy and I have a collection of scars that speaks to the kinds of damage I carry. Knives, chains, shrapnel, bullets, broken bones, you name it. I've had more stitches than most people have had hot dinners. So, that's no big.

But when she gets to the point where lines coalesce into shapes, and shapes take on appearance and meaning, well, yeah, that's when it goes to shit. I try to stay braced, you know? To get ready for that first real hit, but it doesn't always happen at the same time. With some faces, maybe it's the eyes—window of the soul and all that. With others, it might be a chin, a hairstyle, an expression. For Needle, it was his mouth.

Don't think I took particular notice of his mouth, but as Patty shaped it, I remembered. Needle has a small mouth, with plump lips. Almost girlish. No, that's not right. More like a fat baby's mouth.

I can't tell you how Patty knows what these faces look like. She probably couldn't tell you how I find the killers. We each got our thing. We each wince as the pain sinks fishhooks into us. That's how it feels. Like a silver, wickedly barbed hook. You almost can't feel it go in but when the line gets jerked all of your nerve endings shriek, and they go on shrieking because that hook is set. It owns you.

Funny how hard it is to explain pain, to describe it in ways that someone else will understand. There are all sorts of adjectives for it, useful phrases, but none of them ever form a true bond of understanding. I think it's because pain—real pain —is such a personal thing. Maybe more personal than fear. Pain whispers to us with such a familiarity that we must bend to listen, but the secrets it shares can't ever be told because they're in a language only we and the pain know. When we try for empathy with someone else in pain, all we can ever hope to do is define it by pain we've experienced. It's never a perfect fit, and probably never close.

And to complicate the math, our nerve endings try to make us forget that pain. We remember being in pain and we cringe at the thought of new pain, but somehow the sneaky nerves edit out any exact recall. Which sucks, because it allows new pain to ambush us. It's like the nerves are coconspirators. Maybe they belong to that part of each of us that is masochistic.

I don't know, and while Patty got closer and closer to finishing Needle's mouth, I tried to buffer myself against the pain by analyzing it and philosophizing it. Well, here's the kicker —none of that shit works because real pain always sneaks up behind you and hurts you sooner and worse than you expect.

Every.

Goddamn.

Time.

Once the face is inked there's some kind of switch thrown,

and suddenly I was in Needle's head. It wasn't like I was a witness. I was in his head. In there with all of the nerve endings still connected to every part of him.

Suddenly I *was* him …

—10—

I—we—were walking down Granary Lane on the edge of the Corner.

Needles was nervous as hell about his impending court case. The lawyer supplied by Tommy G looked like he was ten years old and right out of some third-rate law school. One of Tommy's countless nephews, and a lawyer hired by nepotism was hardly a comfort.

The thing is, from the thoughts crashing around in Needle's mind, it was immediately clear that he intended to make that court date. He wasn't skipping out on his bail after all. That changed the math for me. It made him a kind of innocent. Or, at least, a potential recoverable soul.

He paused to light a joint and stood in the cold shadows and took several deep hits, holding the smoke for as long as he could. With each drag I felt his tension relax.

Needles was scared, but not of someone looking to kill him. That was clear. And his nerves about the trial were not about his personal safety. He would probably get eighteen months for the third-string crimes he'd committed. Really, what he was most guilty of was being too stupid to live straight, and he admired the power of scumbags like Tommy G. Needles wanted a taste of power, and I could feel in him that if something better came along—something on the straight and narrow —he would leave the clown show at the Corner and fly right.

That was his goal.

He still loved Belle. And he really loved his kids, and the fact that he'd failed them in all the important ways mattered to him. From the intensity of the emotions I felt while I shared his last few minutes, I actually believed he was working his way into a redemption path. Not as a religious thing, but an actual change of heart and of nature.

It does happen, even among the lowlifes.

I started to feel a kinship with him. In the grand scheme of things, I've almost certainly done ten times as much harm in this world than he ever did. All those years pulling triggers and not questioning orders put a lot of red in my personal ledger. Doing the stuff I do is no guarantee I'll ever balance the books. I felt the heat of that all the time. Didn't talk about it much, but it's there.

The ghosts know.

Patty knows, too. At least I think so.

Who knows, maybe even Crow knew.

The path to redemption is a rocky one and it goes through some very dark territory.

So, there was Needles, smoking a blunt, keeping his head down, minding his business.

And then hands came out of the dark and took him.

It was very quick and nasty, and Needle had no time to do anything. One hand clamped over his mouth and used thumb and index finger to cut off air and screams. The attacker kneed Needle in the tailbone, buckling his legs. Then he sat him down on the pavement, pressed moist lips to Needles' ear and said, "You are in the way, little man. You and everyone who works for Tommy G. You are an inconvenience."

The other hand reached around and pressed the cold steel of a very sharp knife against Needles' throat.

"This is a clean sweep, asshole. Tommy and his boys are on my list. I'm going to have you all. Them and theirs. You and yours. That's the play. And nothing you can do about it. Nothing you can do to warn anyone else. How's that feel? Is that delicious? I think it is. Knowing that you're being cleared off the board and leaving behind your wife and kids. She's a hag, so I'll make it easy for her. Nail her to a chair and make her watch what I do with the kids."

By now Needle was screaming and struggling, but the other guy was much stronger, and he knew what he was doing. He made small cuts all around Needles' Adams apple. Scary, because they promised the kinds of terrors that actually happened.

"Maybe I'll fuck your wife while the kids are bleeding out. Fuck her and then let her give me tongue. How's that sound?" asked the killer.

"But I need to take out the garbage first. I'd say no hard feelings, but I have a lot of feelings about this, and I'm hard as a goddamn rock right now." He laughed. "Not as hard as I'll be when I visit your family. Won't be tonight. I want them to know what I did to you first. Get them worked up. Get them all but shitting their pants wondering if someone like me is going to come after 'em. No, man, I'll wait until they start to think they're safe. That's when I'll be there. Yummy wife. Delicious kids. Life's a fucking banquet."

He said more, but by then the knife was doing its work and Needle was slipping away and soon my eyes went dark as the playback of memories ended when his heartbeat stopped.

—11—

When I could see with my own eyes again, Patty was right there. She pushed a drink into my hand. Not a beer. This was mezcal. *Pierde Almas Tobala.* Made from wild tobala agave plants grown in San Baltazar and aged for twelve years. Sweet and floral, with strong vegetal notes of fresh agave, plus some herbs and hints of marshmallow and clove.

Not that I gave a shit at the time. I hammered it back and waggled my fingers for refills a couple of times.

She looked at me. "Bad?"

I wiped my mouth with the back of a trembling hand. "Bad enough."

Patty took a swig from the bottle then refilled my glass a last time. "Enough?"

I had to think about that.

"Maybe," I said.

The clock on the wall said it was north of nine p.m. There wasn't much of the day left and outside it was snowing hard.

"Maybe sleep," suggested Patty. "Go after this man tomorrow."

I said, "Sure."

But we both knew I was lying.

I left Patty's place and walked around in the storm to clear my head.

There was a lot to unpack in Needles' memories.

The killer's comment about taking out the trash was telling. It rang a bell and I wanted to get home and do some net searches. Like all PIs, I have access to a whole slew of useful databases. And I have tons of my own files. Things I learned from both sides of my profession. There was something about that specific phrase that kept telling me it was an actual clue.

But then there was that vulgar, vile threat against Needles' wife and kids. I understood now with total clarity why he came to me. Guilt and terror. Guilt because he believed—and likely rightly so— that all of this was tied to his working for Tommy G. Terror, because the killer wasn't lying. He was sharing his real plan because he wanted Needle to die afraid and helpless to protect those he loved.

So, I went home to get some dry clothes and take a very long shower. I boiled myself under the spray, reaching out now and then for the cold beer I left on my toilet tank. I was more than half in the bag, but I gave exactly zero fucks about that.

Still in my bathrobe, I tucked in at my desk and hit the databases. There are apps that let us search financial backgrounds, family records with accompanying addresses, lists of known associates, lists of properties, vehicle info including plate numbers, and more.

The searches told me that Tommy G lived just outside of town in what used to be an apple farm. It had been damaged by fires during The Trouble and stood empty for a while. Tommy bought it and sank two million into a complete back-to-the-studs rebuild. Lots of security, too.

So, I called Crow. He answered with a mouth full of something and chewed for a minute.

"Monk?"

"Yeah, did I catch you at a bad time?"

He swallowed audibly. "I'm eating. Val cooked. So ... yeah, a bad time."

"I can call back later."

"No. You've had Val's cooking. Save me, Obi-wan. You're my only hope."

In the background I heard his wife say "Hey!" But then she laughed. Val was smart and capable. She could plant and plow forty acres and rebuild a motorcycle from a box of parts, but she cannot cook. Like ... at all. Dreadful stuff. Might account for why Crow is so skinny. And *does* account for why most of their friends, me included, drop by with takeout.

"This is quick," I said.

"Whaddya need?"

"What can you tell me about Tommy G? His outfit here in town. Any issues involving snitches or betrayals that might explain Needle's Colombian necktie."

There was a pause. "You mean aside from the fact that Tommy Go's dead?"

"Wait ... *what*? When? How?"

"Let me start with the *why*, since you didn't ask," said Crow. "Looks like the power vacuum in Philly is being filled. A crew from New York is setting up shop in a big way. You'll see it on the news. Six dead from Tommy G's outfit. Couple of key players from other gangs. Looks like we might be in for a real spring cleaning at the rate it's going."

"Well ... shit. When did this happen?"

"Last night. Didn't happen here in town, though, so I got a report on it just a few minutes after you left. Tried to call, but your cell was off."

I looked at my phone and saw that the ringer was indeed off. I'd done that when I was at Patty's and forgot to turn it on. And there was a notice of a message from Crow.

"I was getting inked," I said.

"I figured."

A short pause on that.

"You said you *got* a report. From where?"

"Tommy G and his goons were at a restaurant in Lahaska. The Cock and Bull. You know it?"

"Sure."

"He and his boys left, crossed the street to a parking lot, and someone took them out."

"We talking car bomb? Hail of bullets ...?"

Crow gave a dark, cold laugh. "No, your ghoul did it quick and quiet. Cut Tommy's throat and then slashed four of his crew into cold cuts before any of them got off a single shot."

I whistled. "Colombian neckties?"

"Only Tommy. And before you ask, Monk, I don't think it has anything to do with him or Needle snitching. That necktie thing is big and splashy and I think he did it for effect. It's become quite the popular method of termination. It's what all the cool kids are doing this season."

"Yeah, I was moving toward that thought, too. Needle wasn't a snitch. I think his biggest sin was orbiting Tommy G, who was in turn overstepping his boundaries by trying to solidify his place in the Philly power vacuum."

"That's my read, too," said Crow. "As for how Tommy's crew bought it, there were some other fan favorites. Two of them with their dicks and nuts in their mouth. One guy had his entire face flayed off. And the other was blinded, had his tongue cut out, and his throat slit."

"Jesus H. Fuck."

"Oh, it's worse," said Crow. "*Then* the son of a bitch chowed down on them. All the vics had bites. Looks like some of the fingers were bitten off rather than cut. There's flesh missing from various parts of all of them. Coroner estimates that a total of about four pounds of meat is missing from the whole group. Our boy is hungry and on a high protein diet. Wonder if it'll catch on. The new Paleo diet except with uncooked meat."

"That's disgusting," I said.

"I didn't say *I* would try it," laughed Crow.

"Forensics get anything at all?"

"Not much. Same shoe prints. So, it's your guy." He paused. "You … um … *learn* anything at Patty's?"

"Some."

"Anything you want to share?"

"Nothing I want to share with an officer of the law."

"What about with a friend?"

I thought about that. "When it's over you can buy me lunch and coffee at the Scarecrow."

"Fair enough," he said.

"There was one thing, though," I said. "The killer said something that keeps trying to trigger a memory that I can't quite catch. 'This is a clean sweep, asshole.' Those exact words. Does it call anything to mind for you?"

He was silent for a moment. "It does, but unfortunately I can't put my finger on it, either. If I can remember what it was, I'll give you a call."

"Text me," I said. "My ringer's going to be off for a few hours."

"Oh? What's your plan?"

"Might go stake out Needle's family and see if Gus the Ghoul was serious about his threat."

"What threat?"

I told him that part of it. The specific threats the ghoul made. Crow did not crack a joke this time. I listened to the sound of his slow breathing.

"I'm resource poor right now," he said at last. "Mike's in the Corner dealing with some shenanigans. Looks like he'll be there for a while. There are two officers with him for backup. And the only other guy I have on shift is out trying to get the snowplow drivers out of bed. This storm is going to go on all night. You want me to call in the off-duty guys?"

I knew how small his department budget was. Calling in off-duty was going to be expensive.

"Nah," I said. "I got this."

"You sure?"

"I'm sure. Besides, we both know I'll be going off-book if that maniac shows up. Cops are complications in this part of what I do."

His answer was a long sigh.

"And Crow ...?" I said.

"Yeah?"

"Lock your doors, brother. This son of a bitch isn't just a hitman. He's way, way off the rails. He's insane and I think he likes doing what he's doing. He's not the type to come quietly because a badge asks him to. So, button up that big ol' farmhouse and maybe keep a piece handy if anything happens."

Crow snorted. "And you feel you need to tell the chief of police in *Pine Deep*?"

"Telling my friend," I said.

We ended the call.

—13—

I dressed in fresh jeans and hoodie and my leather jacket. Beneath it was a Glock 19 and a Gerber Prodigy survival knife hung upside down for a quick draw. The brass knuckles and slapjack were in easy-access pockets.

I looked at myself in the mirror.

"You're a freak," I said.

The reflection offered no argument. On my side I could feel Needles' tattoo squirming.

—14—

Needles' widow lived near the Black Marsh bridge, so it was a short drive. I took my truck instead of the 1940 Indian Chief motorcycle I'd spent two years restoring. Aside from the snowstorm, that ride is hardly subtle. It's loud and unique. Instead, I fired up my old pickup. It looks like a farm truck that's seen too many seasons. Engine's good, though. I had it rebuilt and tuned so it's quiet as a cat, though the snow chains I put on

235

spoiled that effect. The rattle made it sound like the ghost of Jacob Marley doing a beer run in the winter snow.

The storm was getting heavier, dropping an inch of snow per hour with no end in sight. That was both good and bad because it meant that a recently widowed woman with a couple of kids was likely to be home. It allowed me to find her but painted a target on the house for anyone else.

The house was nice enough for cookie-cutter. Two stories with an attic sitting on a quarter acre backed up against part of the sprawling state forest. Two car garage, playset in the yard and, God help me, an actual tire swing hanging from the crooked arm of an old elm. Looked like the kind of place any sitcom family would call home.

I drove past three times, looking for bad guys parked in out of the way places. But there was nothing suspicious. The houses further up the road had Christmas lights on. It was still technically fall, but maybe they listened to the weather man and wanted to catch the spirit of the season. However, the contrast of the brightly colored LED glow and some inflatable Santas and Rudolphs in the yards made the darkened Di Carlo home look desperate and desolate by comparison. It was going to be a bad damn Christmas for what was left of Needles' family.

There was a side road twenty yards north and I pulled in there, my truck completely hidden by shadows. I cut the lights and opened my iPhone to refresh myself on details. Needle's wife was named Isabella, known as Belle. The photo he'd shown me must have been a couple years old, because it listed the older kid, Marie, as five and the younger one, Danny, as two.

Poor bastards.

I wondered if they would grow up knowing what happened to their old man. Would they know he was a criminal? If so, would anyone ever be unkind enough to tell them how he died?

I wish that there was some way I could tell them of their father's sacrifice in his willingness to become a lingering ghost here on Earth, tied to the ambulatory pile of wreckage that was me. Needle could have moved on into the light and left his family up to chance.

He didn't. That mattered a lot to me. When this was over, and if I wasn't some psychopath's midnight snack, then I'd find some way to let them know their father was a standup guy when it counted.

I got out of my truck. The inside light is deactivated for just this kind of moment. I'm a big ape but when I want to move quiet and not be seen, I can. Learned that on battlefields and Spec Ops runs a long time ago.

The snowstorm was wet and heavy, but the cold was less severe. I faded into the fringe of woods and moved only as fast as caution and observation allowed. I had no idea if the killer was even going to be out on a night like this. Or if he was telling the truth about his threat. Could not take the chance, though. Not after Crow told me that Tommy G and his boys were dead.

This is a clean sweep, asshole. Tommy and his boys are on my list. I'm going to have you all. Them and theirs. You and yours. That's the play. And nothing you can do about it.

Those words were still ringing a bell somewhere in my head. *This is a clean sweep.*

As I moved through the snowy darkness, I clawed open all the closets in the haunted house of my brain. It was a phrase I'd heard before and was—I was certain—connected with underworld murders.

Then I felt my phone vibrate in my pocket. Crouching in the shadows behind a big oak tree, I read a note from Crow.

I couldn't let it go. That phrase. Logged-on remotely to the station computer and did a search on variations of that phrase. Got a hit right away.

He followed that with a longer text.

Not sure if you followed the news about the mob hit in Newark five years ago. Three members of the Annucci family were killed. No Colombian neckties, but the murders were particularly savage. The Feds got involved because some forensic evidence tied it to another mob hit in Baltimore seven years back. Footprints of someone wearing Timberlands. Same basic MO—and get this—one of the wiseguys in the Baltimore hit was injured but escaped. He said that the killer wore a ski mask. Description is: Adult male, mid-20s. Caucasian. 5'9" to 5'11". The shoe size from Needle's hit matches the shoes in both previous hits, and the calculation of the killer's gait is consistent with a man of that height. I think it's our guy. And here's the kicker ... the surviving witness testified that the man said, "This is a clean sweep, asshole."

I stared at the text. Then, just as I was composing a reply, Crow added another comment.

These cases are all filed as open-unsolved. I called a buddy of mine in the FBI and asked him if there was anything held back from the press. He didn't want to share until I told him about Needle and Tommy G. He told me that they withheld that the killer is believed to have bitten and possibly ingested flesh from all of his victims. This is our boy.

I texted ...

Shit.

He replied with ...

The profiler who worked on the case believes the killer is a psychopath who likely chose the hit man gig because it allowed him to satisfy his appetites. My friend promised to dig deep and send the entire case file to me. I'll let you know if anything else comes up.

Then …

Be safe. As soon as Mike is done in the Corner, I'm going to send him your way. Watch the Di Carlo house, but don't engage until you have backup. No joking around here. Don't play masked avenger.

I lied and said I'd wait.

And then I ran to Needles' ex-wife's house. I don't have spider sense, but my gut was telling me to hurry.

I ran as fast as I could.

The front door was locked.

The back door stood open; the lock splintered. And there were footprints all over the back porch.

Timberlands.

—15—

I drew my Glock and flattened against the back wall, listening.

The world had fallen silent the way it does during a heavy snow. Except for a car on the road driving with care, there was nothing outside.

Inside, though. Yeah. I heard the kinds of sounds I did not want to hear.

It was faint, coming from somewhere deep inside the house. Children crying. And a woman speaking.

No, *pleading*.

"—do whatever you want to me," I heard. "Just don't hurt my babies."

And then I was inside the house.

I couldn't know what weapons he had. If he had a gun pointed at the kids, then the slightest sound I made could get someone killed.

The kitchen was dark and still. I paused near the doorway to the dining room, but there was nothing. Belle Di Carlo's voice was oddly muffled, and it took me a moment to realize that it wasn't coming from the main house. Not downstairs, and too close to be upstairs.

I squatted down and looked at the floor.

There were visible prints—and some drops of blood—on the linoleum. They came *out* of the front of the house and stopped at the closed door to the cellar. I laid my ear against the wood and listened.

Belle was still begging for mercy for the kids. Not for herself.

That says a lot. She was telling him that she was his for the taking—in however way the killer wanted. She was willing to die for her children.

Her husband had been willing to enter purgatory for them and for her. It saddened me that people with that kind of selfless courage were caught up in the wrong world. Needle had integrity where it really counted. So, clearly, did his wife.

At the same time, she was *still* pleading. I hope that meant there was no unfixable act of commission. The blood on the floor was light, maybe from a torn lip or broken nose. It wasn't the kind of spatter you get from a mortal wound.

It was a slender hope, but it was something.

The cellar door was the usual cheap kind—hollow wood with a Mickey Mouse spring lock. Despite all of my fears making me want to whip it open and charge down the stairs, I could not risk it. Safety lay in stealth, and stealth takes time. If the tone or immediacy of her cries dialed up to eleven, then I'd say fuck it and go charging down.

Not yet though.

Not yet.

I gripped the knob and waited for her to say something else, then I turned it. The click was soft.

"Please, for the love of God and Mary," she was saying. "Not my kids. Not my babies."

"They look so yummy," said the killer. Baltimore accent but soaked with the wrong kind of desire.

"Take me instead," she screeched. "Let them go. I'll do

whatever you want. Anything. Just let them go and I'll do anything."

"You're getting me hard, Bellie-Belle. Rock hard. Want to see?"

"I'll do anything. Just please, for the love of Jesus, let my babies go."

The kids were oddly quiet. Just muffled sobs. That suggested gags. Another splinter of hope in that. This freak was taking his time, letting it play it out so he could get his jollies. Like he did with Needle—giving him a speech and making threats when all he really needed to do was kill him.

The FBI profiler was right. This was a psychopath.

I'm coming, I mentally promised Belle and her kids. *I'm coming. Just keep stalling him.*

With the door open, I moved onto the top landing and squatted down, the pistol in a two-hand grip. Hoping the ghoul came within range at the bottom of the stairs.

He didn't.

Moving with every bit of caution and care I'd learned as a Spec Ops shooter, I began descending the steps. If he was turned toward the stairs at all there was going to be a moment when he would see my feet on the steps. There was nothing I could do about it. There was only a black pipe banister and no other cover.

Step by step.

Moving slow.

Crouching with the pistol pointed toward the sound of his voice. Two steps. Three. Four. Thirteen to go.

And the fifth goddamn step creaked.

Real fucking loud.

Then everything went to shit.

—16—

Belle Di Carlo screamed.

The kids tried to scream.

I jumped down the rest of the steps. Big jump. Landed hard in a crouch but it still sent painful shocks up my shins and into each knee. My right knee buckled, and I went down.

That saved my life. It bought me a second's grace.

Something silver flashed past me as I canted sideways, and instantly a line of white-hot heat exploded along my cheek. The knife he'd thrown hit my cheekbone and bounced off, trailing blood as it clattered to the floor.

I threw myself into a tight roll, but the son of a bitch was fast. So goddam fast.

As I came out of my roll, he flung Belle aside and kicked the gun out of my hand, then did a lightning-fast changeup and kicked me on the right ear. The world was instantly filled with a sound like an explosion and pain shot deep into my skull. He'd caught me on the ear with the toe of those Tims. It was like getting hit with a golf club.

I fell, but even with the cut and the hit I wasn't out. As I landed, I turned the fall into a barrel roll toward him. My hip caught him across the shins. He fell over me but rolled like an acrobat and sprang to his feet with dangerous agility.

My peripheral vision mapped the scene in a microsecond. The two kids were against the rear wall, their hands bound with zip ties and duct tape over their mouths. The killer had wanted them to see what was happening to their mom. Sick fuck. As for Belle, she'd staggered and hit the water heater face-on. If her nose had been cracked before, it burst now. Red and messy. She puddled down to the concrete floor.

The killer rushed at me, wanting to shut me down completely as fast as he could. He did a power-generating little skip and snapped out with a heel kick to my face. I was in motion, but that heel caught the side of my mouth and I felt teeth break.

He reached into his jacket pocket and pulled out a Buck hunting knife and charged me while I was smashed against a stack of plastic bins filled with Christmas decorations. They toppled over me and one of them caught the slash of that blade.

It took him maybe half a second to dislodge the knife, and in that tiny window of time I made my move.

I pivoted on my hip and kicked another plastic bin at him. It did no harm, but he had to avoid it and that gave me the time to rise to a crouch and dive at him. As I did that, I thrust my hand under my jacket and ripped the knife from its drop-sheath. My shoulder caught him on the side of the left knee and there was a *crack*. He cried out in pain and toppled, but I used my free hand to wrap around his legs and rode him down. The knife seemed to move in my hand like *it* wanted to hurt this monster. The arc was short and jerky because we crashed into the remaining Christmas ornament boxes. I felt more than saw the knife bite deep into his hip.

He howled with pain.

But he was not going to fade out easy. As we hit the floor, he hit me in the face with three very fast, very hard punches. My left eyebrow burst apart and all vision on that side of my face was hidden behind a thick veil of dark red blood. I lost the knife.

He tore the knife from his hip and stabbed me in the chest.

I was turning as the blow fell, but the point of his weapon punched right through jacket, shirt, flesh, and muscle and hit bone. A rib snapped with all the abrupt pain of a gunshot.

There was no time to *be* in pain. No time to be the victim. The kids were shrieking as loud as the duct tape allowed. Belle was on her knees, hands pressed against her face, her eyes dull and nearly vacant from pain. And I was nowhere close to winning this fight.

It was right then, at that moment, that the evil son of a bitch bit me.

His head darted forward like an alligator and strong white teeth closed around my forearm. I could see his eyes through the slits in the ski mask he wore, and they blazed with madness and hunger and red delight. He was going to kill me and then kill Needles' family and then he was going to feast on us. There in the basement, with no one to hear or help.

Suddenly, someone yelled, *"No!"*

It was a man's voice. Muffled but loud, filled with fury and fear and panic. And a rage that went miles and miles deep.

The killer whipped his head around, but there was no one else in the fucking cellar. He stared, his lips gleaming with bright blood. He bared his gore-streaked teeth.

There was no one.

I was hurt in a lot of places and a lot of ways and could feel my strength soaking away. I lay in a pool of my own blood, and he sat astride me.

With all of the speed and power I had left, I punched upward with my right hand—the effort tearing the knife wound further open and ripping a scream from me. My fist caught him under the chin, the knuckles smashing into the soft tissue above his Adam's apple. He reeled back, gagging and choking, but still in the fight.

I reversed the same arm and chopped down into his crotch with my elbow.

It folded him in half, and as his upper torso collapsed onto me, I clamped my teeth around his windpipe. He went wild, thrashing and punching and trying to free himself, but I was past feeling what damage he was doing. All I could see was the terror in his eyes and taste hot blood in my mouth. Salty and bitter and awful.

I growled like a goddamn dog as I shook my head back and forth, worrying his throat like a terrier with a rat. Out of the corner of my eye I saw his fist hurtling toward me.

And then it all went red and then black as I sank into darkness.

—17—

I remember thinking that being dead hurt more than I expected.

Then I heard those little clicks and pings of machines. I felt the nasal cannula—those clear plastic tubes with the prongs that stick up your nostrils. Much more slowly and with breaks for passing out, I felt the bandages and the damage they covered. Too many bandages. Huge pain.

Opening my eyes took effort. It was bench-pressing five hundred pounds with my eyelids. There was an uninformative speckled acoustic-tiled ceiling above my head. There were voices somewhere, but I could only hear them with one ear. There was no sound at all in the other ear.

I tried to say something, to call out. That's when I realized my jaw was wired shut. So, I closed my eyes and let the darkness have its way with me.

Next time I woke, Crow was sitting in a plastic chair three feet away.

"You look like shit," he said.

I said nothing. Tried, though. Failed. Grunted.

I raised my one good arm and touched my face and raised inquisitive eyebrows. He took a long pull from a bottle of Yoo-hoo, considered the label for a moment, and set it on the bedside table.

"Short version is that you are a mess. Skull fracture with concussion, broken jaw, cracked cheekbone, broke three teeth, eight stiches in your eyebrow, cracked orbital around that eye, various stab wounds. Worst was the one to the chest. That gave the docs some entertaining moments because the knife broke a rib, and the ends of the rib punctured your lung. You tried your damndest to drown in your own blood. Luckily Mike Sweeney showed up. Belle Di Carlo probably saved your life, though. Compression and a few other tricks. You lost enough blood to float a canoe."

I kept staring at him.

"Mike also found what was left of Andrew Alan Baker, 30, of Baltimore. Has a bunch of black belts in different martial arts. Fought in a slew of off-book cage matches but was tossed out for —want to guess? Yup, biting. No arrests, though. No criminal record of any kind, but DNA from his saliva puts him at the scene of twenty-two murders in seven states. His psych profile from the shrinks his parents took him to when he was a kid reads like a Stephen King novel. It's out in the press now," said Crow. "Baker the Biter. Some idiot at the *Philadelphia Inquirer* hung that on him. And, yes, he's dead as a doornail."

With great effort I pulled up my hospital gown and touched the tattoo of Needle. Crow studied it and I saw some of the smartassery fade from his face. He nodded, though.

"His wife and kids will be okay," he said gently. "Kids are bruised and scared and they're going to need therapy. Maybe a lot of it."

I waited.

"Belle was here for a couple of nights, but she's back home with her kids. Concussion, lacerations, some soft tissue damage from punches and slaps." He paused, reading my face. "Yes, she was in the hospital for days. You, my friend, have been here for a full week. Been out because of the head wounds. Doc says you'll be here another five days or so. Then Val said to bring you home to our place. Oh, don't look so alarmed … I won't let her cook for you."

We shared a long silence as he let me process everything. Then he reached out and touched the tattoo.

"Here's one thing from the witness statements that I haven't yet accounted for," he said. "I have my theories, but …"

I waited.

"Belle and both kids swear that they heard someone yell at just the right time to distract Baker and give you the moment you needed. And that it wasn't anyone down there in the basement. When I pressed them on it, they just looked at each other and said they didn't know who it was. Now, what do you think about that? A sudden yell out of nowhere. Muffled, as if whoever yelled was masked. Or maybe muffled by clothes."

His eyes were penetrating, yet weirdly amused.

"I think we both know who it was who shouted that timely warning, now don't we?"

Even if I could talk, I wouldn't have said anything.

The thing that Crow could not see but I could, were the ghosts who stood around my bed, filling the room. Dozens of them. Mostly girls and women. And in a corner, staring directly at me, was a man. His face was no longer warped by the wounds that had killed him. He smiled at me.

If I could have, I'd have smiled back.

Crow saw me looking and turned to see. But he saw nothing. And understood everything. He reached over and gave the unbruised and unbandaged part of my arm a squeeze. Then he rose, took his bottle of Yoo-hoo and finished it, bent and placed it quietly in the trashcan, and went out.

I lay there, still awake, for a very long time. All around me, the ghosts were quiet. Even the ones who are normally screamers. They were all smiling, too.

ABOUT THE AUTHOR

Jonathan Maberry is a *New York Times* bestselling author, 5-time Bram Stoker Award winner, 4-time Scribe Award winner, Inkpot Award winner, editor, and comic book writer. His vampire apocalypse book series, V-WARS, was a Netflix original series. He writes in multiple genres including suspense, thriller, horror, science fiction, fantasy, and action; for adults, teens, and middle grade. He is the editor of many anthologies including *The X-Files, Aliens: Bug Hunt, Don't Turn Out the Lights, Nights of the Living Dead*, and others. His comics include *Black Panther: Doomwar, Captain America, Pandemica, Highway to Hell, The Punisher*, and *Bad Blood*. He is the editor of *Weird Tales Magazine*, and the president of the International Association of Media Tie-in Writers. Website: www.jonathanmaberry.com. Find @jonathanmaberry on Instagram, Twitter, and Threads; and facebook.com/jonathan.maberry.5/

OTHER WORDFIRE PRESS TITLES BY JONATHAN MABERRY

Empty Graves

Midnight Lullabies

Shadows & Verse

A Fantastic Holiday Season 2: The Gift of Stories

An Antarctic Mystery

Decision Points

Empty Graves: Tales of the Living Dead

Gilded Glass: Twisted Myths and Shattered Fairy Tales

Midnight Lullabies: Unquiet Stories and Poems

Monsters, Movies & Mayhem

Mystic: The Monk Addison Case Files (Coming December 3, 2024)

The House on the Borderland

The Narrative of Arthur Gordon Pym of Nantucket

The Wolf Leader

Weird Tales: Best of the Early Years 1923-25

Weird Tales: Best of the Early Years 1926-27

Our list of other WordFire Press authors and titles is always growing. To find out more and shop our selection of titles, visit us at:

wordfirepress.com

PREVIOUSLY PUBLISHED

"Ink" was published in *Urban Fantasy Magazine*, Vol 1 issue 11 (Sept 2015).

"Mystic" was published in *Peeling Back the Skin* (Grey Matter Press, June 2016)

"Grit" published in *Dark Cities*, edited by Christopher Golden (Titan Books, May 16, 2017)

"Faces" published in *Wind Through the Fence* and other stories (JournalStone Publishing, 2017)

"Job Description—a Poem" published here for the first time.

"Reflected Image" published in *Gilded Glass* (Western Colorado State University/WordFire, 2022)

"We Wear the Masks" published in *Joe Ledger: Unbreakable* (JournalStone 2023)

"Dead to Me" published in *Dead Detectives Society* (Monstrous Books, 2024)

"On Lonely Roads, A Poem" published in *Long Past Midnight* (Kensington, 2023)

"Needles" published here for the first time

Printed in the USA
CPSIA information can be obtained
at www.ICGtesting.com
LVHW091811061224
798422LV00006B/1226

* 9 7 8 1 6 8 0 5 7 6 9 8 6 *